CAUGHT UP IN YOU

"I never said anything about a relationship," he countered, offended she'd already shut him down. "This tension between us is strictly chemistry. It's not going away."

"If we keep ignoring it, it will," she said, sliding her hand from his.

That soft tone held no conviction. "I feel the opposite," he informed her, pleased when her brows shot up in surprise. "I say we tackle this head-on and then we can move forward."

"And how do you propose we do that?"

Oh, all the ways he wanted to answer, but Braxton went for the safer route. Leaning just his face toward hers, he came within a breath of her lips.

"Cora," he murmured. "I'm going to touch you again."

That was all the warning he gave before he closed his mouth over hers. As much as he wanted to back her against this wall and kiss her good and hard, he kept his touch light. Because even though every part of him was wound tighter than a coil ready to spring, he wanted to remember this, wanted to have her taste, her touch embedded into his mind. . . .

Books by Jules Bennett

WRAPPED IN YOU

CAUGHT UP IN YOU

Published By Kensington Publishing Corporation

CAUGHT UP
IN YOU

JULES
BENNETT

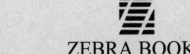

ZEBRA BOOKS
KENSINGTON PUBLISHING CORP.
http://www.kensingtonbooks.com

ZEBRA BOOKS are published by

Kensington Publishing Corp.
119 West 40th Street
New York, NY 10018

All Kensington titles, imprints and distributed lines are available at special quantity discounts for bulk purchases for sales promotion, premiums, fund-raising, educational or institutional use.

Special book excerpts or customized printings can also be created to fit specific needs. For details, write or phone the office of the Kensington Sales Manager. Attn.: Sales Department. Kensington Publishing Corp., 119 West 40th Street, New York, NY 10018. Phone: 1-800-221-2647.

Zebra and the Z logo Reg. U.S. Pat. & TM Off.

First Printing: December 2016
ISBN-13: 978-1-4201-3910-5
ISBN-10: 1-4201-3910-X

eISBN-13: 978-1-4201-3911-2
eISBN-10: 1-4201-3911-8

10 9 8 7 6 5 4 3 2 1

Printed in the United States of America

*To everyone who has embraced this series and
encouraged me during the process . . .
thank you.*

Chapter One

Just try it, she said. *It will be fun,* she said.

And that manipulative conversation with Sophie, his soon-to-be sister-in-law, is how Braxton now found himself wearing nothing but his boxer briefs and a towel, waiting for a massage.

A massage. He may as well turn in his man card now and go ahead and sign up for a facial and a pedicure while he was here.

Braxton Monroe and his brothers were gearing up to open a women's-only resort and spa, in honor of their late sister, Chelsea. The business had been her dream, so how could they ignore something she'd been so passionate about?

With the resort set to open at the first of the year and the open house just a week before Christmas, they were needing to hire a masseuse. In the beginning, they weren't sure if they needed one on hand the first day the resort was open, but they finally decided they wanted to do this up right and do it up big, just like Chelsea would've wanted.

Sophie had just sold a house to a new lady in town and, after some apparent girl bonding, Sophie wanted the guys to check out this prospect for the masseuse position.

Because the woman was new to the small town of Haven, Georgia, and not currently employed, Braxton was now in this stranger's home. He'd been half naked in a strange woman's house before, but usually under much different circumstances. Braxton hoped like hell Sophie hadn't lied when she'd said she'd checked out the woman's credentials.

Thankfully, Sophie had driven him to help with the awkwardness of the situation. Though he'd questioned her in the car when she started acting weird. She never gave him a straight answer when he asked about the naughty grin on her face and he was almost afraid to see how this was going to play out. Okay, he wasn't almost afraid, he was flat-out terrified.

He also had no clue why he couldn't meet the potential employee before she came in and rubbed her hands all over him. But Sophie insisted he was to undress and wait in the room because he needed to have the full "client experience." Yet again, how the hell had he ended up with his ass up and his head in a doughnut-shaped hole?

Braxton groaned as he realized how foolish he looked lying here. For all he knew, this was a prank orchestrated by his brothers. No doubt Zach and Liam were back at the resort laughing their asses off at his expense. There would be payback.

The door behind him clicked, and footsteps shuffled across the glossy wood floor. Braxton didn't lift his head, didn't want to see whoever had just walked in. He'd had more than enough of pampered rich girls to last him a lifetime. He'd seen the designer bag by the front door, Prada if his ex had taught him anything.

The last thing he wanted was to deal with another label-snob.

Bitterness was a pill he'd been trying to swallow for months . . . it still wasn't going down.

Braxton wanted to get this humiliation over with so he could go back home to his punching bag, drink a beer, fondle his remote, and try to regain some of his masculinity. First, he had to get this damn warped interview process over with.

The pocket door to the room slid open, then shut with a soft *whoosh*. Braxton attempted to mentally prepare himself for the next hour of the unknown.

"Good morning, Mr. Monroe." The soft, almost angelic voice washed over him, hitting him straight in the gut with a punch of lust. That was definitely something he hadn't prepared for. "My name is Cora. Have you ever had a massage before?"

Braxton grunted out a laugh. "First, call me Braxton. Formalities aren't necessary when you're going to have your hands on me. Second, no, I haven't, but I lost a game of rock, paper, scissors with my brothers and my so-called friend drove me so I wouldn't be able to back out."

Her soft laugh seemed to caress his bare skin. "I assure you, by the time I'm done, you'll be glad you lost that game."

Between that laugh and her sultry tone, he was getting more turned on than he should. Seriously? That was new to him. For the past several months he'd been a bit . . . social with the ladies. Normally it was a flirty smile, a heavy-lidded lingering gaze, or a blatant touch that set him in motion.

Did Cora have a sultry smile or bedroom eyes? Tall, short? Did she have curves or more of an athletic build? Did she dress classy to match that Prada bag or was she more laid-back?

He gritted his teeth. He was here for a job interview, not to visualize the body that belonged to that sexy voice. He shouldn't care because the last thing he needed was to be tied in knots over a woman . . . any woman. Physicality was his best friend lately and he was just fine with that.

Braxton closed his eyes, listening to the soft movements, the subtle clangs of containers being opened, closed. He had no clue what to expect, but when something small and warm rested against the top of his spine, he stiffened.

"What's that?" he asked.

"Hot stones. I'll be placing them down your spine. Would you like me to explain each step as I go so you're more comfortable or do you prefer quiet? Each client is different, but since this is basically an interview, I feel I should tell you everything so you understand better what it is that I can offer."

What she can offer? With a voice like that . . . Braxton bit the inside of his cheek. He couldn't start hitting on a potential employee. Yes, he'd gotten a bit more outgoing since his engagement debacle, but there was a time and a place. This was neither, nor.

Cora carefully rested the stones down his spine, which he had to admit was rather nice. Damn it. He refused to like this. He was here under duress. Why was he already thinking of her on a first-name basis? Oh, yeah, because she was about to rub him.

"While I'm working I can tell you about myself."

Yeah, something he should've thought of. This was his chance to interview her for the position and they desperately needed someone to fill the role. Sophie absolutely swore this woman was the one for the job, but she'd insisted one of the brothers interview her to make sure. Focusing while getting a rubdown was a bit difficult, in his defense. Damn it, that felt too good. Should he be enjoying himself this much?

"I've been a licensed masseuse for two years." Her calm, relaxing voice cut off his thoughts. "Not very long, but I went to college first and I have my degree in accounting."

Okay, so that told him two things: She had her head on straight for getting a degree, which the nerdy professor in him admired. And she was still young, almost a decade younger than him if he were to wager a guess, which was just another reason he needed to keep his lustful thoughts out of his head. Just because her voice was silky smooth didn't mean he had to react to it or start to fantasize what she looked like.

While the rocks stayed in position, Cora's hands started gliding in short, smooth strokes from the middle of his back down to his side. Braxton had to catch himself from groaning. No, he wasn't here to enjoy the process, he was here to see if she would work out in their spa. In his defense, though, he could see how women would eat up this type of pampering. And that's precisely what they needed for this women's-only resort and spa he and his brothers were going to open.

Bella Vous was a vision of their late sister, Chelsea, and the Monroe boys were fighting like hell to make sure this resort was unlike anything around. They didn't want to just open their doors and hope for the best. They wanted to make the business thrive and flourish, just like their beautiful sister. They wanted this to be a place women came to relax from work, from family, from life in general. Chelsea had wanted that because their adoptive mother had put her life on hold to ensure they all had an amazing life. The woman had never asked for anything for herself, everything was for her family. Chelsea's dream was to cater to those women who were constantly giving.

"Why aren't you working as an accountant?" he asked, impressed he could form a coherent sentence while she worked her magic. Oh, man, those hands of hers were talented. And he had no idea why there were rocks down his back, but this was absolutely amazing.

Fine. He was enjoying every second of this, but that didn't mean he had to admit it to anyone.

Her hands stilled for only a split second before she replied. "Personal reasons. Being a masseuse gives me more freedom. I love making people relax. In a world when everything is rushed and hectic, I think people need to take more time for themselves. To work at a resort as unique as this one would be perfect."

Something about her passion, her need for freedom, reminded Braxton of Chelsea. His late sister would already love Cora for this position in the spa. And Braxton had to admit, he could get used to this treatment . . . still without anyone knowing, of course.

"I'm going to use some oil now," she told him, still in that soft, made-for-the-bedroom voice. No, damn it. She wasn't made for a bedroom, at least not his. "Do you prefer a scent or unscented? I keep both for allergy reasons and for men who prefer not to smell like flowers or fruit. Everyone is different and I like to please each client."

Oh, man. She was killing him. Killing. Him.

His mind drifted to areas it shouldn't be. He didn't need to think about being pleased in any other way than to find the perfect employee.

Braxton laughed at his wayward thoughts and how

quickly he'd strayed off course. "Unscented is fine. Do you have many male clients?"

"I did where I was working," she replied easily. "I had quite a variety, actually. CEOs, blue-collar workers. Granted, most of them were private about their guilty pleasure, but that's fine. I understand the need for them to feel masculine. I've learned how to keep secrets and every client has them."

Her hands slathered together seconds before the warm, oily glide took over. He had to swallow back the groan that threatened to slip out. Mercy, he didn't expect to really enjoy this. Braxton didn't know if all massages were this sensual or if he'd hit the masseuse jackpot, but this woman and her clever hands could rub him all day.

Best. Interview. Ever. Maybe he needed to hold more interviews for possible masseuses. Or not. That was one thing he'd never live down if either of his brothers thought he actually liked this.

"Why the move to Haven?" he asked. "I was told you lived in Atlanta."

Her hands traveled easily to the other side of his back. The oil slid effortlessly between her palms and his skin, making him think of other, very nonprofessional thoughts.

"My family is in Atlanta, but I've never wanted to stay there. I'm not a big-city girl. Too rushed, too chaotic for me." She finished his back, then moved to shift the towel over his backside as she placed more oil on the tops of his thighs. "I love Savannah, always have. Several summers ago I came to Haven with a friend and instantly fell in love with the small-town charm."

Was she trying to get away from the city or her family? Or both? There was a story there, but right now Braxton was having a hard enough time controlling his urges with her digging into the backs of his thighs . . . he couldn't delve into her personal issues.

"Can you tell me more about the resort?" she asked, shifting down the table to work on his lower legs. "Sophie told me enough to have me interested in what three guys would want with a women's-only resort."

Braxton chuckled, lifting his hands to settle on either side of his face on the cushy doughnut pillow. "We're either really smart or we're about to make total fools of ourselves."

"Personally, I think the idea is brilliant. Working moms; young, single women looking for a getaway; sisters; moms and daughters. You'll have a whole host of women flocking to this resort."

He didn't know why her approval pleased him. Cora with the sultry voice and the talented hands had clearly taken control of his mind and every single thought. Who knew a masseuse held so much power?

"Our sister, Chelsea, bought this house a few years back. She always loved to travel and take off on a whim. The one place she always wanted to see was Paris." He focused on the story, not on the fact she was now on his thigh up near very personal territory. "She had a vision for this place that none of us knew about until she passed away almost a year ago."

Cora's hands froze. "I'm so sorry. I had no idea you'd lost someone that close."

Braxton still couldn't believe it himself. Not a day went by that he didn't want to send Chelsea a text, but just as quickly as that thought would hit, the pain of the emptiness would replace it. That ache, it hadn't lessened one bit. The pain was just as fierce, just as crippling; he'd just grown accustomed to living with a hole in his life. He didn't like this new chapter without her, but he would go on living and honor her memory.

The alternative of letting his grief consume him wasn't an option. Chelsea was a strong woman and he'd be damned if he'd let her down.

"We're getting along." The simple reply for emotions that were anything but. "We're doing this for her, to keep her alive the only way we know how."

Cora smoothed the towel back in place. She brushed against the side of his leg as she moved toward his feet. "You must be a strong family to support one another like this."

There was a wistfulness to her tone, almost a longing. None of his concern. Sexy women were one thing, baggage and anything personal were a whole other level he ran fast and far from. Being jilted by a so-called love could make a man a bit jaded . . . or at least wake him up to how careless people were with others' hearts.

"We have our typical moments where we don't agree, but we know we can always depend on one another."

"Sounds perfect," she murmured.

Oh, yeah. There was a story. A story he had no reason to care about. Even if she came to work for his family, getting personally involved on any level would be a mistake.

"Chelsea left behind several binders with notes and pictures, detailing exactly what she wanted out of this new property she'd purchased." He still couldn't believe the whirlwind they'd been on over the past year. "She wanted to name it Bella Vous, which means 'beautiful you' in French."

"She must have been an amazing woman," Cora replied. "This idea, it's all so perfect."

"That's what we're holding on to," he said honestly. "We want every woman who hears about the resort to have that same reaction. We figure at first there will be all kinds of interest, but we don't want that newness to wear off."

"Tell me more about my position," she went on as she gripped the arch of his foot with her fingertips. "Will there be appointment times given like at a spa or would you prefer someone there all day to be ready for spur-of-the-moment clients?"

Sticking to the reason he was here, Braxton replied, "We will have set hours for the spa, but you will be doing your own appointments. We want the spa workers to feel like they have control over their schedules while still meeting the needs of the clients."

"Smart."

Braxton smiled. He'd be sure to tell his brother Liam that, since Liam wanted all spa employees to be there all day and all evening. Braxton and Zach had finally talked some sense into him. They'd burn out their staff in the first few months working them to death like that. Growing could come later. Right now they needed a good, solid base to keep things running smooth without being so overwhelming they missed out on catering to the guests.

By the time his massage was over, Braxton didn't know if he could move. Would it be unprofessional to lie here and take a nap now that he was all relaxed?

"I'll let you get dressed," she told him. "Just tell me when you're done and I can come back in so we can talk more. I just have a few more questions and I assume you have more for me."

He should, but with his loose muscles all he could think of was *When can you start?*

The door opened and closed. Braxton sat up, twisting his neck from side to side. Damn, he felt pretty good. After working on that house, getting everything fixed and repaired, he'd had his fair share of aches and pains. He wasn't twenty anymore and his body was reminding him with each crack and cramp. Not to mention he was used to working at a college and not a construction site.

He quickly dressed because now he wanted to see the woman behind the magic. Would her tone match her appearance? For all he knew someone's elderly grandmother had just felt him up and he'd liked it.

Wouldn't be the first time he'd found himself in the company of an older woman. Unfortunately, Zach's overeager neighbor had been a one-night mistake he still couldn't dodge.

But Cora wasn't a grandmother, of that he was sure. She'd sounded young, she'd given him a hint as to her age when she'd discussed her education. Regardless of how attracted he instantly was, that was only because of her voice, her talented hands. What man wouldn't be instantly turned on? He was human.

He needed to get into professional mode fast because he refused to be taken off guard again by this woman.

Fastening his watch, Braxton glanced to the closed door. He'd been in here for all of an hour and he'd never felt this calm. She truly was a miracle worker and perfect for the spa. As usual, Sophie was right.

Braxton turned the knob, easing the door open, but stopped short at the sight of Cora standing in the hallway talking with Sophie.

Swallowing his shock, Braxton stared at the beautiful woman who'd just rubbed his body to complete relaxation. The long, rich auburn hair tumbling down her back, the petite build, the way she tipped her head toward him but didn't meet his gaze.

Sophie smiled. "I'll let you two talk. I'll just wait in the living room."

Braxton noted the large yellow Lab sitting obediently next to Cora. He hadn't seen the dog when he'd first arrived, which was strange. Didn't all dogs bark and run like mad toward the door when a visitor arrived? Zach's dogs certainly did . . . all eight of them. Well, the seven puppies did. The poor mom tended to remain still as if she didn't even have the energy to greet a new guest.

"Would you like to go in and sit or stay in the hallway?" Cora asked, a wide smile spreading across her face, her gaze still locked over his shoulder.

Braxton returned her infectious smile. "We can go back in here. I only have a few more questions."

"Great."

Braxton watched as she reached her hand out. He thought she was reaching for him, but realized she was feeling her way. She also hadn't looked him in the eye. And she had a very obedient dog who stayed by her side.

Nothing much shocked him, but the fact Cora Buchanan was blind and had just given him the massage of a lifetime sure as hell left him utterly speechless.

He followed her into the room, but remained standing until he saw where she wanted to go. Propping his hands on his hips, Braxton stared down at her where she'd taken a seat on a small accent chair in the corner of what most likely used to be a bedroom. Her dog right at her side.

"Why didn't you tell me you were blind?"

* * *

Cora ignored the accusatory tone. "Does my sight change how you felt when you were getting a massage? When you were completely comfortable and talking about the job?"

"No."

His feet shuffled against the wood floors and Cora kept her hand on the back of Heidi's neck. "I asked Sophie not to tell you. I wanted to be interviewed and judged on my abilities and my professionalism, not my lack of sight."

Because she'd come here to prove she could be alone, she could work and not worry about being judged or discriminated against by those who were supposed to support her the most. Why did her condition disturb so many when she was the one who lived with it?

She was the one who'd been robbed of her sight, she was the one who had to rebuild her life, to rediscover who she was after the accident that ultimately led to a life-altering diagnosis. And damn it, she refused to let any obstacle stand in her way. Independence was hers, she just had to reach out and grab it.

There was a time when she'd been too afraid to grab hold of freedom—a time when she'd reach out and only encounter darkness. She had no idea what all she'd lost until everyday actions became difficult.

With each passing day her world had grown dimmer and dimmer. She waited for the anxiety, the panic attacks, but they never came. What consumed her had been so much worse. There was an emptiness she couldn't even put into words. There were places she wanted to see in this world, but once the diagnosis hit, her family started to withdraw and Cora feared traveling alone.

"I don't like being manipulated," he told her, pulling her back into the moment. Why did his tone have to be so low, so sexy? And why were her hands still tingling? She'd given countless massages, many of them to men, but there was something about Braxton's taut muscle tone beneath her fingertips that would have them zinging for days.

Focus. No zinging.

"I don't manipulate people," she defended with a tilt of her chin. "But I also wanted a fair shot at this position."

The air shifted as Braxton moved. Material slid together in a smooth yet quick motion. She pictured him crossing his arms over what she knew was a broad chest. Her heart beat so fast, she had to force herself to take deep, calming breaths. She couldn't let this opportunity pass her by. She needed this position and the women's-only resort sounded absolutely amazing. Financially she didn't need this at all, but for her sanity, for the life she longed to have, she wanted this job and she wasn't letting it slip from her hands.

Cora wasn't going to hide behind her lack of sight, wasn't going to use it as a crutch to have people help her through life. Even when she'd been at her lowest point, she'd fought to get back that independence. She'd come so far and she had no intention of slowing down.

She literally had all the money she could ever want, had a multimillion-dollar company at her disposal . . . but it came with a price and Cora had to at least try being on her own before deciding what to do with the rest of her life. She wanted, no, needed to stand on her own two feet—and she damn well would or she'd go down fighting.

"If you need to think about it, or discuss with your brothers—"

"How would you get to work?" he asked, cutting her off.

Cora pursed her lips. She'd thought of this when first approached by Sophie for the potential job. "If you give me the job, I'll figure it out. I know I'm only a couple miles away."

Silence settled in the room once again. Braxton wasn't moving, she could barely hear him breathing, but tension filled the room. Cora slid her hand down Heidi's back, taking comfort in her best friend . . . the only being she'd been able to depend on the past three years.

At first Cora had wondered just how much a dog could help, but she and Heidi clicked instantly. Cora recalled that moment when she didn't feel so alone. When just the slightest brush of fur reminded her she had a companion who understood and maybe, just maybe, they would get through this together.

"You'll need to see the resort first," he stated, then muttered a curse and shifted again. "Sorry. I wasn't thinking."

Story of her life. Everyone was sorry, which only made her angry. Why was everyone sorry? Had they caused the condition her doctors had overlooked for years? A condition her parents were still in denial about. There was nothing to be sorry about. Her condition was something she'd learned to live with, was still learning to live with. Adjustments came every day, but in the three years since she'd lost her sight, she'd become a stronger woman. Just because life threw her a major curveball didn't mean she would give up on what she wanted, on what would make her happy.

"Please, from here on out, don't apologize. Don't

try to watch your wording, don't try to coddle me. I would love to see the house because I can see without my eyes."

"I'm sorry . . . what?"

Cora smiled. Typical reaction from a stranger and just one more way she could show him that she was not some blind woman who planned to sit on the sidelines and have life pass her by. Yes, she'd had to make some major adjustments and in the beginning it was easier to feel sorry for herself. But Cora wasn't going to live her life engulfed in self-pity and she sure as hell didn't want pity from anyone else, either.

"You'd be surprised how much your other senses are heightened when one is taken away." Nerves swirled around in her belly, but she pushed forward. She couldn't afford to be nervous now. Strength, independence, and a strong will were her new best friends. "I'm guessing you're about six-three. You either work out quite a bit or you're into manual labor. You're nervous since you found out I was blind because you're shifting more now than you did before."

His soft laugh slid all over her. "When you were rubbing on me I was relaxed."

That gravelly voice shouldn't make her body have such a severe response . . . but it did. "Well I'm not rubbing anymore and you'll just have to adjust," she retorted. "So. When do I get the tour of this new resort?"

Because backing down wasn't an option. She was good at her job and that coveted independence was within her reach. Her parents doubted her, her pseudo fiancé doubted her. The only person with faith in Cora was Cora.

"I'll pick you up tomorrow morning. This afternoon I'm meeting with an inspector to go over all the wiring in the guest cottages."

Shocked he'd just volunteered to be her chauffeur,

she concentrated on what else he was saying. "Guest cottages?"

"Besides the main house, there are two small cottages on the grounds." His feet slid across the floor, his breathing grew a touch louder, which meant he'd moved in closer to her. "The main house is done, other than some minor touches. The cottages have a bit more work, but nothing we can't handle in the next couple weeks. Once we tour, I'll need to know how you'll want your space set up and what needs to be ordered for your room. We'll have to get that taken care of, first thing."

Cora nodded as she exhaled a breath she'd been holding since they'd walked into this room. Finally, she was getting the break she needed. Being a Buchanan had normally gotten her everything she wanted out of life. She could buy anything at any time . . . except her sight and her freedom. Her parents still didn't understand why she wanted out, why she'd felt trapped in that office day in and day out. But she'd prove to them, and to herself, that she could live on her own, have a job she loved, and be the happiest she'd ever been. It wasn't about money, it never was. It was about finding who she was, not who she'd been molded to be.

Cora offered him what she hoped was a grateful smile. "Thank you."

"If this works out, I'll be thanking you."

Coming to her feet, she took a step forward. Instantly Braxton's hand gripped her bicep. "There's a towel on the floor. I didn't want you to trip."

"Oh."

His protective hand remained in place, giving her that zing once again. She couldn't afford to zing or tingle or any other verb associated with his touch. That voice alone was enough to have her hormones on high alert. Touching couldn't be added into the mix.

"Did I drop it? Usually I'm good about knowing when something falls."

"I think it was the one I used," he said, removing his hand. "I've put it up on the table. All clear now."

Cora slid her hand to Heidi's head and patted. "You can go ahead. I'll follow you out to the living room."

He didn't move and Cora hated the thought of him studying her. She wasn't self-conscious of her sight, but she didn't want to be analyzed, either.

"You're staring," she accused.

"I won't apologize."

Cora ignored the punch of lust at his soft yet powerful voice. At least he'd listened to her and wasn't saying he was sorry. That was something.

"Do you live here alone?" he asked after a moment. "Not that it's my business, I'm just amazed, I guess."

Amazed? That was a first for her. Her parents certainly hadn't been amazed at her decision to move away and be on her own. Her wannabe fiancé had been stunned speechless . . . so much so he didn't even ask her to stay, which was fine with her since she wouldn't have anyway.

There was just something about the way Braxton delivered such a simple sentence that warmed her. To know a total stranger didn't find her actions ridiculous— her mother's words—was refreshing. The need to be seen as an equal by anyone was overwhelming and she hated that she allowed herself to feel this way. She knew in her heart she would be just fine, but a little encouragement along the way was something she wouldn't turn down.

"I live with Heidi," Cora replied. "She's all I need."

Again, silence settled heavily between them. Uneasiness slid through her. What was he thinking now? Was he staring at her, looking around the small room? Replaying that massage that her hands may never recover from?

"Was there something else?"

"We never did decide how you'd get to work."

Cora shrugged. "Let me worry about that. If I want something, I don't let little things stop me and I want this job. Are you sure you don't need to talk things over with your brothers?"

"Trust me on this."

Cora thought to the dynamic family who always posed a strong front, but once rough times hit, they were nowhere to be found. Her parents were all about pretenses. Look good on the outside no matter the turmoil inside. Ignore it and it will go away. "It" was an umbrella term for whatever her parents didn't want to face at that moment. With their money, they'd truly believed they could buy happiness. Unfortunately for their daughter with a health issue, they could toss out any dollar amount and nothing could change the fact.

They ignored the issue once they realized every specialist called in had no cure. So they moved on with their lives, their parties, their business deals and jet-setting, leaving Cora to work everything out on her own. The loneliness taught her so much. Hard life lessons learned had made for some deep scars.

Swallowing, she replied, "I don't trust anyone."

Braxton let out an audible sigh. "We all have our own baggage," he muttered, telling her a bit more about the intriguing man. "You'll see my brothers won't disagree with Sophie's opinion or mine. Actually, Sophie pretty much rules our lives and we're afraid of her, but don't tell her I said that."

Cora breathed a slight sigh of relief and laughed. "Good to know. Let me walk you and Sophie out and I'll be ready in the morning for that tour."

Chapter Two

"Say that again."

Braxton leaned against the rail on the newly renovated porch and stared at Zach. "I said the new masseuse is coming to check the place out tomorrow."

"After that, dumbass," Zach grumbled, shaking his head.

"I said she's blind."

"How in the hell can she do this job, then?" Zach's arm flew out, his tone raised. "You needed to run this by me and Liam before inviting her here and all but handing her the position."

"Ignore him," Sophie stated, coming out the front door. "He's in a mood because he didn't get enough sleep last night."

She threw Zach a wink and Braxton held up his hands. "I don't want to hear about bedroom habits. You left the final judgment call up to me and I think she'll be great for the job."

"I never said you had the final word," Zach stated.

"Since I was the one chosen by default to go get a massage, I'm the one making the final decision. Cora is hired."

"I agree," Sophie chimed in, wrapping an arm around Zach's waist. "The other employees we've hired all have a trial period once we open, so Cora will be no different. Sixty days is the perfect time frame for all parties. Who knows, Cora may end up not liking it in Haven and want to move back to the city. It's a risk we have to take. But, for that matter, any of the employees we've taken on may decide they don't like it. It's just one of the many perks that come along with owning a business."

Braxton kept his thoughts to himself, but he seriously doubted Cora would leave Haven. She'd seemed adamant about getting away from her family, away from the city life. He'd also heard that wistful tone of hers when he'd been discussing his brothers. She didn't have the bond, didn't have the stability family provided. In a brief time, Cora had made him extremely protective and defensive.

Damn it. He hadn't allowed himself to be so exposed to vulnerability in over a year. Now all of a sudden because some stunning stranger gave him a massage he was ready to get possessive and take charge. How the hell had this happened?

He quickly reminded himself of how she'd reminded him a bit of Anna. Polished, poised, a bit of sass behind the class.

But there was something about Cora that was a far cry from Anna. The determination to prove herself, to stand on her own two feet. Anna would rather stand on someone else's feet and have them carry her where she wanted to be.

And why the hell was he comparing the two women?

"You knew from the start that she was blind and didn't say a word to any of us." Zach turned an accusing eye on his fiancée. "I'm not trying to be rude here, but I'm just concerned for obvious reasons. This is a brand-new resort and we can't afford to take such big risks."

Sophie shrugged. "I'm not concerned one bit. I checked out her past employer and they were sorry to see her go. She had the most clientele of the entire day spa. That tells me all I need to know."

Cora's popularity with her clientele didn't surprise Braxton at all. Her hands were magical. Damn it, why did he keep using that word? Why did he keep reliving those sixty minutes her hands had been nearly all over his body? He seriously needed to get a grip.

"You can meet her in the morning," Braxton stated, circling back around to the point of the conversation. "Liam should be back this weekend to talk with the new cook we hired. He can meet with Cora, too, if you still have reservations. But please, I'm begging you to be nice when she comes. She doesn't need you to be your usual grouchy self."

Zach growled. "I'm nice. Just because I don't smile all the time or try to make everyone in my life see puppy dogs and rainbows. You're the peacemaker, not me."

Guilty, but the peacemaker hadn't been able to come through when it had been most important. His life had changed forever, but he was still just as determined to keep those around him in calm waters.

Braxton pushed off the newly installed post. "Since the inspector passed the cottages, I need to get those porch swings up soon. I'm going to be moving in some of the furniture tomorrow afternoon. I'll need to borrow your truck. I found some end tables and a kitchen set in town at Old Days Antiques."

Zach nodded. "If you'd get rid of your fancy SUV, you could get yourself a truck."

"I prefer something classier when I take a woman out."

Speaking of which, he had a date tomorrow. He hadn't had a date for two weeks. A dry spell for him since he'd revamped his social life after Anna publicly ripped out his heart and handed it back to him in shattered pieces.

He'd pined for her for a while, he wasn't ashamed to admit it. He was human, he had been blindsided and crushed. But he'd made a promise to himself never to let a woman get that close to him again because he wasn't sure he'd live through more heartache. The deaths of his biological parents, the deaths of his adoptive parents, then Chelsea, then Anna deciding she deserved better . . . there really was a breaking point in everyone and he'd nearly exceeded his limit.

"Whatever," Zach replied. "Just don't put a ding on it."

Ignoring the pang of betrayal that accompanied any memory that had just flooded his mind, Braxton forced a laugh and headed down the new, wide porch steps. "That rusty deathtrap?" he asked, throwing a look over his shoulder. "One more ding and it would fall apart."

"Trust me," Sophie chimed in. "He knows all the scratches and dents. He'll know if you put in another. Don't ask me how."

Zach merely raised his brows at her affirmation. Braxton shook his head and moved down the newly designed walkway that curved out around the landscaping he and Liam had spent hours sweating over. Now they were transitioning into the holiday season and all too soon Sophie would have lights, garland, and wreaths all over the house, inside and out. Braxton couldn't wait until Zach saw that expense. Zach wasn't known for his . . . holiday cheer.

The place was coming along better than any of them had hoped, even with Zach's sunshine attitude. Since Zach and Sophie had found Chelsea's secret notes regarding this property, the Monroe boys along with Sophie and Brock had done some serious renovations to this house. Brock had been a runaway teen who was lucky to have landed where he did when Zach discovered him hiding in the unfinished resort. He was now just one of the family.

Chelsea would be so proud, so excited. Granted, nearly everything they'd done had been lined out in precise detail, logged in thick binders. She'd been meticulous with the color palettes, the landscaping, the layout of each guest room. She'd thought of every single thing.

Sophie added her own touches, knowing her late best friend would approve. Apparently, Sophie was a master at pencil sketches and she'd done some amazing pictures for each room. They'd themed the resort to stay in tune with Chelsea's favorite place, Paris. There was classy elegance, café-style seating, and a charm that was both Southern allure and European flair. They'd had to be careful that the decor didn't lean toward tacky, but all of that fell to Sophie, for obvious reasons.

Braxton settled behind the wheel of his car and let his mind drift to his late sister. He could still see her infectious smile, hear her laughter. He prayed those memories never faded. He needed to keep hold of them, needed to keep her alive if only in his mind. Braxton had lost those images of his mother. Her face, her smile, they would start to slide into his mind, but each time he tried to grasp the memory, they vanished. Too many years had passed, added to the fact he'd been young when she was killed. But that didn't stop the ache he had that clawed at him to remember something about her, something he could hold on to.

But Chelsea's death was still fairly recent, the hurt still fresh. She may have been a free-spirited drifter, but whenever he'd needed her, she'd always been right there. He needed her now. Hell, they all needed her.

More than once she and Braxton had broken up altercations between Liam and Zach. Braxton never liked angry fighting, and Chelsea only wanted her brothers to get along.

So many times she would sit on their back porch with him and they'd try to figure out what they could do to get Liam and Zach to actually be friendly toward each other. But the type A personalities with chips on their shoulders simply weren't interested in family bonding moments when they'd been teens.

Fast-forward a few years when Zach, Liam, and Sophie had been in a serious car accident that left Sophie with a limp and Liam physically scarred and the two brothers only had a bigger wedge between them.

Since Chelsea's death, they were coming around. They'd all pulled together, Liam reluctantly at first, to get the old Civil War–era mansion fixed up and ready to turn into Chelsea's dream, her vision. Now they were all pitching in when they could. Braxton had taken the next semester off from teaching and Liam would come in on the weekends from Atlanta.

Bringing his engine to life, Braxton knew without a doubt that Cora and Chelsea would've already bonded. Chelsea wouldn't care one bit about Cora's inability to see and Braxton didn't either. Once the initial shock had worn off, he'd been in awe and more than impressed with a woman who had so much drive, so much determination. Braxton admired her already for her streak of independence.

But that didn't mean he wouldn't keep his eye on her. She was new in town, she was vulnerable whether she would admit it or not, and Braxton had appointed himself her . . . what? Guard? Keeper? He was nothing but a potential boss. He needed to keep that in mind because no matter how amazing her hands felt on him, no matter how much of a stunner she was, and no matter how her breath had caught with arousal when he'd touched her, she was going to be working for him and his brothers, which meant hands off.

Besides, he had enough ladies to keep him busy as it was. Why add another? His date tomorrow with the very curvy, very outgoing Lola would get his head back on straight. Braxton didn't do relationships, didn't do even second dates. He purposely found women who were after the same thing he was . . . no strings and a good time. His social life could be summed up as: dinner, yes—breakfast, hell no.

As he steered his SUV from the drive, Braxton cranked up the radio to his favorite heavy metal station. Why the hell was he even thinking of Cora and dating and relationships at all in the same sentence? Relationships were for fools. The only exception being his adoptive parents and Zach and Sophie. Out of all the people he knew, the percentage of those who actually found this so-called love was obviously low and there was no way in hell he would risk his heart again.

So, no. No more thinking of Cora and her magical

hands on him because she wasn't one of those women who was out looking for a good time.

Damn that massage that had his mind all twisted into a fantasy that could never be.

"Are you too cramped?" Cora asked as she felt for the latch to her seat belt.

Braxton brought the vehicle's engine to life and laughed. "Not at all. We're fine."

Even though they had put Heidi in the backseat, the dog always liked her head between the passenger and the driver. Cora assumed her loyal pup was trying to stay close or she just really liked to watch the world go by.

"Are you sure?" Cora asked, worried she wasn't making the best impression. Today was pivotal in her turning her life around and back in the direction she needed to go. "She will lie down back there if I tell her to. It's just, she really likes to be near me and—"

A hand settled across her knee, radiating warmth throughout her entire body. "She's fine, Cora."

Okay. There went those sensations once again. Even when he removed his hand after reassuring her, she still felt him. She knew firsthand how powerful a simple touch could be, she made her living off of that promise. But she'd never experienced someone's simple gesture the way she had Braxton's. She'd never actually craved more.

"Tell me about your work," Braxton stated as he turned the vehicle toward the right before picking up the speed. "That rock thing you did to me. Is that popular?"

Cora laughed at his description. "The hot lava rock

massage is quite popular, but there are various types of massages. I chose that one for you in particular."

"Really?"

Cora smiled wider because his tone indicated he was impressed. "Sophie had told me how hard you guys were working on fixing up the house. I figured you had some abused muscles and the heat is the perfect way to relax them."

"My muscles weren't abused," he stated with that rough, sexy tone of his.

When Heidi's hair tickled the side of Cora's face, she reached up to rub her pup's silky ear. "Ahhh, so you're that type of man."

"What type?"

"The one who thinks he's too masculine to get a massage or admit he needs pampering. I've had your type before, but they always come back for more." Cora cringed when she realized how that sounded. "I meant—"

"I know what you meant," he laughed. "Is that awkward for you? You know, to massage men?"

"Not for me." Cora patted Heidi's face before settling her hands back in her lap. "All of my clients become my friends. It's an intimate bond, which sounds strange, but when it's just you and one other person in a room for an hour, you get to know them pretty well. Pretty much all of my clients were regulars. I had the occasional client who walked in or wanted a spur-of-the-moment massage."

They drove for a bit in silence before Braxton spoke. "What other types of massages are there?"

Pleased that he wanted to know more about her work, Cora went through the most popular: the Swedish massage, aromatherapy, deep tissue, reflexology, and the pregnancy massage. Then she proceeded to explain the differences, why some of her clients choose one type over another, and how she decided what would work best for each person.

"Wow, I had no idea," Braxton muttered as he steered the car around another curve. "I know you're licensed and everything, but I guess I didn't realize how extensive it was."

"The schooling was a bit tougher for me since I had to do everything through a voice recognition program and the training was definitely all hands-on, but I love my job. I didn't realize how much I would enjoy it, actually."

Much more than the office, the potential husband, and the plump salary with the 401K waiting for her. The last thing she ever wanted to be was the co-owner of Buchanan Chocolates—a subsidiary of Buchanan Enterprises—with Eric Cutler as her husband and business partner. Her parents had been all too ready to hand over that section of their company to her.

The thought sent her into a crippling fear because, while that lifestyle might sound ideal to someone else, to her it sounded like a prison sentence. Unfortunately, it took a life-altering accident and diagnosis to wake her up and force her to see that she didn't have to fit into this perfect mold.

Cora knew she blew her parents' carefully laid plans all to hell when she proclaimed she was not getting married now . . . or ever. She wanted to be on her own, have her own freedom. She couldn't do that if she was with a man who kept treating her as if she were helpless and couldn't take care of herself.

Besides, she'd grown up beneath two of the most loveless people ever. They lived and breathed work. Cora had never once heard them say they loved each other, never once did she utter those precious words to her, either. And Eric? Yeah, he might as well be their son, as detached from emotions as he was. Cora had made the mistake of sleeping with him, wondering if maybe he'd be warmer in the bedroom. Nope. Still just as boring and lackluster as always. Why would she want to be married to a business and a man she didn't love? He was all career, all the time.

And since she'd lost her sight, they'd all acted so differently. Sometimes smothering her so much she couldn't breathe, other times treating her as if she had the plague. That accident changed everything, but Cora was determined to get her life back on track on her own, thank you very much.

"Hey. You okay?"

Cora smoothed her hair behind her ear and nodded. "Yeah. Just drifted off in thought for a second."

When he made a slow turn and cautiously moved forward, Cora's heartbeat increased. "Are we here?"

"We are. Zach is in town with Sophie today. Their dogs had vet appointments."

"How many do they have?" she asked.

"Eight." Braxton laughed. "If you knew my brother, you'd know how laughable it is that he has eight dogs, seven of them still puppies, a fiancée, and a child he's now legal guardian over. He's what you'd call . . . a moody loner."

Cora unfastened her belt when the vehicle came to a stop. "Doesn't sound like a loner at all."

"Yeah, his world got turned upside down about six months ago. But that's a story for another time."

She knew all about worlds turning upside down. She was still hanging there waiting on her world to right itself.

Braxton hopped out of the car as Cora was feeling

for her door handle. Suddenly her door opened and Braxton gripped her hand. "I got you."

"I can do it," she replied. "Why don't you open the back door and let Heidi out."

"Let me help you first."

Cora squeezed his hand to get his attention and looked in the general direction of the tone of his voice. This needed to stop now because she wasn't going to start her new life in a new town and get into the same pattern as her old life.

"Don't coddle me. That is the last thing I need. I appreciate your help, but I'm fine."

"You're not used to people helping you, are you?" he asked, still holding on to her, only now he'd stepped closer.

She pulled her hand from his, ignoring his question. She wasn't getting into what she'd been used to, what she came from or who she was. This was the new Cora and the old one . . . well, she didn't exist anymore.

Heidi nudged her from the back and Cora's body shifted forward . . . straight against a hard wall of muscle. Why did he have to be so charming and helpful? And why did his body have to feel so amazing against hers?

Braxton's other hand came to her shoulder. "I'm going to help you so Heidi can get out. She obviously wants out this door."

What was Heidi doing? Cora hadn't known her to be so pushy . . . literally. Maybe Heidi saw something in Braxton. Maybe she already picked up on the fact he was genuine in wanting to assist. His actions were almost sweet as if he truly cared as opposed to seeing her as a burden. He didn't come across as being put out and he sure as hell didn't have to do any of this.

He could've had her find her own way to the resort to show her around, but he'd volunteered to pick her up and bring her, and he'd treated Heidi as if she wasn't a huge beast in his backseat. What man would allow a strange dog to take up such space in his vehicle? Eric certainly complained each time they had to go somewhere and he'd gripe about having to get the seats cleaned to clear out the dog hair.

Another reason she needed to move beyond that life. Even her parents had tried to steer her away from a Seeing Eye dog. They'd told her a walking stick would be just fine, especially since she'd always be with someone. The image they painted for her of a life without sight wasn't one she wanted to continue. Breaking away, starting fresh was the only way she was going to have a happy life. She'd never wanted to be a suit-wearing corporate moneymaker or the wife of one. So here she was . . . not doing any of those things.

And until she figured out what to do about her place in the company, she was here building on something she knew would be the refreshing change she needed. She wasn't worried about Buchanan Chocolates. They would get along just fine without her and no doubt her parents would pass the reins to Eric . . . just like he wanted.

Reluctantly accepting Braxton's help, Cora stepped from the car, but immediately backed away from his touch once she was on solid ground. He would learn soon enough she hated being treated like she couldn't take care of herself. Being dependent on someone at this point would be working backward. She'd been trying for nearly three years to stand on her own two feet.

When she'd first been diagnosed and knew what the future held, Cora feared she'd forget what she looked like. Silly as that may seem, she would stand in front of a mirror, memorizing her features. Suddenly all that stuff that she hated about herself didn't matter. The brows she wished were more arched, the chin she'd always thought too round, the nose with the slight tilt on the end . . . she soaked it all in because she hadn't known when she'd wake up and not be able to look at her own reflection.

Binge-watching her favorite shows and rereading her favorite books had also become a priority. She'd logged in so many hours, laughing, crying, running through a gamut of emotions because her entire life had taken on a whole new outlook. She'd tried to cram in as much of her life as possible.

Taking walks, enjoying the sights of the city, even though she'd never loved living in the city. Suddenly when you know something will be taken away, your entire opinion changes. She'd driven out to the country a couple times just to look at the bright blue sky with no skyscrapers blocking her view. Butterflies became more stunning, the lush plants seemed more vibrant. Everything she could soak in, she did. Until the day she couldn't take in any more.

The darkest day of her life was her rock bottom. Nothing could put her back down there again. She refused to be that vulnerable and crushed.

Immediately Heidi was at Cora's side and Cora reached for the stiff collar. "You can lead the way. Heidi will follow."

"Actually, I have a surprise inside. I hope it's okay with you."

Cora pursed her lips. "A surprise? I'm intrigued."

Braxton's shoes scuffed against the concrete, so she knew he'd turned to walk away even before the gentle tug from Heidi leading the way. Cora wasn't sure what she expected in terms of this unexpected surprise, but the fragrant scent of apricots hit her and she stopped, immediately forgetting all about anything beyond right now.

"Do you have fragrant olive planted out here?"

"We do. How did you know?"

Cora closed her eyes and took a deep breath in, wanting to take a moment and enjoy the beauty she knew was around her. The sun shone down on her face, warming her, her hair slid around her shoulders as the soft breeze sent her long strands dancing and that fragrant plant just made this first experience even more perfect.

"I love that plant. I've always wanted one, but living in the city doesn't make much space for thriving plants." Cora started forward again, gently nudging Heidi that she was ready. "There's nothing like the sweet scent of apricots. Your guests will love that too."

"We're going to put lilac bushes around back near the patio," he told her. "Watch your step here."

Heidi hesitated, angling her body just in front of Cora's, letting Cora know there was an obstacle. Raising her foot gently, she started up the step and Heidi carefully guided her up the three steps to the porch.

By the time Cora reached the front door, she hesitated when she heard the distinct sound of hinges squeaking. "You have a nice, wide wooden porch and you've put porch swings on each end. I can hear them swaying in the breeze. I love this place already."

She inhaled the various mixture of floral aromas, listened to the swings, and couldn't help but feel a sense of belonging. Had this happened before? Had she ever craved for more of the moment? She'd been thrust into meetings, deadlines, marketing, and so many other business-related things since the day she'd been born. She'd been forced to grow into the person her parents desperately needed her to be. She never would be that girl—what a disappointment for them.

Heidi remained at her side and Braxton hadn't moved or said a word. She'd lost herself in her own thoughts and hadn't taken into consideration he may be waiting on her.

"Sorry." She released a deep breath and offered a smile. "I didn't mean to hold you up. My mind traveled. Bad habit."

"You're fine," he retorted. "I'm just . . . you're so in tune with everything around you."

Cora shrugged. "I have to be. I can't see, so my other senses pick up on every single thing."

"You told me that yesterday, but I didn't realize how sharp your other senses were."

"Pretty sharp. Why don't we go inside and I'll see what else I can impress you with." Not that she wanted to show off, that certainly wasn't her intent, but she couldn't stop herself from wanting to prove to Braxton just how capable she was.

The soft *click* of the front door had Heidi easing forward and Cora excited with anticipation. Right inside these doors could be her new life, her new career with a local business that had a fresh, new idea. What better avenue to start the next chapter than with a place that was also looking to prove itself to the community and surrounding cities?

The Monroe guys and Sophie all had so much invested, financially and personally, in this resort. Cora couldn't imagine how anxious they were because she was a bundle of nerves herself.

She was interested in meeting the other brothers collaborating on this women's-only resort. The Monroe clan was bringing a piece of the European life to

Haven, Georgia, with Bella Vous and Cora couldn't wait to be part of this experience. And word would get out that this resort was run by three guys and women would flock to see what all the hype was about.

Braxton was such an easygoing guy. Fun to talk with and he didn't treat her like she was an invalid. He did treat her with care and there was a vast difference. Would the other guys be as understanding about her lack of sight? Would that bother them? She wasn't naïve or stupid. She knew her blindness was considered a disability to others, but all she needed was one great chance to prove herself and she'd show them just what an asset she could be. Sophie and Braxton were giving her that chance.

He'd said to trust him, but she didn't take that action quite so easily. Trust was earned and sometimes even then it wasn't foolproof. First thing she'd wanted to do was get settled into Haven and she'd gotten a good start with her new house. Once her job was in place, she could start thinking about growing more roots, making friends, and having a social life.

And then she would think about the position in her family's company. She couldn't just walk away from it, but she needed a break until she knew if she wanted to sell her shares or . . . well, the other option made her cringe. CEO or CFO or any other title that came with running a multimillion-dollar company just didn't appeal to her.

Cora stepped into the house, the cool air hitting her as she came in from the hot Georgia sun. Heidi kept moving forward at a slow pace because she too was taking in her new surroundings.

"Stand right there and I'll give you the layout," Braxton told her. "The entryway is open and the stairs to the second floor are straight ahead about eight feet.

They're wide and curve up toward the left. Sophie has plans to put the biggest Christmas tree she can find in this spot."

Cora could practically see in her mind this beautiful, historic home all decked out in garland, wreaths, pinecones, and live trees. The true spirit of the South at Christmastime would shine through and make every guest feel the warmth of the season.

"To the left of the base of the steps is the hall leading to the kitchen and dining area, plus a half bath and dressing area. It's actually across from a large room, which I think we will use for your space. Any questions so far?"

"Sounds great."

"You guys can follow me."

When Heidi maneuvered in front of Cora, Cora turned to her left.

"Does she always do that?" Braxton asked.

"Do what?"

"Get in front of you like that?"

"Oh, yes. That's how I know when to turn," she explained. "She keeps me from running face-first into walls."

"You're quite a team." The smile in Braxton's tone had her smiling as well.

"She's my best friend." There was no other explanation. Eric never understood the bond between Cora and Heidi. There was a level of trust there that Cora knew she'd never have with anyone else. But being with Heidi hadn't always been easy. They had to get to know each other and Cora had to get used to actually putting all her faith into Heidi . . . that was the hardest obstacle to overcome. Now Cora couldn't imagine her life without Heidi. No walking stick could give her the sense of security that Heidi did.

As Braxton led her into another room, the smell of fresh paint and a hint of sawdust hit her. Heidi led her around and Cora noted quickly how spacious the room was and that it was absolutely empty.

"We haven't bought any equipment yet," he explained from behind her. "We wanted to wait until we hired someone and could get what they specified. We did just finish painting and getting the crown moldings back up to keep that Southern charm this house already had. Even though we're throwing in some of the Paris themes, we wanted to keep this old house as close to the original state as we could. There's too much history here to ignore."

"I'm really impressed with how much you all have done and how much you've thought things through. You've catered nicely to the feminine clientele."

Braxton laughed, his shoes echoing in the room as he walked across the wood floor. "Don't be too impressed. Chelsea had nearly everything mapped out. Apparently, she'd been planning this for some time. But what she didn't have notes on, the guys and I asked Sophie. There's no way we could come up with half this stuff."

Cora smiled as she turned toward his voice. "That's a smart move. In terms of equipment I will need, I actually have several things already at my house. I was keeping them there for now, but I'm more than happy to move them here. With having a real job, I won't need them taking up my spare bedroom anymore."

"Let me take you to the surprise and then we can talk more," he suggested. "Follow me."

Follow me. He said the simple words, knowing Heidi would follow and Cora would be right there with her. She couldn't get over how he treated her, how he saw her need for independence and kept her wishes by letting her do things on her own. She wanted to hope this new start for her would be just what she needed. Yes, she was still young. Yes, she had a handicap according to society, but she was a regular person and she wanted to live as such with a few modifications.

By the time Heidi came to a stop, Cora could tell they were still on the left side of the house. "Are we in the kitchen or dining room?" she asked.

"The kitchen. I have a bowl of water, some food, and a pad for Heidi to lie on. Will she let me give you the tour and stay here?"

Shocked at the abrupt request, Cora gripped the collar tighter. "Um . . . you set up a space for my dog?"

"Well, yeah." Braxton's tone almost sounded as if her question was absurd. "I wanted to be the one to show you, to guide you, but if you're not comfortable with that, Heidi can stay. I just thought we'd give her a break and I could be your guide."

Cora bit her lip, unsure of how to respond. Eric had always wanted to be the one to do everything for Cora, as if her depending on him gave his overinflated ego another boost. He never liked Heidi in his car, his house, his life, basically. Her parents had never been keen on the idea of a "smelly, furry animal" in the office building. If Heidi was going to be a problem here, maybe this wasn't the place for Cora, either.

"It's fine if you want her to come with us," Braxton stated, breaking into her thoughts. "I just figured I'd do something for her. We can wait until she's done with the snack if you want her with us."

Wait. He was doing all of this . . . for Heidi? A surge of emotions swept over her. In the past three years, the only person who had done anything at all for this loyal dog was Cora.

"No." Cora held up her free hand. "We don't have

to wait on her. I'm just speechless. I had someone in my life who wasn't so keen on the fact I came as a package deal."

"Then that person is a fool." His feet shifted across the floor, growing louder as he neared. "Your call."

She had complete and utter control, something she'd craved but hadn't had before. "Heidi will probably be happier here with snacks and a bed. Or she may follow me and not give us a choice," she laughed.

Braxton's hand slid over hers on the collar. "I've got her," he said softly. "She's already spotted the organic snacks I bought her."

Organic snacks. Did the man think of everything or was all of this perfection just an act?

Cora nodded and eased her grip. "Go ahead, Heidi. Nap time."

Her dog liked to rest while Cora would listen to her audiobooks or do work on the computer, so she definitely knew the command "nap time."

Now standing alone, Cora wondered how she'd let this virtual stranger talk her into this. Was it the way he'd been concerned with Heidi's needs? Was it the smooth way he talked to her?

Before she could fully think of what an impact this man had on her, his rough hand slid against hers.

"Is this okay?"

Chapter Three

Hell no, this wasn't okay. Braxton didn't need her to answer, he knew everything about this moment was not okay. He was pushing boundaries he shouldn't be and all for the simple fact Cora intrigued him like no one else had.

"This is fine," she replied, giving him that high-voltage smile he'd come to associate with every thought of her. He shouldn't be having any thoughts of her, and he especially shouldn't be thinking of her enough to be able to make inferences about her smiles or other actions.

Damn it. Why was he letting her tie him up in knots? He did not authorize any of these mental shenanigans. Yet he refused to let anyone else help Cora, because he was more than capable. Besides, she'd had her hands all over him. Surely, they'd reached some weird relationship level that gave him full access to any crazy emotions.

Clearly, he was out of his element. He had no clue how to feel, how to act. He'd never been this way around women. Normally, they were the ones getting all worked up. Braxton didn't do "worked up"—he did sex. Nothing more.

Braxton glanced back to see Heidi curled up on the pad he'd bought yesterday evening when he'd had this insane idea to be the one to guide Cora. How ridiculous he'd been jealous of a dog, but well . . . he was. Not that he didn't fully understand why she needed the Seeing Eye dog, but because he wanted to be the one to introduce this new world to her. He was selfish when it came to his desires and he most definitely desired Cora Buchanan.

Braxton's hands were rougher than usual since he'd been working on this house all summer, quite a contrast to her smooth, silky skin. The difference between them constantly showed its ugly face. He knew she came from money, could tell by the way she handled herself, the extra-polished look with her clothes, the defiant tilt of her chin and squared shoulders and the designer bag he'd seen—which he confidently assumed was just one of many.

In his defense, Cora wasn't one hundred percent like Anna. Cora didn't appear to be high maintenance, she was more low-key and she was actually yearning for a change and a laid-back lifestyle. She wanted away from the city life and all the hustle it had to offer. She seemed determined to make it on her own without help from anyone, especially and including her family.

Anna on the other hand had longed for bigger, better, and obviously someone with a more prestigious job than a college professor with a fallback career of construction. In hindsight, Braxton could admit that Anna didn't deserve him.

Holding on to Cora stirred things within him he'd sworn could never be stirred again.

Yeah, this was a bad idea. He needed to focus on

giving her the tour, not on how amazing her skin felt against his. He was holding her damn hand, not lying naked with her.

"You're tensing up on me," she commented as he led her down the hall toward the foyer. "Are you okay?"

"I'm good. Just thinking maybe this wasn't smart. I don't want you to trip or get hurt."

She gave his hand a reassuring squeeze. "I don't think you'd hurt me on purpose and it's not like I haven't tripped before."

He didn't like the thought of her vulnerable and hurt, didn't want to think of her struggling in any way. "We'll walk slowly and we don't have to go upstairs if you don't want to. It's all guest bedrooms and a library. The salon, dining room, patio, and sitting room are all down here. We also have a small area where we've designated a wine-and-cheese room for the guests each night. It's off of the dining room."

"Sounds like you guys have thought of everything."

Because he felt like a junior-high geek the way he was awkwardly holding her hand, Braxton slid her hand around his arm. There. Escorting her didn't seem to feel as ridiculous, but now she was closer and he could feel just how petite she was. And with each shift of their bodies, his arm slid against the side of her breast.

Man, he needed to get a grip. He'd not been this mentally worked up over a woman since he'd started dating Anna, and he'd sworn the moment she cheated on him only weeks before their wedding that he would never, ever let any woman have that kind of power over him again.

He'd been completely blindsided by her betrayal. Never once did he believe she'd be that cold and heartless. Braxton had been so trusting, caught up in love—or what he thought love was. Love wasn't one-sided and Anna had definitely not been in love with him.

The piercing pains he'd had at the time had vanished. He'd gone numb, but ached to feel again. He didn't want her to have such power over him that he stopped living. So he turned the total opposite direction and lived life to the fullest.

Hence the outgoing lifestyle he'd adopted since. He was perfectly fine with how his life was going, thank you very much. One date with one woman, then on to the next. Hell, they didn't even have to go out on an actual date, but it was a onetime event. He didn't do seconds and he didn't do sleepovers. And any type of promise was a major no-no because he wasn't about to give any woman false hope . . . not when all his hope had shattered right along with his heart.

He'd been naïve enough to believe he and Anna would have a happy marriage, children—all things he never had. But her selfish act robbed him of his dreams of that picture-perfect family.

Just call him the man of steel, because he'd pieced himself back together and had shut out all emotions. Never again would a woman penetrate his soul.

Yet another way they differed. Cora was a breakfast type of woman. She wouldn't be one out looking for a good time and nothing more, so he had no reason to keep having such thoughts about her. Yet, he did. He saw delicious, sweaty, dirty images. He couldn't help where his mind went. He was a guy, his mind was supposed to travel to the dirty side.

Braxton would much rather whatever he was feeling go away and leave him alone because he sure as hell didn't have time to be in a jumble of thoughts and nerves around a new employee.

"Your mind is wandering." Cora's soft tone pulled him back to reality. "Do I make you nervous? I know some people are uncomfortable around me."

Braxton came to an abrupt stop, cursing when she stumbled slightly over his sudden movement. "Who the hell is uncomfortable around you? Simply because you're blind? Then that's their problem, not yours. And no, I'm not uncomfortable. I just have a lot on my mind and it's stealing our time."

Damn it.

"I mean, our tour. That's all," he assured her.

Her brows drew together. "I haven't met a man like you. You're pretty bold in what you say. Most people try to dance around the obvious."

"I believe in total honesty at all times. Sometimes my brothers and I can be a bit harsh with our words, but we'll never lie to you. That's one thing I can guarantee."

Cora turned her face away as she chewed on her bottom lip. He didn't know what to make of her actions. Maybe she didn't believe him or maybe she had secrets she was keeping. Either way, they didn't know each other well enough for him to question her, and her personal life sure as hell wasn't his business. Yet he still wanted to make it his business.

Why the hell did he have to have this invisible pull toward her? He hadn't felt an ounce of desire or pull toward the stylist they'd hired. He didn't give the new cook a second thought after they'd brought her on board. Yet this particular employee was turning him inside out.

"Let's get the layout down for the first floor so you're comfortable here and we can discuss what other items you'll be needing for your space," he suggested.

Without looking back up, Cora nodded and gripped

his arm a bit tighter. Braxton showed her around the entire first floor, even taking her onto the patio, which wasn't quite done but he and Zach planned on tackling the rest once Liam got back into town. Cora lifted her face to the late-summer sun, her auburn hair danced around her shoulders, and Braxton had a hard time pulling his eyes away from the sight that literally stole his breath.

There was something so refreshing, so simply elegant and sexy about Cora that he'd not seen in many women. Sophie was an elegant beauty, but Braxton never had this punch to his gut when he looked at her.

But Cora . . . something about her gripped him and wouldn't let go.

"This house has a bit of history to it that you may want to share with your more chatty customers," he told her once they came back inside.

"I love history," she said, beaming. "Sophie mentioned this home was built before the Civil War. That is so fascinating. I'm such a nerd. In school I would always add more to my history papers because I enjoyed studying so many different eras, I tended to throw in more details. And, I can't believe I'm going to admit this, but I used to watch documentaries for fun. I know. Total geek."

She loved history? Of course she did. He didn't need another clink locking into place as to all the reasons he found this woman attractive and intriguing. She was beautiful, smart, had a good business sense, and now she confessed to loving the exact topic he taught in college. Perfect. Simply . . . perfect. He was screwed.

"We have a really cool feature in the house, but it's in the basement. You up for it?"

Her brows shot up, those violet eyes seemed to shine even brighter. "I have a feeling this has something to do with that history you just mentioned, which will exalt my geek status even more when I get excited and possibly squeal."

"Bring out that inner geek. I rarely hide mine." Gripping her hand over his arm, he led the way toward the basement steps. "Every old house has a secret area, you know. This one just happens to be so damn cool."

When he opened the basement door, he paused. "How should I do this? Do I go first and you behind me? The steps are narrow, so we can't do side by side."

"I'll be fine," she assured him. "My old house had steps, I just need to know how many there are and I'll need to keep hold of either you or a rail."

Braxton flicked on the light leading downstairs. "There are twelve. I know this because I'm the one who replaced them. I made the actual boards wider, someone with bigger feet will still feel stable, but the actual width going down is narrow. There's a rail on the right. You hold on to that and I'll hold on to your left hand. I'm not taking chances."

Cora shook her head and held her hand back. "I swear I'm fine with the rail. You lead the way, then if I trip you can save me by cushioning my fall."

Braxton laughed. "You've got a mean streak, Cora."

With a shrug, she reached out with her right hand to feel for the rail. He stood directly in front of her but didn't touch her. He wanted her to find her way, because she'd insisted. But if she lost her balance, he would definitely catch her. When her hand gripped the rail, he started down sideways to keep an eye on her. She came down slowly and he held his breath, worried over the simple act of her on the stairs.

"You can go faster," she told him, as if she knew he was staring and not moving as quickly as he normally would. "I've got the rail and I'm on step four. I'm quick with the math."

Braxton couldn't help but admire her witty attitude, her ability to practically hear his thoughts. She'd been adamant about doing things herself and that little insight she gave him earlier about not having freedom before told him how serious she was about finding that independence.

He moved on to the last step, but waited for her until she reached the bottom. Just because she was doing everything on her own didn't mean he wouldn't be watchful. This was new territory for him. He'd respect her wishes, but he was sticking close.

"You didn't finish the basement," she said immediately. "There's a coolness to the space, almost a damp smell, but not musty. Tell me there's brick or stone walls."

She'd proven how stellar she was with her senses, and she kept enforcing that fact over and over. He shouldn't be surprised anymore, but he was.

"Stone. That's why we didn't finish the space down here. We wanted it to be the original. But that's not what I wanted to show you."

When he reached for her hand, she jumped. Braxton cursed. "Sorry. I wanted to lead you to the secret spot."

"It's fine. Just warn a girl when you're going to touch her," she joked.

He didn't want to conjure up an image in his mind of touching her, but too late. It just popped in there. Definitely a bad idea to show her this place all by himself. Maybe Sophie should've done this. Maybe anyone else in the freakin' world should have done this because the more time he spent with her, the more inappropriate thoughts consumed him. And it wasn't just the thoughts, it was everything. The emotions that came along with all of these lustful feelings. Something beyond lust was taking over and if he didn't get a damn grip on this soon, he was going to find himself exposed, vulnerable, and at the mercy of another woman holding all the control over him.

"There are tunnels," he told her, getting back to the point. He watched as her face lit up and she turned her head toward him. "They lead to the two cottages on the property. Apparently, they had been used to hide slaves during the war. Being that I'm a nerd, too, I did some research and I'm pretty sure this was part of the Underground Railroad."

Cora gasped. "You're kidding? That is the coolest thing ever. Of course you can't be from this area and not be thrust into that part of history, but to know this exact spot helped free slaves . . . I'm getting chills just thinking about it. Can we walk through the tunnels?"

The excitement in her tone, the elation on her face matched his own. Yup, he needed to get control over his emotions before this innocent woman became trapped in his world. Or he trapped in hers. Either way, they weren't meant for anything beyond employee/employer. And friends. Friends would be fine. Nothing else.

"I was hoping you'd want to go through."

Braxton had never met a woman—outside of work—who got this excited over history. Anna sure as hell hadn't. She found it boring and even when he'd planned a getaway trip, she'd complained because there had been no mall nearby, only historical sites.

And why was he comparing the two women? One was out of his life and the other he barely knew.

Braxton led Cora toward the wide opening. "We left this open for the guests to use, just an extra something cool for the clients who bump up their stay and use a cottage. We ran a small strip of theater-style lighting along the ground so they could see to get through, but we wanted to keep the overall feel of the stone passageway."

Cora reached her left hand out to the side, feeling for the wall. Braxton steered her over a few inches so she could touch the stone. Her unpainted fingertips ran over the ridges as she took careful steps. Braxton loved this house, Chelsea had loved this house, but seeing Cora actually experience the house in an entirely different way was something he hadn't expected. He found that he wanted to really take his time, to let her see things the way she knew how, to be the one to show her all the newness around her. He continued to watch as she familiarized herself with the area.

The fact she could see through her fingertips, in a sense, was absolutely mesmerizing and fascinating. He didn't say so, he didn't want her to feel insecure because that was definitely not his intent. He was just so in awe of how she adjusted with her inability to physically see. Cora Buchanan was one intriguing woman, no doubt about it.

She'd been in his life for one day and he already had this possessive streak he'd not experienced in a long, long time. Actually, he'd only felt that way about three other women: his mother, Chelsea, and Sophie.

Cora removed her hand from his and took a step forward. Reaching her arms wide, she shifted side to side. Braxton stood back and watched in amazement. She was measuring the width. Slowly she reached her arms up, the tips of her fingers brushing along the stone ceiling. And that gesture brought the hem of her pink T-shirt up just enough for him to catch a glimpse of creamy skin above the top of her designer jeans.

Braxton fisted his hands at his side. Cora turned to face him, her eyes darting over his shoulder. "How much farther does this go?"

"It's pretty long." He wanted to close the miniscule gap between them, but he remained still. "It's one passage and then up a bit it forks off and leads to the two different cottages. Each cottage has a hidden door in the kitchen."

"This may be the coolest house I've ever been in."

Braxton shifted closer, unable to stay away any longer. He actually wanted that feel of her hand in his, wanted to continue to show her all around. And it was all of those wants that was going to get him into trouble. There were too many and they were piling up higher and higher. His defenses were crumbling where Cora was concerned.

She was their new employee, which meant he had to keep his hands to himself. The last thing he needed was to scare her off or have that added complication and tension at the resort.

His foot scuffed against the concrete floor as he came to stand before her. Cora's eyes widened, landing just over his shoulder. He shifted so he was in her line of sight. Not that she knew it, but he did. He wanted her eyes on him.

"Are you going to touch me?" she asked. And why the hell was her tone breathy?

Braxton gritted his teeth. "Yeah. I am."

But he didn't reach for her hand. He smoothed her auburn hair back behind her shoulder, keeping an eye on her face as her breath caught. For a woman who wore no makeup, nothing fancier than a T-shirt and jeans—granted, they were perfectly molded to her frame—Cora Buchanan was the most stunning woman he'd ever laid eyes on. And speaking of . . .

"Your eyes are the most beautiful color," he murmured before he could keep the thought locked away.

"They used to be my favorite asset. Now they're . . ."

His heart clenched. This was the first time he'd heard a glimpse of her sadness over being blind. Her eyes were her best asset, and she had some great assets.

"They're violet. I've never seen anything like it."

Cora closed her eyes and turned her head away. "You can't say things like that to me," she whispered.

An invisible band around Braxton's chest tightened. Damn it. He knew he shouldn't have opened his mouth. Now that awkward tension thickened and that was exactly the opposite of what he wanted.

"Sorry I made you uncomfortable." He forced himself not to take her hand because he didn't want her to jump or feel threatened. She didn't know him and here they were in a basement and he was flirting. If Zach or Liam could see him, they'd kick his ass and he'd no longer be allowed to interview or show the new employees around again.

But Braxton didn't care about the other employees the way he did Cora.

Cora shook her head and faced him. "I'm not uncomfortable. I know my eyes are unique. I used to love the shade they were, playing around with makeup and getting compliments on how expressive they were. But since my accident, I know they're not expressive. I know they look lifeless and I wish . . . damn it."

He watched as a myriad of emotions washed over her face. She battled so much, more than she'd let on so far.

"My mother told me they weren't bright like they

used to be," she whispered, hurt lacing each and every word. "I don't know if that's true. I mean, she's . . ."

Cora shook her head and whatever she was about to say regarding her mother was locked inside now that she'd thought better of it. Braxton wanted to know. He wanted to know why a mother would say such things. Why anyone really would be purposely cruel.

Whatever issues Cora had with her family, her parents in particular, were vast. He wasn't going to ask, still none of his business, and especially because the subject of his birth parents was definitely not one he'd ever want to explore with anyone. If she wanted to talk, she would, but he knew that need to keep things private, to hold on to the ugliness and not let it creep out and affect your new life.

The large black hole he carried deep inside him was always on his mind. One day he'd break and he felt sorry for whoever was around then because there was only so long someone could hold so much hurt inside. Cora was the same way. He could see it in her eyes. While he didn't know the severity of her past or what she was hiding, he knew a wounded spirit when he saw one.

"I'm going to touch you," he warned before reaching for her hand. As soon as he stepped against her, she trembled beside him. Her frustrated sigh matched his own mood.

"You want to continue to ignore this or do you want to get it out in the open?" he asked, knowing he was seriously on shaky ground but he hadn't been lying when he'd said he valued honesty.

"I'm fine ignoring it," she told him, her fingers laced through his. Wasn't threading the fingers together more intimate than just regular holding? Braxton nearly groaned. He was analyzing how she held on to his hand. Great.

"Are you?" he retorted, taking another risk by closing that final gap until her body pressed against his. "Because every time I've touched you, your body has trembled, your breath has caught, and your eyes are too expressive. They're bright, they're beautiful, and they don't lie."

Cora swallowed and gave a brief nod. "Fine. Maybe I do respond to your touch, maybe my eyes are just as expressive as they've always been. But ignoring whatever is between us is the only thing we can do. I need this job, I'm not looking for any type of relationship. I already got out of one and the last thing I need is another."

"I never said anything about a relationship," he countered, offended she'd already shut him down. And why was he offended? Her verbiage matched his thoughts; he just didn't like to be the one on the receiving end of that rehearsed speech. "This tension between us is strictly chemistry. It's not going away."

"If we keep ignoring it, it will," she said, sliding her hand from his.

That soft tone held no conviction. "I feel the opposite," he informed her, pleased when her brows shot up in surprise. "I say we tackle this head-on and then we can move forward."

"And how do you propose we do that?"

Oh, all the ways he wanted to answer, but Braxton went for the safer route. Leaning just his face toward hers, he came within a breath of her lips.

"Cora," he murmured. "I'm going to touch you again."

That was all the warning he gave before he closed his mouth over hers. As much as he wanted to back her against this wall and kiss her good and hard, he kept his touch light. Because even though every part of him was wound tighter than a coil ready to spring, he wanted to remember this, wanted to have her taste, her touch embedded into his mind.

Those delicate hands came up to his biceps and slowly roamed up over his shoulders. Cora pressed herself fully against him and sighed into him. The woman was beyond potent as she returned his kiss with more force, more intensity.

Braxton was never one to deny a woman, so he did exactly as he'd wanted to and cautiously backed her against the wall as he framed her face with his hands and cocked her head so he could claim everything she offered. He needed more. So much more. But this was all he could have and he was a selfish bastard for taking it.

So much for getting her out of his system. He wasn't even finished with this kiss and he was ready for an encore.

Cora's palms went to his shoulders and pushed slightly. Braxton pulled his mouth from hers, looked down into her striking eyes, and realized what he'd done.

"Damn, Cora. I'm sorry." With a shaky hand, he smoothed her hair from her face. "I didn't mean . . . well, I meant to kiss you, but that . . ."

Great, now he wasn't even able to form a coherent sentence. Taking a step back, he tried to focus on his breathing, but he licked his lips, tasting her once again, and all other thoughts vanished.

Cora closed her eyes and Braxton's heart clenched. He'd gone too far. No, kissing her was going too far. Backing her against the wall like he'd lost all control was out of line and grounds for her to walk out of here and slap a lawsuit on his ass.

Fists clenched at his sides, Braxton cursed himself for being like the man who instantly took what he wanted, not giving a damn about the repercussions. Braxton vowed to never be like his biological father, but his mental thoughts and the fact he'd lost control were exactly like the man he hated.

"Cora—"

She held up a hand and brought her eyes up to his. "No, don't apologize. That kiss was bound to happen. But we can't do that again."

She didn't sound angry. If anything she sounded . . . turned on and frustrated. At least he wasn't alone and maybe she didn't hate him.

"I need this job," she stated. "I'm flattered you're attracted to me, but I'm new in town. I don't want to have a reputation and I certainly don't want to start any type of relationship."

Braxton crossed his arms as he let his ego take a beating. Was she brushing him off? Not that he planned on getting involved, but what if . . .

No. There were no "what-if" scenarios here. She was right. She would be working for his family and they needed to keep a professional mind-set about this.

"We got that out of our systems," she went on in that prim tone he'd come to appreciate from her, though it drove him mad. "Now we can move on like you'd said."

Before he laughed in her face at the absurdity of her speech, because there was no way in hell she was out of his system, he heard footsteps overhead.

Cora's head jerked at the heavy footfalls too. "Company?" she asked, lifting her brows.

Was she really so unaffected by their kiss? She didn't

even look flustered, she wasn't breathless, no pink cheeks . . . nothing.

Clearly, he was out of her system. Too damn bad she'd just settled deeper into his.

"My brother and Sophie, most likely. Let's go back up so you can meet him."

Maybe that kiss was all she needed to move forward, but he didn't think so. She was good at lying, he'd give her that, but she'd also admitted she couldn't go further . . . not that she didn't want to. She was battling the same war with herself as he was. Braxton couldn't wait to see who won.

Chapter Four

By the time Cora made it back upstairs on her shaky legs, she'd almost gotten her breathing under control. She'd been able to fake control in the basement after Braxton had kissed her in a way she'd never been kissed before. She'd even managed to sound convincing when she'd told him it couldn't happen again. But on the inside she'd been a quivering, trembling mess of emotions.

Mercy, that man had a power over her she couldn't quite process. Letting someone in at this point in her life wasn't smart, she didn't have the energy to focus on anything other than standing on her own two feet.

And she certainly didn't have time to dwell on the basement events. She needed to remain poised and professional, just the way her parents had drilled into her from birth. She was a Buchanan. No matter that she didn't want the name or the company that came along with it. She'd left that life behind until she could fully focus on how to handle it and if she weren't careful, she'd screw up this new start before she fully got settled.

Heidi's nails clicked across the hardwood floor. Relief settled into Cora now that she was getting back to her normal comfort zone.

Just as she reached for the collar she knew would be on her left side, Cora's phone went off in her pocket. She knew from the tone who was calling. Her mother. Again.

"Do you need to get that?" Braxton asked.

Cora shook her head. "They'll leave a message. I'd like to meet your brother."

"We're in the kitchen," Sophie called out.

"Follow me," Braxton told her.

Cora reached into her pocket, flipping her phone to vibrate because when her mother called once, the woman always called a second time, and most often a third. Barbara Buchanan did not like being dismissed, put on hold, or told no. Cora would call her mother later. She'd called when she'd settled, but didn't tell them the town because she knew full well they'd send Eric to talk sense into her and try to convince her to come back.

Of course they wouldn't come themselves, because they were too busy, but they'd send the man who was more like their child than Cora was. The son they'd never had. Those words were said so often, Cora just wish they'd adopt him and stop screwing with the preposterous idea of marriage to form the "perfect union."

And if she were honest with herself, a little bit of that truth stung. She didn't like being second to a man who could've been cut from the same cloth as her parents. He was everything Cora wasn't, and Victor and Barbara Buchanan never let her forget it. Granted, they weren't blatant, but their veiled put-downs and not-so-subtle hints that she was flawed always sliced her deeper than she'd ever admit aloud. There was only so much a woman could handle before she had to take charge of her life and stop letting everyone else control it.

"Hey," Braxton murmured, his fingertips lightly brushing her shoulder to get her attention. "Everything okay?"

Pasting what she hoped was a convincing smile on her face, Cora nodded. "Sorry. My mind drifted. Go ahead. Heidi and I will follow."

She knew he hesitated since he didn't move right at first, but finally his foot slid against the wood and he moved down the hall. She was getting the first-floor layout pretty well; now she needed to keep Heidi going over the floor plan so she'd remember how to get to certain places.

"Are you getting the grand tour?" Sophie asked.

Cora came to a stop when Heidi did. "I am. This place is amazing. I cannot believe how perfect it is for a resort and spa. Women will absolutely love it."

"That's what we're counting on," Sophie stated with a smile in her tone. "I want you to meet my fiancé and one of Braxton's brothers, Zach."

Cora didn't know which way to angle her body until Braxton whispered, "Left."

Thankful for the tip and stunned at the fact he was already in tune with her, Cora extended her hand. "I'm so excited to meet you," she told him as he gripped her hand and shook. "Braxton has shown me around and my room is more than sizable. I can't wait until you guys open."

He released her hand and she heard someone

shift in their place. Heidi remained diligent at Cora's side and Cora tried not to fidget. She'd grown used to being in a room with near strangers, given her upbringing and her parents' various parties. Cora had learned to smile, be polite, and keep her mouth shut at times. Something about this meeting put her a little more on edge than usual. She wanted to make the best impression and she wanted to fit in. Besides, all of those other meetings in her life had been when she'd been able to see who was looking at her. Now when people analyzed her, she had no idea . . . and she didn't like that empty, uncomfortable feeling.

Story of her life as of late. Trying to fit in.

"Sophie told me you came from another spa in Atlanta," Zach stated. "She also said you left behind quite a clientele."

Cora nodded in agreement. "I did. I loved the salon I was at, but I was ready to get out of the city. Haven is a great little town that I visited years ago and fell in love. When I wanted a change, I knew exactly where I wanted to be."

Silence settled into the room and Cora wasn't sure what else she could say. Thankfully, Braxton chimed in before she had to revert to the dreaded small talk.

"You'd be amazed at what all she can do with her other senses," he told them. "She's more in tune with everything around her than most people."

While she appreciated his chivalry in coming to her defense, she wanted to do this on her own. No, she needed to do this on her own.

"You learn to work with what you have," she explained. "Besides, I knew if I wanted to be independent, I needed to learn how to do everything all over again. I refuse to be defined by the fact I'm blind."

"And that's why you'll be such a great asset," Sophie

chimed in. "You're determined. You fit right in with this bunch."

Cora breathed a sigh of relief. She wanted to fit in, damn it. She hated that she allowed herself to feel so left out, but she couldn't ignore the truth. She hadn't fit with her family before her accident and after . . . she might as well have been invisible. She'd been nothing but a burden to them for the past three years. Ignoring her and pretending everything was fine wasn't going to make her sight reappear. They figured if they just found someone to "take care of her" that everything would be perfect in their flawless world. She hated to be a disappointment to them, but she refused to stick around any longer and live a sheltered life.

"Brax, did you get a list of what all we needed to order for her room?" Zach asked.

Those familiar nerves balled up in her stomach. Yeah, they were supposed to discuss that, but the whole boss/employee chat got put on hold when Braxton had kissed the hell out of her. Okay, fine. She'd kissed the hell out of him right back. Who could blame a girl? That man had more charm and sexiness in just his voice than Eric had had in the past several years she'd known him . . . and one year was a pseudo engagement. Though she knew in her heart that was a pity ploy cooked up by her parents, who insisted she needed a keeper and someone to help her run the company.

Why did she let that hurt so much? Why did she give them the power to control how she felt?

Oh, yeah. Because she wanted that sense of belonging and she'd assumed family was a good place to find that. She'd been wrong.

Cora didn't want to think of Eric or how perfect he

was for her parents but not for her. Whatever mess she'd
left behind she'd deal with later. Right now, she wanted to
be Cora the masseuse, not Cora the millionaire daughter
to the world's largest chocolate importer.

Besides, she and Eric didn't have chemistry. They
got along well enough in the boardroom, but to take
it to the bedroom until death do them part was not a
good decision. She didn't want to be married to her
job and that's exactly what would've happened had
she married Eric per her parents' orders.

There wasn't an ounce of chemistry with Eric like
she had with Braxton. Now, that man . . .

"We got distracted by the tour," Cora finally admitted,
hoping her entire face wasn't showing that she was lying.
"This house is amazing and Braxton was showing me
the tunnels and explaining the history."

"I'll make sure we get a detailed list by tomorrow,"
Braxton promised.

Cora's face heated. Part of the reason she was here
was to go over what was needed for her room, not so
she could kiss her potential boss. Kissing Braxton had
been a mistake. A wonderfully delicious, toe-curling
mistake. And she'd been right to tell him it couldn't
happen again. Besides, she didn't need a replay; she'd
been feeling the aftershocks of that encounter for a
good while. Had she ever experienced an aftershock
before? Nope. Not even an after-tingle. Braxton was a
man who, once he entered your system, may very well
never leave.

Just when she thought she could run from trouble,
she found a new set of issues to deal with. Though an
issue like Braxton wasn't necessarily a bad thing.

"How does your dog do while you're working?"
Zach asked.

"Heidi is great at following commands." Cora patted her head, rubbed her ears, and took hold of the collar again. "At the old salon, she would stay in a designated area while I worked, in case there were people with pet allergies. I'm extremely careful about sanitizing and most everything is new with each client. I clean the table and the massage chair, though. Nearly all of my clients loved Heidi. I actually only had one person with an allergy, but that was only if she touched the animal. I can be accommodating to whatever clientele you have in here. Just let me know in advance. Plus, her breed is selected for blind people with an allergy issue. I don't have one, but she's the dog I was paired with."

"Can you tell us what types of massages you will want to offer?" Sophie asked. "Strictly for selfish reasons," she added with a laugh. "After dealing with these guys, I'm going to need some pampering."

Cora heard Zach mutter something, then Sophie laughed again. Okay, clearly these two were in love and if she had to guess, she'd say they were new into this relationship.

Cora couldn't help but smile. She admired people who were brave enough to venture into a romantic commitment. Now they were throwing in a business relationship as well. Cora couldn't even imagine what type of bond those two must have.

"I had a hot stone massage," Braxton chimed in. "That was pretty cool."

Zach laughed. "Seriously? You know the terms? I can't wait until Liam hears all about your day of relaxation. He'll never let you live that down."

"Please," Braxton grunted. Cora imagined Braxton rolling his eyes or shaking his head. "The day my brother makes fun of me over a massage, I'll gladly throw back in his face how he pipes frosting all day."

Cora nearly choked when an unexpected laugh escaped her. "Excuse me?"

"Ignore them," Sophie stated, her tone softer as she drew closer. "They bicker at each other about everything. Liam is a very talented pastry chef in Atlanta. He's an amazing cook, but he focuses on desserts now."

Interesting. She wondered what restaurant he worked at. Most likely she'd been there, but she didn't want to seem too nosy.

Cora hoped he didn't think of her last name and start putting two and two together. Though Buchanan was a household name for anyone who loved chocolate or to bake with chocolate, it was also a common Southern name, so she should be fine. Besides, it's not like she was in the limelight very much. When she'd been young, maybe, but since growing up and staying behind the scenes in the company, she wasn't exposed like her parents were. They actually thrived on the press and the attention.

Her accident had made news, but that had been a couple years ago and it wasn't like she was actually a celebrity. Far from it, thankfully.

"Back to those massages," Sophie added. "I'd really like to hear about them."

Cora spent the next several minutes discussing the five main types she preferred to offer. Suddenly the nerves, the kiss, the new town and people didn't matter. Okay, the kiss definitely mattered, but she'd have to think more about that later when she was alone and could give it the attention it deserved.

Discussing what she loved doing was something Cora could get lost in. Working with people, talking to them, making them feel better about taking time for themselves. All things she felt would help her parents if they would've ever opted to put business second in their lives just once.

But whatever. She couldn't make them into different people any more than they could make her into the child they wanted. They were mismatched from the start and the accident had only put things into perspective. She'd let other people control her life for too long; no way would she let this continue. She may make mistakes, she may even fail at her attempt, but Cora refused to go down without a fight.

"Our open house is coming up in a couple weeks," Zach informed her. "We plan on having everything in place. The entire staff will be here so the people of the town can see exactly what it is we're doing. I'm sure people will have their own questions."

Sophie groaned. "You know Ms. Barkley will show up with her five-inch heels and her six-inch cleavage, right?"

"If she spreads the word about the resort, I don't care," Zach retorted.

Cora gripped Heidi's collar. "I take it there's a story there. Is this a woman I need to be warned about?"

"Only if you have a man in your life," Sophie answered quickly. "She'll try to sleep with any man between the legal age and the grave. No lie. And the legal age may not even be an issue for her."

Braxton and Zach both laughed. Odd they were brothers, yet they sounded absolutely nothing alike. Even their laughs—Cora could definitely tell which one was Braxton. That low, throaty tone wasn't something a woman could ignore. He literally demanded space in her mind without even trying. How did he have such power?

But she had to ignore all the tingles and other feelings that accompanied Braxton and his sexy ways. She'd already scolded herself; now she just had to keep reminding herself that he might turn her inside out, but she had to remain in control or she'd find herself plastered against another wall and being kissed within an inch of her life. Not that the experience hadn't been pleasurable, but still.

"I'd like to take a walk around a few times a week over the next month so Heidi can get used to the place and learn to guide me properly." She wanted them to know she was more than competent and would be nothing but professional. "Once she knows the layout well enough, we will be ready to go. She learns quickly and so do I."

"No problem at all," Braxton stated. He still stood so close, close enough that when he talked, his elbow would occasionally brush against her arm. "I'm here nearly every day now that I'm not in school."

"In school?" Cora asked. "Are you going back for a degree?"

"Hardly," Zach interrupted. "He's the family nerd. He teaches history and economics at the local college."

And there went her last shred of self-control. The man was sexy, kissed like his life depended on that one act, and he was intelligent. Did he have a flaw? Flatulence attacks in public? A third nipple? Ear hair? Surely, Braxton Monroe had something that made him not so perfect.

"I'm on break," Braxton added. "I can bring you here anytime you want to come over. In fact, I'll be the one to make sure you get here for work and back home."

Cora's grip tightened on Heidi. "Oh, no. I'll work it out. You don't have to go to any trouble."

"Cora." She jumped as he whispered in her ear. "We'll discuss it later. No arguing."

Later. She'd have to be alone with him later when they were supposed to discuss the equipment needed for work; now they were adding her transportation, which would no doubt lead to an argument. Great. If they argued, that would drive up the sexual tension and that was the last thing she needed.

Then again, if she let him chauffeur her all the time, they'd be alone then, too. There really was no good answer.

"We need to get back home to the dogs," Sophie stated. "We left Brock in charge. And while he loves them, he also lets them get away with murder."

"They only shredded one pair of your panties on his watch," Zach added.

"Each. Those seven puppies *each* shredded a pair."

"Fine by me," Zach laughed.

"All right," Braxton interrupted in a louder tone to cut off any more panty chat, and Cora couldn't help but laugh at the banter. "I'll get Cora back and I'll make sure to get a list of everything we need. You two go check on Brock, the dogs, and Sophie's underwear situation."

Once Cora said her good-byes, she hoped she'd made a good impression on the moody brother . . . though he didn't seem moody to her. By the time Braxton had led her and Heidi back to the car, Cora had her nerves under control. She could handle this tension between them. Granted, she'd never had such chemistry with a man before, but how hard could it be to keep control over? All she had to do was keep her hands, and her lips, off of him and do her job. Piece of cake.

"Zach seems nice," she commented after they'd pulled out onto the road. "When your other brother is around, do you all just harass one another?"

"Pretty much," Braxton admitted with a slight grunt.

"May I ask what happened to Sophie?" She hoped she wasn't stepping on too personal ground here, but she'd been curious since she'd met her initially when they'd been on the house hunt.

"What happened to her?" Braxton repeated in reply.

"Her gait isn't smooth," Cora explained, reaching up to pat Heidi's face when her head came to set on Cora's shoulder. "I wasn't sure if she'd been in an accident or what. None of my business, so just ignore me."

"It's okay," he assured her. "Sophie wouldn't mind. She was in an accident a little over ten years ago. She was severely injured, tore up her hip and thigh. Liam was in the car too. He's physically scarred on the right side of his face."

"Oh, my word," Cora gasped. "That's scary."

"Zach was the driver."

Those words hung between them as Cora processed all of that information. There was so much backstory there, she knew there was, but none of this was her business. Still, she wanted to know more because it was clear this family had overcome tragic obstacles. Her family, on the other hand . . . never would.

"Was Zach hurt?" she finally asked, dropping her hand back into her lap.

"His hands are all scarred. He punched out the glass to go get help."

"I don't even know what to say," she muttered.

"It was a long time ago." Braxton paused before

adding, "Zach and Liam were always butting heads before. After the accident it got much worse, but since Chelsea's death, they've come to some sort of silent agreement that we're all doing this for Chelsea."

Cool air filled the car as Braxton turned on some vents. "That okay?" he asked.

"Fine."

"Zach and Sophie have obviously let the past go," he continued. "They'd danced around each other for years. I'm glad they're finally together and planning a wedding."

They drove in silence a bit more until her cell vibrated once again. Groaning, she knew she couldn't keep avoiding her mother.

"Everything okay?" he asked.

"Yeah," Cora muttered, pulling her cell from her pocket. She didn't want an audience for this, but she'd try to keep this as simple and as short as possible. "Just a call I'd rather not take."

Answering, she put the phone to her ear and tried to shift closer to the door as if she could use her body as a sound barrier.

"Hello."

"Corinne, ignoring my calls is no way to act," her mother huffed, totally bypassing the traditional "hello, how are you" greeting. "This makes my fourth call today."

"I'm aware of that, Mother. I've been busy."

"Too busy for your mother? Well, Eric is worried and he would like to know where you are."

Resting her elbow on the arm of the door, Cora rubbed her forehead, hoping to ward off the impending headache. Of course her mother would never admit to wanting to know where her daughter was—that would indicate she actually cared about something other than spreadsheets and financial numbers. And Eric didn't give a damn either. He only wanted Cora as a stepping-stone to get to the top of Buchanan Chocolates.

Did anyone stop to think about what she wanted? No, which was precisely why she'd left. Her family was in constant denial about her health, which was how she ended up on a path that couldn't be reversed. She may have been stuck living without her sight, but she didn't have to be stuck living in a loveless lifestyle where she felt as if she were a marionette being jerked around and manipulated.

"I'm still in Georgia," she explained, knowing that still wouldn't appease her mom. "I have a house and a new job. I'm actually quite happy."

"You can't seriously be staying?" her mother asked, shock lacing her hoity-toity tone. "We need you here. The holidays are always an exciting time for the company and you know we have our annual ball coming up just before Christmas. I sincerely hope you'll be in attendance. I've already ordered your gown."

"I haven't decided on that event yet," she stated, cringing at the fact her mother ordered her a gown, just as she'd done the previous year and the year before that.

"Of course you will. Darling, who is taking care of you there? I'm worried someone is going to take advantage of you. Do you even care that I'm losing sleep over your move?"

The guilt card had been played so much throughout her life, Cora was immune. She closed her eyes, refusing to feel bad for wanting to live her life, for wanting to break away from the chains and control she'd lived under for years. And as far as who was taking care of her? She wasn't even getting into that right now because for once in her life, she was taking care of herself and making the best decisions for what made her happy.

"I need to go, Mother. Assure Eric I'm fine."

If Eric even wanted to know. She wasn't even going to ask about her dad. Cora's father maybe gave her a passing thought between holes seventeen and eighteen at the country club. He'd given her attention after her accident, but that loving period didn't last long.

Cora ended the call before her mother could say any more. One had to be in the right mind-set to fully take on Barbara Buchanan and Cora was most definitely not in that mood.

"I'm going to venture into territory I shouldn't and assume you and your mother have a strained relationship?" Braxton asked.

Cora kept rubbing her head as she let out a sigh. "'Strained' would be a kind way to put it. We're nothing alike and that has never gone over well with her. My parents and I had a difficult relationship before I went blind. Having an imperfect daughter only added to the mess."

She'd never admitted that out loud to anyone, but now that the words were out, she didn't regret them. The truth had glared at her for years, so why run from it?

"I doubt they think you're imperfect."

Cora smiled. "You don't have to defend them. I wish the situation were different, but it is what it is and I'm dealing with it the best way I can."

"By fleeing to Haven?"

The vehicle turned to the right, pushing Cora a little more against the door. "I didn't flee," she corrected. "I wanted a fresh start."

"Fleeing," he muttered as if agreeing with himself.

"Do you want to go over that list of supplies or did your mother drain your energy?"

Cora was tempted to tell him she wanted to be alone and they could go over the list tomorrow. But, in doing that, she would give her mother the control and Cora was done letting that happen. Besides, her mother always drained her energy and would most likely do it again tomorrow when she called. Cora might as well focus on the life she had going for her, the future she wanted to start building.

"We can go over it." The vehicle came to a stop and Braxton killed the engine. "Are we back at my house?"

"Um . . . no. I'm hungry so I pulled into this little burger place that's popular in town. Since I had you out all day, we didn't get lunch."

Part of her was irked he didn't ask and assumed she wanted to eat lunch with him. Another part of her, the part that was still reeling from his kiss, was pretty excited he'd thought to take her to lunch.

"Fine by me." Her stomach was growling and she wasn't about to throw out her pride simply because in his mind he was being a gentleman. "Will they let Heidi in?"

"I graduated with the owner. They'll let her in," he assured her. "I'll come around and get you. Don't argue. This is a busy street. You hold on to Heidi, and I'll hold on to you."

She wasn't going to argue, but he didn't even give her the chance as he hopped out of the vehicle and shut the door.

"Well, guess that solves that issue," she muttered to Heidi, who simply breathed heavy and hot against Cora's cheek.

The back door opened first and Braxton let Heidi out. Then Cora's door opened and he slid his hand into hers. Would there be a jolt every single time he touched her? Mercy, she hoped so. She liked knowing that someone could cause emotions in her. At least now she knew she was normal.

She was twenty-four years old and had never been jolted by a man before . . . her would-be fiancé included.

Braxton led her across the street. Cars whirring by, people chatting and laughing, and one person calling to Braxton in a friendly hello all greeted her as they walked together.

His entire body froze, his hand gripped her just a touch tighter, enough to alert her that something was wrong.

"What is it?" she asked quietly, not knowing what was going on since he hadn't said a word.

"Good afternoon, Braxton."

The unfamiliar voice had Braxton shifting his body and she knew he stood slightly in front of her now, still holding on to her hand. She didn't have to ask again, she knew this man wasn't one of Braxton's friends.

"Rand." The cold greeting intrigued Cora. What had this man done to Braxton?

"And who is this lovely lady you're with?" the man asked.

"Cora Buchanan," she offered with a smile. "We were just heading in to have some lunch. If you'll excuse us."

"Oh, but I haven't had the chance to properly introduce myself," he went on. "I'm Rand Stevens, the mayor of Haven. I'm so glad you're visiting our little town."

Braxton's rigid shoulder brushed against hers. She didn't need any more encouragement to try to break away from this guy. His cocky attitude shone through in his tone and if Braxton was irritated by the guy, that's all Cora needed to know.

"I'm actually living here now, so I'm sure we'll run into each other again," she told him, attempting to brush him off but not be terribly rude until she could form her own opinion. "Have a good day."

She urged Heidi along, tugging on Braxton's hand in the process. "I have no idea if I'm heading the right way," she muttered once they'd taken a few steps. "I just wanted away from that man."

"Why? Did he steal your fiancée, too?"

Cora stopped for a second before she started again. "I'm sorry, Braxton. I could tell he wasn't your favorite person, but I had no idea why. I just wanted to get away. You were so stiff and . . . cold."

"He has that effect on me," Braxton replied, a bitter tone she hadn't heard before lacing his voice. "And you are going in the right direction. You must've smelled the grease from the world's best burgers."

Cora laughed. "That must be it."

As soon as they were inside and seated, Braxton started telling Cora the best items from the menu. He wanted to forget the incident outside and enjoy his lunch.

With two menus in hand, the waitress came up to Braxton's side, eyed Cora, and quickly dismissed her. Her eyes ran over Braxton in a look he recognized all too well. At one time he may have been interested, but not today.

"Hey, sugar. What can I get ya?"

"You trust me to order what I think you'll love?" he asked.

Cora nodded and he was warmed by the idea that she wanted to express her independence in everything, but she didn't mind letting go at times . . . with him.

As Braxton placed their orders, he didn't miss how the waitress was completely ignoring Cora and purposely eyeing him like he was the lunch special.

She bent down, ripped off a sheet from her pad, and laid it facedown on the table. Quickly giving him a wink before sauntering off.

Braxton groaned. Coming here was a mistake. Even though he wasn't on a date, the fact that he was with a woman made this situation awkward. Though Cora didn't see anything that happened, Braxton didn't like the fact the waitress ignored her, then blatantly passed her number.

"Everything okay?" Cora asked.

Braxton settled back into the booth and sighed. "Fine."

"Are you still angry about what happened outside?"

Braxton ran a hand over his jaw. Damn, he needed to shave. Being off his big-boy job had made him lazy.

"I'm not angry. I'm immune to those feelings now."

Okay, well, maybe not immune, but he was no longer jealous. He was quite happy he saw Anna for who she was before he'd placed a permanent band on her finger, because marriage was a big deal. He wasn't one of those guys who figured if things didn't work out divorce was a fallback plan. No, when he'd proposed marriage, he'd planned on it being a forever thing. Now he knew better than to believe in some ridiculous notion.

"Let's discuss what you need to get started. We want everything done and in place for the open house so people can see exactly what you will be offering."

Cora leaned forward, placing her elbows on the tabletop. "You dodge the subject nicely, but I won't make you discuss your ex. I'm happy to order the items needed. I already have an account set up at the online store I always order from. That might be the simplest way. I just need the address and I'll have everything shipped to the resort."

"That's fine with me. I'll keep the invoice and reimburse you."

The waitress came back with their drinks. Braxton purposely didn't glance in her direction.

Unfortunately, she leaned down and whispered, "I get off at six tonight if you want to meet me."

"Yes, Braxton. Would you like to set up a booty call? I'm not able to meet your needs this evening since I'm still busy unpacking."

Cora's sweet tone delivered the bold question and it was all Braxton could do not to burst out laughing. And he couldn't even get into the fact she'd mentioned meeting his needs. She had no idea just how much he'd like to take her up on that.

The waitress stood back up and glared over to Cora.

"Actually, I'll pass," he told her before she could say anything in response. "I've already got plans."

Throwing a sultry look his way, the waitress replied, "If you change your mind—"

"I won't." Braxton was done playing games. "We'd like another waitress."

With a huff, she turned and marched in the direction of the kitchen. She stopped by another waitress and pointed in their direction.

"Maybe we should go," Cora suggested. "I have a bad feeling there will be spit on our burgers."

Braxton laughed. "There won't be. Excuse me just a second."

He was going to find Beth, who he knew would be in the kitchen or back in her office. No way would he put up with the way Cora was treated and Beth needed to be aware of her employees. Had he been alone and the waitress had hit on him, that would've been one thing, but to be so blatant and so dismissive of his companion was something he wasn't going to tolerate.

Once he settled this issue, he planned on making it up to Cora . . . somehow. The peacemaker in him couldn't handle the friction, the turmoil that was instantly thrust against them. Although she'd not acted irritated, unless she was just a great actress. She'd been quick with her wit and hadn't seemed hurt at all.

Regardless, he still found himself wanting to overcompensate for the attitude of a stranger. Even though he and Cora were . . . what the hell were they? Employee/employer relationships didn't have scorching kisses like they'd shared.

Whatever the label, Braxton wanted this taken care of now.

Chapter Five

"That was amazing."

Braxton pulled into Cora's drive and killed the engine. She'd eaten every single bite that she had ordered. That was a rare experience, not just when he'd been engaged to Anna, but the women he'd been with since. They all picked at their food for various reasons—wouldn't eat red meat, were vegan, didn't do carbs, wouldn't do fried foods—the list was endless. But Cora had eaten her greasy burger, her fries, and a high-octane, sugary pop, not the diet variety.

He wasn't sure how the rest of their lunch would go after the extremely awkward situation, but Beth had assured him she'd take care of the aggressive waitress. In the end, he'd gotten their things to go and they'd eaten at the park just down the street near Sophie's office.

"Glad you liked it." Braxton reached up to pat Heidi. In just the trips today, he'd had already gotten used to the yellow Lab's head right near his shoulder. "That's my favorite place to eat."

"Seriously?" she asked, shifting in her seat to face him. "You eat there often? Because you're so toned,

I can't imagine how you'd stay in such great shape eating junk. And . . . wow, that was out of line."

Braxton laughed. His ego didn't mind one bit that she was discussing his toned body, which he worked his ass off to keep in shape. If she was talking about his body, that meant she was thinking about his body and he was definitely okay with that, because he'd thought about hers more than he had a right to.

"Can I just go inside and we'll forget I just discussed having my hands all over you?" she asked. "Because this could get more awkward and we'd already decided not to go into that territory anymore and the more I'm talking, the deeper I'm getting. This is a new level of unprofessionalism."

He reached beneath the dog's head and patted Cora's hand. When she jumped he pulled away. "Sorry. I keep doing that."

"It's okay," she sighed. "I need to get used to the fact that when I'm around you, you're a bit touchy."

Not nearly as much as he wanted to be. But Cora was indeed an employee and she was remarkable with her hands, she knew her stuff, and she would be a great asset to his family's business.

And Chelsea would get such a kick out of Braxton wanting a woman and not being able to have her. Somewhere, Chelsea was laughing her ass off at his expense. The thought warmed him and he actually didn't care that he was going through this sexual tension charged with a layer of humiliation.

"I just wanted to tell you that you're more than professional," he stated. "This attraction isn't one-sided, so don't take all the blame."

"Maybe so, but it will go away if we ignore it and that's what we'll have to do." Her hand reached out toward the door, patting along the panel until her fingers hit the handle. "Thanks for lunch and I'm sorry if I caused more of an issue than necessary back there."

"Don't apologize," Braxton scolded.

"I shouldn't have said that about the booty call." She chewed her bottom lip, something he noticed she did when he guessed her nerves kicked in. "That was rude of me and I wasn't brought up that way."

He stroked the back of her hand. "No, I imagine you were brought up with manners and taught when to keep your mouth shut."

"You have no idea how close you are to the truth," she muttered, and he hated the sadness in her voice.

"Anyway, thanks again for the tour and for lunch. I'm excited to get my stuff ordered and get the space set up."

There was no way he was letting her go yet. For reasons he didn't want to explain, he enjoyed spending time with her and he wanted more. And more time would only lead to trouble. Wasn't he supposed to be avoiding temptation, not walking face-first into it?

Braxton gave a mental shrug and jerked on his door. "I'll come in and help you get everything ordered."

Before he climbed out, he heard her mutter something about him being stubborn and not taking no for an answer. He smiled as he rounded the hood and opened Heidi's door first. The dog stood right by Braxton, waiting obediently for Cora to step out of the car.

Braxton hated for her that she couldn't see, hated how she'd been treated earlier, but he didn't think that was all due to her condition. Damn it, he wanted to protect her from being hurt in any way, but it wasn't his place to do so, and she certainly wasn't asking for his help.

As she gripped her hand in his, Braxton knew he was growing too used to her touch. If he was already this comfortable with her after such a short time, how would he feel once she'd been here awhile? The ache and need clawing at him were growing stronger each moment he was with her and he either needed to take a page from her book and ignore this attraction or . . .

Yeah. He was more of the "or" type of guy. No way could he ignore this. He'd be gentlemanly enough to let her catch up. But something was going to make him snap and he knew crossing the employee/employer line was inevitable. They'd already done it once; not much was keeping him from doing it again.

Everything about Cora had his possessive instincts on high alert. Other than the obvious desire to shield her from pain, he wondered about her family life and what made her flee. From the little pieces she randomly threw out, he was starting to put the Cora puzzle together. If he had to wager a guess, he'd say she had a strict, wealthy upbringing and this free-spirited woman didn't want to be molded into the person her family wanted her to be.

Whatever turmoil she had with her mother had to have played a part and he'd heard her mention some guy named Eric. Braxton already hated the guy.

Cora reached out for Heidi and the two started up the walkway. Braxton watched in awe as Heidi guided Cora up the steps toward the porch, but Cora's foot missed the step or got caught on something because one minute she was up and the next she was down. Braxton cursed as he made two quick strides to reach her.

"Let me help you," he said, sliding his hands beneath her arms to haul her up.

"I've got it, Braxton. I'm fine. Just stepped wrong."

Braxton helped her up, though she pulled away from him the second she was on her feet. The woman was maddeningly independent. Damn if he didn't admire that. But the fact of the matter was she was blind and if he saw she was heading toward danger, he was going to step in no matter how angry she got. She could deal with it.

Braxton glanced down to make sure nothing had spilled from her purse and noticed the board loose where she'd fallen. Maybe a half inch raised above the next one, but enough for a foot to get caught if you didn't see it.

"Let me have your keys."

Her hand shifted in her purse and lifted a gold key chain with Sophie's real estate logo on it. Odd to see a set of keys without more than one key, but he figured she didn't need anything else. There was no car in her life. Odd how the simplest things in his life were absent from hers.

"I can let myself in," she told him, attempting to do just that. Her hand slid down the door to the keyhole and efficiently inserted the gold key. The lock snicked and she pushed the door open, gesturing him inside with a snarky grin. "After you, sir."

He stepped over the threshold and looked at the house differently than he had the first time he'd been there. This time he saw how a person without sight would live. Before he'd been too busy wondering why the hell he'd landed here for a massage and he hadn't taken in much of her surroundings. Last time he'd walked in, he'd zeroed in on that Prada bag hanging by the door, but now he knew Cora wasn't that snob he'd been expecting. Damn it. He hated when people stereotyped, but he hadn't been able to help it. He was still jaded, but spending time with Cora was making him a better man. He actually wanted to figure her out because her layers were so complex and fascinating. Now all he had to do was convince her to let him in.

Braxton moved on in and took his time surveying the surroundings. The living area was sparse with just a leather sectional sofa taking up the majority of two exterior walls. No coffee table, no pictures on the walls. The fireplace had a short vase full of colorful potpourri on the mantel and nothing else. Granted, the room was small and she'd just moved in, but there wasn't much by way of furniture or decorations. She also didn't have a television, but there was a small desk with a computer in the opposite corner.

No Christmas tree, no stocking, no wreath on the door. Nothing about this house said holidays. He hated that tug on his heart. He didn't want to be tugged emotionally in her direction, not when the physical pull was more than enough to deal with. But still, he didn't like the fact she was in a new town alone only weeks before Christmas. Who purposely leaves her family during the holidays and why was he letting himself care so damn much?

"You know, I really can handle all of this on my own." Cora crossed to her sofa and took a seat, sliding out of her sandals and pulling her feet beneath her. "I'm new to living alone without my sight, but I think I've got the hang of it. You're worrying for no reason."

"I'm not worried at all. I have nowhere else to be." He moved farther into the room to sit at the opposite end of the sofa. "How do you use your computer?"

"I have a voice recognition program. I speak my commands and most of the time it listens to me." She laughed and shrugged. "I've had a few hiccups, but overall it's great. The key was finding the one that worked best for me."

He didn't know why he was still amazed, but everything about her was so damn motivating. She acted as if there were no stumbling blocks in her life. If she wanted something, she'd find a way to get it. Simple as that. If she had insecurities, she kept them hidden. She'd lost her sight three years ago, which just went to prove how adaptable and determined she was.

"Why don't we go ahead and get things ordered. I can use my card while I'm here and you won't have to worry about anything."

Jaw set, she stared in his direction. "You know one reason I moved? Because my family constantly believed I couldn't do things on my own. That I would fail or get hurt. I know it's a natural reaction for you to want to help, but I'm not your responsibility."

Braxton settled into the opposite end of the sofa, resting his elbows on his knees as he stared over at her. Yes, he wanted to help everyone around him. His default was set to assisting others in making their lives happier and calm. His messed-up childhood had reprogrammed him and set him on a different path and there wasn't a damn thing he could do to change who he was. That terrified little boy still lived inside him and Braxton could only shut him up by helping.

And this woman didn't want any hand extended to her. Too damn bad.

"I never thought of you as my responsibility," he corrected. "I think of you as a friend and an employee and a woman I'm attracted to more than I have a right to be. I'd offer to help whether you were blind or not. And I know it's not really me you're angry with."

She waved a hand in the air before placing it back on Heidi's head. "I don't know who I'm angry with," she admitted. "Myself, my family. This situation. Part of me wonders what the hell I'm doing, but the other part is so determined to do this on my own. I refuse to fail. I refuse to go back home and give them the satisfaction of knowing they were right."

Red flags waved furiously in his mind. He figured she'd let out more than she intended, but he wasn't going to question her further. Clearly, she wanted to stand on her own two feet. She was young, craving independence, and he couldn't fault her for needing to prove that she could overcome the doubts and negativity placed in her life.

"Then consider me here as your employer and let's get this stuff ordered."

Cora laughed and shook her head. "You're aggressive."

"Only when I want something."

The smile froze on her face, her eyes widened, and that swift intake of breath told him she completely understood what he was saying. She may try to ignore this attraction, but he wasn't that good at hiding his feelings.

"Let's focus on work instead of your wants," she countered, swinging her legs back to the floor. "Why don't I pull up my account and we can look at what all I'll need."

"Fine by me."

She made her way cautiously over to the other side of the room and settled into the desk chair. Even though she didn't go far, Heidi followed close by and steered her away from the edge of the desk. Cora's fingertips slid over the desktop until she found the power button and turned on the computer. In no time, she'd verbally pulled up her account and was already loading up her cart. Clearly, she'd done all of this before.

Braxton moved in behind her and stared over her shoulder. "Holy shit. Are those massage chairs always that much?"

Laughing, Cora glanced over her shoulder in his vicinity. "They are, but don't worry. I already have two different styles."

"We can get new," he corrected once he caught his breath again. "It's not a big deal. I'm just . . . speechless. This isn't something I've ever shopped for."

"I would hope not."

Cora proceeded to school him on the style of massage chair she'd recommend and the brand of oils and lotions she used. The sanitizer was already in her own personal stash. Towels, robes, pillows, and table coverings were next.

"We'll need robes for the clients," she explained. "Maybe something with the resort name on it. An emblem of sorts."

Mentally he agreed with everything she was saying, even nodding as she was speaking, though she couldn't see him. He continued to stare at the screen, surprised how fast the bill was racking up, but they'd budgeted more than enough for this portion of the resort. Everything was costly and he hoped like hell they all weren't putting their savings, their retirement, their entire lives on the line only to lose it all.

Fulfilling Chelsea's dream was worth the risk. And that right there was the main reason he didn't want to fail. The money was just paper, but honoring his late sister was everything.

"Sorry." Cora cut into his thoughts. She shifted in her chair and stared beyond him, but kept her head low as if she were truly sorry. "I didn't mean to tell you what to do. I just thought robes would be nice. But it's your business."

"No, don't apologize. I was lost in thought for a minute. Just run that kind of stuff by Sophie, though I'm sure she'll think it's a great idea."

Cora shrugged, bringing her eyes up a bit in an attempt to reach his face. "You were so quiet, I thought I'd overstepped."

Gripping the back of the chair, Braxton dropped to his knee beside her. "Don't worry about crossing the line. There is no line."

A slight gasp escaped her. "Braxton—"

"I meant in the professional setting." From this viewpoint her wide eyes were even more vibrant with dark purple rims. "There is a line personally, but we've already crossed it."

Cora's lids fluttered closed as she let out a soft sigh. "I need a friend right now, Braxton." She opened her eyes, turning her body more to face him. "I have to discover who I am before I can discover what I want out of life. And as attracted as I am to you, I can't trust my feelings. I've been through some emotional times the past few years and . . ."

Braxton shifted closer. "Don't say anything else. I understand. I have my own demons I battle."

Her fingertips slid over the back of the chair, bumping into the edge of his hand. When she lifted his hand and laced their fingers together, he forced himself not to overreact.

"Everyone has something they want to hide," she murmured. "Some ugly, some shameful. I respect you and that's not something I offer to everyone I know."

Braxton said nothing. What could he say? She'd pretty much told him he was important to her and he knew they were both wading into uncharted waters. All he could do was take one day at a time because Cora deserved to have someone who actually cared. And he cared . . . more than he ever wanted to again.

"Those curtains in the guest rooms are hideous."

Zach glared across the room as Liam stepped out onto the back patio area. Braxton held up his hand before Zach could say anything. These two were always looking for a reason to argue, fight, nitpick at each other. They were like two bulldogs at times, other times they were bickering old ladies and Braxton figured he'd always be playing referee.

"What's wrong with them?" Braxton asked.

Liam shrugged, picked up a bag of dirt, and carried it near the fat, round pots they were filling along the edge of the brick patio they'd just finished early that morning.

"They look dated and boring," he replied.

"They're simple and classy." Zach tore the bag open with more force than necessary, thus flinging dirt everywhere. "If you have a problem, you can choose the ones that we put in the cottages. I didn't realize you were so up-to-date on style."

"I'm pretty sure I know more than a man who thinks a clean flannel is dressing up," Liam retorted.

With a mental shrug, Braxton sighed. These two were actually getting along. For years they were at each other's throats, literally. They'd scrap as teens, throw an occasional punch until their mother saw, and then they'd go their separate ways. Then the accident happened and they hated each other. Now that Chelsea was gone and they'd all come together for this project, they were talking, arguing, and bickering, but overall, they were doing all right.

"Where's Brock?" Liam asked.

"Sophie took him for his driver's test. I can't handle the pressure," Zach admitted. "That boy reminds me of me and the thought of him behind the wheel of a car . . ."

"He'll be fine." Liam picked up the plastic pot of ornamental grass and carefully pulled the plant out. "Don't worry where it's not necessary."

Zach nodded. "I'll remind you of that when you have a kid who is getting a license."

Liam snorted. "I'm not having kids so your threat is invalid."

Braxton let the two argue once again over children and parenting. He'd ignore their harmless verbal sparring and let them get it out of their systems. If they wanted to discuss parenting, have at it. None of them knew a thing about raising a child. Not one of them had ever had any aspirations about having children since they'd all come from some sort of tragic, broken childhood. Braxton sure as hell wasn't doing the kid thing, because he refused to turn into his biological father. Using fists instead of words, using anger instead of guidance . . . that wasn't parenting. That was control. And it was that control that ultimately took his mother's life.

"I hear we have an official masseuse," Liam said, swiping his damp forehead with the back of his arm. "Macy tells me she's blind and that you're smitten with her. Macy's words, not mine."

Macy, the local hardware store owner and longtime friend. And clearly something to the closed-off Liam.

Braxton froze, his hands in the dirt of the pot he was working on. Glancing up, he quirked a brow. "First of all, I'm not smitten with anyone. Cora and I are friends. And second, since when are you and Macy talking privately for her to tell you this and who the hell told her?"

Both men turned to Zach, who shook his head. "Not me. I'm building a house for her, not gossiping while we get our hair done. If I had to guess, I'd say Sophie said something, but I never discussed Braxton or Cora's status with her. She's picked up on something all on her own."

Braxton shook his head, silently vowing to speak with Sophie later. "Let's circle back to you and Macy."

Liam turned, crossed the patio, and brought another empty pot over to the corner. "There is no me and Macy. She contacted me about catering something, I returned her call to tell her I couldn't, and we started talking. Lasted all of five minutes and that's the end of it."

Braxton glanced at Zach.

"Stop it," Liam growled. "You two are like a bunch of women. Quit looking for something that's not there. I'm friends with Macy. We're allowed to talk."

Braxton was keeping his opinion to himself. He'd always had his suspicions about Liam and Macy, but the two never did more than dance around each other, so maybe there was nothing to see. Still, Liam would rather eat nails than talk on the phone, especially with a woman, so the fact that he'd called Macy back spoke volumes because he could've easily texted her.

Granted, if Liam had feelings for anyone he was good at hiding them. The man had always been a bit standoffish, but after the accident he did everything he could to close in on himself. When Zach had gone to prison for a year, Liam didn't even make an attempt to visit him. To Braxton's knowledge, Liam didn't do relationships of any kind. Whatever demons he faced from his past, they were giants and Braxton had his own occupying his mind. While he cared for Liam and loved him, Braxton didn't have the mental capacity to dig too deep into Liam's heavy backstory.

Zach jerked up from his squatting position and pulled his cell from his pocket. Apparently, the vibrate setting is what sprang Mr. Moody into action. He gave the screen a brief glance before answering.

"Tell me he passed." Zach cringed. "No, tell me he

failed and we have to drive him everywhere and keep an eye on him."

Liam snorted and shook his head as he packed the dirt into the pot around a freshly planted spray of blood grass. While Zach pinched the bridge of his nose and let out a groan, Braxton went around the patio area and picked up their trash, shoving it all inside a deep contractor bag. From the look on Zach's face, Brock had passed his driver's test. Poor Zach. No doubt he was already figuring up the insurance, another car, gas. He'd have Brock working even more to help pay off those added expenses.

Brock was exactly what Zach needed and Zach was exactly what Brock needed. The two couldn't be more alike. Besides the eighteen-year age difference, the two could've been cloned. Brock was damn lucky Zach had taken him in, gone through the proper channels, and was now his legal guardian. A piece of Braxton's heart broke thinking how cold and heartless Brock's biological father had been. The man signed away his own son as carelessly as making out a grocery list. Braxton hated that for Brock, but the teen was in a much better place now and Zach could easily relate to the broken childhood.

Braxton shoved another empty container into the trash. Not all childhoods had to be broken to be bad. Braxton had parents who were married and a mother who adored him. It was his controlling father who had destroyed any happy childhood, any chance at a family life they could've had. Things were always strained, but toward the end, when Braxton kept trying to fix all the cracks in their relationships, to help calm the currents crashing through their home, his father had gotten violent, accusing Braxton of meddling, of trying to take over as man of the house.

When Braxton's mother came to his defense, his father turned on her.

Swallowing the guilt, closing his eyes against the flashback of that horrendous day, Braxton wondered yet again if he'd actually caused his family's downfall.

The moment Zach hung up, he dropped to the closest chair. Elbows resting on his knees, head dropped between his shoulders, he sat there silently gripping his phone between his hands.

"You do know that all sixteen-year-olds typically get their license, right?" Braxton asked. "It's how things work. In two years he'll vote, too."

Zach swiped his hat off, raked a hand over his sweaty head, and slapped his hat on his knee. "Shut up."

Liam crossed the patio and slapped Zach on the back. "Brock is a smart kid. He's going to be fine and so are you. But you better act happy for him when he gets home or I'll kick your ass. That kid is a teen boy and he's finally gotten his first taste of freedom. He deserves for all of us to be happy and not automatically thinking the worst."

Zach came back to his feet, shoved his hat back on, and shook his head. "It's the fact he's a teen boy that scares me. I was a teen boy, I know how they think. Cars, sex, booze. I think I'd rather have the toddler stage of parenting. I'm pretty sure I could handle toys being flushed down the toilet before I can handle this."

Braxton laughed as his phone vibrated in his pocket. Pulling it out, he cringed.

"Not again," he muttered. Why did this woman have to harass him?

"Problem?" Zach asked, raising a brow. Braxton wanted to punch that smug smirk off his face.

"Kiss my ass," Braxton replied before shoving the phone back into his pocket. "I had a moment of weakness one time and damn if I'm not still regretting it."

"Better you than me," Zach replied.

Evelyn Barkley was a divorcée who also happened to be Zach's neighbor. She was blatantly horny. There was no other way to describe the woman who was constantly on the prowl. And in a time where Braxton wasn't thinking clearly, after coming off a life-altering breakup, he'd lost his mind and taken Evelyn out . . . he may have stayed around for the proverbial nightcap, too.

Braxton didn't regret many things, but giving this woman any attention was ranking high on his short list. He wasn't a long-term man, not anymore. Not that Evelyn was looking for a relationship. No, she somehow got it into her head that he was her go-to booty call guy.

Hell. No.

"If you want to call her back, we'll give you privacy," Liam joked with a wink. "Don't let us come between you and your lover."

"She's not my lover," Braxton ground out. "And I don't need any damn privacy. We're not talking about my life here, we were talking about you and Macy and then Zach and the teen driver he's responsible for."

"Damn it." Liam slapped down his hand onto the back of a wrought-iron chair. "There is no me and Macy. Lay off. Zach sees her more than me. He's the one building her a house. Harass him."

Braxton shrugged, crossing his arms over his chest. "Zach has Sophie. I know he's not interested in Macy."

"Neither am I," Liam ground out through gritted teeth.

Oh, yeah. He was. A man wouldn't get that fired up over it if there were no feelings whatsoever. Braxton only hoped if Liam did make a move that Macy reciprocated the feelings because Liam couldn't handle any more hurt in his life. He'd been treading on careful ground for so long that Braxton truly feared one more heartbreak and Liam would snap.

Braxton wiped his hands down his jeans. "Ladies, I'm sorry, but I have to run. I have plans later and they don't involve you two losers."

"When are you going to take one of those puppies off my hands?" Zach asked.

Braxton really didn't want a dog, but he felt sorry for Zach being stuck with the mommy and seven rowdy, chewing, pissing puppies. Braxton was gone so much when school was in session, he didn't feel it fair to take an animal into his house just to ignore it for hours upon hours.

"I never said I was," Braxton retorted as he headed toward the side of the house. "Ask around town. All you have to do is find a kid and a parent who can't say no. They'll take a puppy in a heartbeat."

Zach nodded. "I know they will, but I don't want just anyone to have them. Whoever gets them needs to know how to care for a puppy properly. It's a commitment."

Liam snorted. "Don't tell me you actually care about puppies. Grumpy, snarky, grouchy Zach has gone soft over fur balls."

Zach shrugged, apparently his only defense. "You could use one to make you a more chipper person, too. I can't keep them all. Thor already chewed Brock's new tennis shoes and Hulk keeps pissing in my work boots."

Braxton shook his head. "Names are cool, but I still can't take one. Sorry, man."

As he rounded the house, he heard Zach calling out to him, but Braxton kept walking. He loved the dogs when he visited his brother, but Braxton really didn't need one and there was no way Zach would just turn them loose. The pups were in good hands, as was Brock.

Braxton laughed as he climbed into his SUV. His disgruntled brother who had been a loner for a decade now managed to have a fiancée, a teenage boy, and a houseful of animals. Their mama always said God had a sense of humor.

Before he could start his engine, his cell vibrated once again in his pocket. When he pulled it out, he stared at the screen, sure he was seeing things wrong.

He'd taken Anna's contact information out of his phone, but he still recognized the number. Whatever she had to say, he didn't care. That may be cold, but whatever. Why the hell would she be calling him at this point? They'd been broken up for nearly a year and she'd moved on. He wasn't wasting another minute of his time on her.

He had another date tonight and didn't want his day ruined with a call from his ex.

As he headed down the long, curved drive, a niggle of doubt settled into his chest. He'd never doubted going on a date before, never questioned them at all, actually. So why now did going out seem so wrong? Why did he want to call and cancel, coming up with some lame excuse?

Braxton knew the answers, he just didn't want to admit it. He was hung up on their new employee and he had no idea what the hell to do about it. Liam and Zach would kick his ass, or give it their best shot, if

Braxton opted to see Cora on a personal level. But she'd made it clear she needed a friend. He had female friends, Sophie and Macy. He could add Cora. Sure, no problem.

Except that he'd never kissed Sophie or Macy and he sure as hell had never wanted to explore anything further with them. Cora, on the other hand, he wanted way too much. He'd just met her and he was already finding himself thinking of her, wondering what she was doing, replaying that kiss in his head, her hands on his bare body when she'd massaged him.

Damn it. Braxton headed home with a new purpose in mind. If she wanted to be friends, so be it. This may be an all-new test to his self-control.

Chapter Six

"No, Eric. I'm staying. I love this town and my new house." How many times did she have to tell the man? "I highly doubt this will put a damper on your plans to head up the company."

Silence filled the line. Yeah, she'd called him out on the reason for his misplaced concern. He sure as hell didn't care about her needs so much as what it would look like if they didn't marry and grow into the next generation of CEOs. No thank you.

"Corinne, please."

Cora rubbed her head and leaned back on her sofa cushions. The only people who insisted on calling her by her full name were her parents and Eric, and he most likely did it to appease them. At one time she'd truly thought he had to be the man for her because he gave her attention, she knew they were compatible in the business world, but then she'd slept with him. That's when she knew there was no way they could spend their life together. The sex wasn't terrible, but it was . . . lackluster. She'd felt nothing and Eric didn't seem to mind the fact the encounter was short, lifeless, and no fireworks went off.

Okay. The sex was bad. Surely it had to be better . . . right? Maybe not so far as to have the fireworks, but at least a little toe-curl would've been nice.

"I do care," he went on in that soft tone that was borderline demeaning. "I also think we'd make a great team here at Buchanan. I know you have a rift with your parents, but don't let that interfere with us."

"A rift?" She laughed, unable to hold it in. "What I have with them is more than a rift. Eric, I moved to get away from the business, to find a piece of myself that's been missing. I have no idea what I'm going to do regarding my place in the company but my parents love you and I highly doubt you and I not tying the knot will hinder your position."

Silence once again greeted her. She'd just let him process all of that . . . apparently he needed yet another explanation. Besides, even if she knew what she would end up doing with her part of the company, she didn't need to run it by him. Regardless if he were to become the CFO like her parents intended, this was between her parents and her.

Loud banging outside her house interrupted her thoughts. The steady beat of a . . . hammer? What on earth? Heidi started barking, but it wasn't a warning bark, more like a happy, excited bark. Her tail swished back and forth, smacking Cora's leg with each sway.

"Eric, I need to go," she told him before he could reply to her statement of moments ago.

Cora hung up her phone and slid it back into the pocket of her summer dress. Barefoot, she stood and snapped for Heidi. "Let's see what that noise is all about."

Cora gripped the collar and moved slowly toward

the front door. She'd been here long enough to no longer need to count the steps, but she still moved with caution. Cora reached for the lock and flicked it open. The instant she eased the door open, the hammering stopped. Thankfully, her screen door had a lock.

"Hello?" she called. "Who's there?"

"It's me."

That familiar tone of Braxton's washed over her and she wished she weren't so affected by a man she barely knew. Now she knew why Heidi was wagging her tail so enthusiastically. She'd known who their guest was.

"What on earth are you doing?" Cora unlocked the screen door and pushed it open before moving onto her porch. Heidi blocked her from going any farther, so Cora stopped.

"I'm fixing this step where you fell earlier."

He . . . what? Cora didn't know what to make of that simple statement. She had already made a mental note to watch that bottom stair and not step right on the edge of it. To stay safe, she always had to remind herself about quirky things like that, but she never dreamed he would come and fix it. Didn't he have things to do? It was a Saturday night. No date? No social life?

"Thank you," she told him. "I don't know what to say, really."

The hammer pounded three more times. "Thank you works just fine."

She pulled in a deep breath and froze. "What's that smell? Is that . . . pine?"

"Yeah. Sophie sent a Christmas wreath for your door. I tied some twine around the back of it and the knocker. Hope that was okay."

Speechless, Cora reached back to the door and felt

her way up until the prickly needles of the evergreen poked her. She lightly moved around the wreath, feeling the pinecones, finding a fat bow at the top. Emotions clogged in her throat. She didn't even know this family, but they were taking her in and doing things for her without asking for anything in return. Did people like this truly exist?

"Please tell her thank you. I love it."

"She wanted to send a tree, but I didn't know if you'd want one in your house or not."

Cora started to tell him that she'd love a tree, but stopped. Crossing her arms over her chest, she drew her brows in. "What made her think to send a wreath to me? She already got me flowers for a housewarming present after I moved in."

Silence. Even the banging had stopped.

"Braxton?"

"I may have mentioned it to her."

Cora pulled in a breath at the same time her heart swelled. Damn it. Swelling hearts were not invited to her new life.

"So I should be thanking you for the wreath?"

"You don't owe me thanks, Cora."

Braxton shifted around, the hammer beating the wood once more, then Braxton sighed heavily. She assumed by the slight grunt and shuffle of boots he'd come to his feet.

"That should do it," he stated with a long sigh. "Anything else you need done while I'm here?"

Cora let go of Heidi's collar as the dog sat next to Cora's leg. Crossing her arms, she thought to all the miniscule things that she'd like fixed in her new home, but there was no way she was asking him to do anything. She could hire someone to come in and fix them.

He'd already fixed a step and brought her a wreath. Just what kind of man was Braxton Monroe?

"The wheels are turning in that head of yours," he declared, his voice growing louder as he approached her. Again, boots scuffed against the porch floor and Cora remained still, waiting to see if he'd reach for her or just drive her madly insane with wonder. "What is it that needs fixed? Don't be stubborn. I'm here and I'm all yours."

Okay, the man found ways to make simple conversations sound so amazingly erotic. "Don't you have somewhere else you should be?" she asked.

"Why would you say that?"

With a shrug, she said, "Because it's a weekend. You're a single guy. Just curious why you're here."

"Because I don't want to be anywhere else."

Cora shivered despite the warm winter evening. He was making this whole not-crossing-the-professional-line thing hard to maintain. Was he trying to get under her skin on purpose? Most likely. Was it working? Absolutely.

"And you said you needed a friend," he went on. "I would do the same for any of my friends. Then I'd expect payment in the form of pizza and beer, but since you're new in town and without a steady income for the next few weeks, I'll treat this time."

This time. He made it sound as if there would be many more times to come. Fine. Pizza and beer worked amongst friends . . . right? So what slot did she place that kiss she was still reeling from?

Diving back in over and over to relive that kiss wasn't going to make this situation any easier. *Focus.*

"I happen to love pizza, but I don't have any beer."

"Let me take care of everything. But I'd like to take you somewhere."

Cora jerked, surprised they weren't just ordering something in. "I'm not really dressed for an outing and the lunch the other day kind of ruined my mood for going out."

"Forget what happened the other day," he scolded. "And you're fine for what I have in mind. Just throw some shoes on and I'll call in our order. What do you like on yours?"

"Pizza is amazing no matter how it's served," she stated. "I can't remember the last time I had it, actually. Just surprise me."

"Go get your shoes and meet me back on the porch."

Cora took hold of Heidi and headed back inside. She had no clue why she was so giddy. This wasn't a date, this wasn't even close. It was two friends getting together for pizza and beer. Couldn't get much more casual than that.

After finding her simple ballet flats right where she left them at the back door, she and Heidi went back through the house, feeling her hand along the hall wall. She wondered where Braxton was taking her, but since she really hadn't met too many people in town and she was so comfortable with him, she was just excited to be getting out. She grabbed her key from the hook right beside the door.

"Ready to go?" he asked when she stepped back out onto the porch.

Cora nodded. "Will I need my purse?"

"Not tonight." Braxton brushed by her and pulled the door shut. "I got it."

When his hand slid over hers, she jumped. Stupid to be that way, but old habits and all that. Eric never liked Heidi and would often grab her to get her attention. Eric and Braxton were on opposite ends of the male species spectrum.

And why was she comparing the two? She refused to marry one and the other was her new friend and boss. So, no. No more comparing because both men were off-limits in the personal territory.

And definitely no comparing of the two men and how differently they kissed her. Nope. Not going there.

By the time they picked up the pizza and beer, Cora still hadn't gotten out of him where they were going. But the windows were down, her hair was blowing in the comfortable breeze, and Braxton had cranked up a familiar heavy metal tune . . . her parents would absolutely hate this entire scenario.

Part of her wanted to throw caution to the wind and act on this attraction simply to spite her parents. But she was realistic and she wasn't vindictive. She liked Braxton so she could never use him in such a catty way and she had more self-respect than that. The next man she got involved with would have nothing to do with her parents' approval. As of right now, she wasn't looking for anyone to fulfill her life. She was loving being on her own, loving how independent she could be.

Ignoring those insecurities was becoming easier. They still hovered in the back of her mind, but she had to take everything one day at a time. And right now, this evening was turning out to be absolutely wonderful.

"That's a good look on you," Braxton commented.

Cora shoved her hand in her hair to pull it away from her face as she spoke. "What look?"

"Your hair all wild, your smile. You act like you haven't a care in the world. Much different from the woman who answered her door earlier."

Cora laughed. Yeah, that's because earlier she was dealing with her past that wouldn't let go.

"Maybe it's the company. You're really the only friend I have here. Well, I would consider Sophie a friend. She's gone above and beyond what a Realtor should do."

"Soph is pretty awesome," he agreed. "She'd do anything for you."

They drove a bit in silence and Cora found herself remembering what this area looked like. Was it still covered with mossy trees? Were all the old, charming homes adorned with lights and garland? Maybe a Christmas tree in the living room window? When she'd get away to Savannah before she'd lost her sight, she would fantasize about living outside the city and in a beautiful town where ladies wore hats on Sunday and had tea on Saturday. Haven was the perfect Southern town. Small, beautiful, so much to offer tourists who wanted that relaxing vibe and charm.

Sometimes she'd just get away and drive, trying to figure out where she wanted to be in life. So many women would have loved to have been in her shoes. A guy who wanted to marry her, though they weren't in love, they were compatible in the workplace. She had all the money she could ever want, homes in Hawaii and Italy, and more chocolate than any woman could ever eat in a lifetime.

Yet it had all been given to her by her parents. Handed to her without any work on her part and she'd felt so completely empty. While some would think she sounded ungrateful, that wasn't it at all. That lifestyle of the fast-paced grind with overloaded schedules, boring meetings, multiple deadlines, fake smiles . . . none of that worked for her and she wanted to make her life her own.

Cora knew her parents loved her in their own way, but they truly had no idea how to express emotions. They'd both been born into money, not that money was a bad thing, but her mother and father were shipped off to boarding schools and rarely spent time with their own parents. Cora had heard enough stories to know that her mom and dad had mirrored upbringings and perhaps that's why they fit together so well. She just wished they would've tried a little harder with her. Surely they realized what they'd missed out on and that a child needed love and attention, not money and objects.

"What are you thinking?" Braxton asked.

She didn't want to get into the whole ordeal spinning around in her mind. "It's been three years since I drove a car." She laughed, trying to play off how ridiculous that must sound to him. "I think of the silliest things sometimes. I mean, you want to go somewhere, you hop in your car and go. I miss that sense of being able to go anywhere at any time."

Braxton reached over and squeezed her hand. "You're getting your freedom back," he told her. "You've moved out on your own, you're going to start working, and you're doing a damn fine job of being independent. Let's focus on all of that and the fact we're about to have an amazing picnic."

Braxton let go of her hand and guided the car around a sharp turn. Cora held on to the door and waited for him to tell her where they were. She had a pretty good idea where he'd taken her, but she didn't want to ruin his fun. "Are we here?"

"We are."

Braxton brought the car to a stop and Cora waited for him to come around. This was one area where she was definitely independent, but she had to admit, she liked having him get her door and escort her. Hey, she was a lady and appreciated a man who treated her as such because he actually cared, not because he thought she was incapable.

As soon as she stepped out, she inhaled the sweet, familiar fragrance of the olive plant. With one hand holding on to Heidi, Cora extended her other one. "Let me take a bag or something."

"I've got it all. Will Heidi follow me?"

"Just keep talking to me and she will know we're together," Cora commented.

"I wanted to bring you back to the resort," he told her as they began walking.

Her sense of direction was impeccable and they were heading away from the front of the house. What did he have planned?

"Since everyone is gone, I thought we could sit by the pond and eat our dinner. That way we can talk, relax, and do absolutely nothing at all. Once Bella Vous opens, this opportunity will be gone."

The fact he'd put so much thought into this truly amazed her. She was used to the fast-paced lifestyle of the city and forced luncheons with rubbery food posing as a delicacy. Pizza, beer, a good friend, and a breeze by the pond sounded absolutely heavenly. She'd wanted a new, laid-back life and she was well on her way to getting it. This was just another layer in building her confidence. Less to worry about meant she could learn to truly be herself. Adding in some Braxton time on the side was a definite perk she hadn't expected.

"Here we are," he told her. "Let me spread this blanket out."

"You carried our food, drinks, and a blanket?"

Braxton laughed and said nothing because clearly he had done just that. Still, she wished he would've let her help him when she'd offered.

She waited while he situated everything. The breeze kicked up, sending her hair spiraling around her shoulders and tickling her exposed skin. Even the air smelled better here. There was something about being out in the open, not surrounded by buildings and cars and people. Everything about Haven was refreshing and exactly what she needed.

As for Braxton. Well, she could admit to herself she needed him, but on what level she still wasn't quite sure. She wasn't naïve and she couldn't ignore this pull toward him, but she needed to go slow. As much as she'd love to just let her emotions guide her, she couldn't risk this new start by getting involved with a guy who was technically her boss. Her sexy, caring, intriguing boss.

"I'm going to take your hand," he warned her. "I didn't want you to jump."

Cora had to bite her lip as her eyes started to burn. Why was he so perfect? Why did she have to find him now when she didn't want anyone, when she wanted to break free and live her life without commitment to anyone? And why did he have to be her boss?

She knew he was a ladies' man. She didn't need to be told. He was sexy, kind, and there wasn't a woman who wouldn't take notice. She had no clue what he looked like, but she knew he had a killer body.

Braxton's rough palm slid against hers as he led her down onto the blanket. Thankfully, her old dress hit right at her knees so she wasn't showing too much . . . she hoped.

Heidi settled in beside Cora, the dog's fur tickling Cora's thigh. The breeze continued to toss her hair around her shoulders. Cora grabbed the thick strands and pulled them over one shoulder as she lifted her face to the warm winter air. She slid her feet from her shoes and stretched her legs out in front of her on the thick blanket. With her hands braced behind her, Cora relaxed and enjoyed the fact she had nothing at all to do right now. She didn't have to dress up, have someone come in and do her makeup so she could be presentable for a business gathering, she didn't have to pretend to be interested in importing talk, and she didn't have to play the role of a doting fiancée simply to appease the public.

Right now she was Cora Buchanan, masseuse. Not Corinne Buchanan, potential CEO of Buchanan Chocolates.

The scent of pizza had her groaning. "Please tell me there's a big slice with my name on it."

"I got a large," he chuckled. "There's about five pieces with your name on them."

Cora shook her head. "If I ate five pieces, I'd have to waddle to the car. Two is probably my limit."

"I'm going to hand you a treat for Heidi. Hold out your left hand."

Shifting, Cora held out her hand. "What did you get Heidi? You didn't have to do anything special for her. She's used to being around me at meals. She's not like typical dogs who beg."

Braxton dropped several hard treats into her hand. "I know she's used to it, but that doesn't mean I can't get her something. I feed you, I feed her. You guys are a package deal, right?"

Wow. The man totally got her in ways others didn't. When she'd first brought Heidi home, her parents hadn't exactly been welcoming of a dog in their home. Cora had moved back in because the fear of living alone while unable to see had terrified her. She'd been vulnerable and hated that she'd been robbed of her independence.

In the days when her sight was starting to go, she'd researched how to live with blindness. Counting steps to maneuver around her home, using her other senses to heighten awareness of her surroundings and slowing down. Nothing was rushed anymore, another reason to get out of the city. The country life called to her long ago, so it was only fitting she stay here.

She had grown so much in the last three years, had pushed her fears aside because she wanted to thrive, she wanted to live. Heidi had helped in the recovery both emotionally and physically.

Much like her parents, Eric hadn't been very welcoming of Heidi. But the instant Cora had been matched with Heidi, she'd felt such a connection and that solitary feeling she'd had was gone. Heidi may be just a dog to some, but to Cora she was her friend, her connection to the world.

She had that same feeling when she was with Braxton. She didn't have to explain herself, he just knew how to make her feel part of everything going on around her and he completely embraced the fact she and Heidi were a package deal.

Cora knew she was sliding deeper into a territory she wasn't ready for and she had a feeling she better hang on tight because this journey wasn't waiting for her mind to catch up.

"Yeah," she replied, gripping the treats. "We're a team."

Cora adjusted so she faced Heidi and hopefully would not make a fool of herself if the emotions became too much to handle. Braxton said all the right things, did all the right things, yet she couldn't trust her feelings where he was concerned. She wanted to enjoy their time together, keep it simple and not analyze every aspect of their new relationship to death.

She'd told him she wanted a friend and that's exactly what he was doing.

They ate in silence and Cora wasn't even the slightest bit embarrassed that she had three pieces. Her maxidress was stretchy and, well . . . she just wanted to.

Once they were done, Cora crossed her ankles, leaned back on her elbows, and listened as Braxton picked up their mess.

"Tell me what the evening looks like right now," she requested. "I know that's such a silly request, but sometimes, like now, I wish I could see what's around me."

The rustling of the trash stopped. "Trust me. The most beautiful sight right now has nothing to do with the atmosphere around us."

Cora's breath caught as Braxton shifted, the blanket gave a slight pull, and he stomped away. His car door opened, then slammed. She heard him mutter a curse and he clearly was battling some war with himself. Just another thing they had in common.

Fighting whatever was happening wasn't working because she couldn't say no to the man and he couldn't seem to keep his distance. She had a feeling, sooner rather than later, all of this friction and tension would consume both of them.

When he settled in beside her, the warmth from his body washed over hers. He sat close; she knew if she reached her hand out he'd be right there. So she remained still and told herself that was the smartest way to go about this.

"So tell me about Chelsea." She wanted to stay here, in this moment, but at the same time she balanced a fine line between what was right and what she truly wanted. "From what little I've heard about her, she was an amazing woman."

"She was," Braxton agreed softly. "I've never met

someone with such a free spirit and a love for life. She would sacrifice her own happiness to see someone else smile. She and I had that in common. We were always worrying about everyone else. I always worried for her because she'd constantly move from one adventure to the next. Sometimes I wondered if she was trying to fill a void left by her biological parents, but she never would open up about them."

Cora heard the love in his tone. Selfishly, she found herself wanting someone to speak of her in such an adoring manner. What Braxton and his siblings shared was a beautiful bond. While the guys may have obstacles, they were winning every single day. She wanted to be winning in her life. She wanted to overcome her hurdles and figure out exactly where she was meant to be.

"Was Chelsea the youngest?" Cora asked.

"Yes, but she came to live with the Monroes first."

Confused, Cora turned her head to face where Braxton sat. "She's adopted?"

"We all are," he replied easily.

Stunned, Cora tried to process the fact that this set of siblings had a stronger bond than nearly any family she knew. Which just went to prove how dynamic, how strong and determined they were. She was going to love working for them.

"I didn't mean to be nosy," she told him.

"You're fine. Everyone in town knows all about the saints who took in four unruly kids. If it weren't for the Monroes, I have no clue where any of us would be. They put up with a lot of baggage."

Cora smiled. "They sound like wonderful people. No wonder you all turned out so well."

Braxton shifted on the blanket, his leg brushing

hers as he repositioned. The silence stretched between them and Cora had so many questions, but what was appropriate to ask? Yes, she was his employee, but they were already so much more than something so formal.

"Did you grow up around here?" she asked.

"About an hour away," he replied. "I came to the Monroes when I was nine after my mother was killed."

Cora gasped. "Oh, Braxton, I'm sorry. I didn't mean to bring up bad memories."

In an instant, he flattened his hand across her thigh. Tremors shook her at the possessiveness of his grip, the warmth of his already familiar touch.

"You didn't do anything," he stated in that soft, reassuring tone of his. "The memories are always there. Every day I see what my life was, how it all turned, and how I ended up here."

When he made no attempt to remove his hand, Cora resigned herself to the fact he wanted it there and she had to admit, she wasn't ready to sever that simple touch. She was relaxing, enjoying the evening and learning more than she thought possible about her intriguing new boss.

"Is the sun setting?" she asked.

"It's almost down."

Sunsets had always been something she loved to look at, especially when she'd been out of the city. There was just something so peaceful about a sunset in the country. The way the orange and pink would spread across the horizon always calmed her. Of all the sunsets she'd missed seeing in the past three years, this one may be the one she longed to see most. To fully embrace this moment with Braxton would be . . . what? Romantic? She needed to omit romance from her mind.

"Describe what you see." The words slipped out

before she could fully think them through, but now that she'd laid out the request, she wanted to know what the world looked like through his eyes.

Braxton's hand moved from her thigh and she wondered what he was doing until he scooted closer, his legs stretching beside the full length of her own, their shoulders completely touching. He leaned back on his hands. When his pinkie intertwined with hers, Cora couldn't help but smile. There was something so refreshingly simple about Braxton. He may have been a bit of a player, but he clearly knew the game and maybe she was just ready for some fun. Flirty, friendly fun.

"The sky is orange and the reflection on the water is just as vibrant. There are a few ducks wading through the water. They like to swim around the dock Zach just built."

"What color are the ducks?"

"Yellow."

Cora sighed. "I bet they're adorable."

She could easily imagine little fuzzy ducks gliding across the water, making V-shaped images behind them.

"Is the pond large?" she asked, needing to get the full mental image of this beautiful land.

"It's a pretty good size. Fairly deep, too."

Cora closed her eyes, letting the picture flood her imagination. This property would be a huge draw for women who wanted to escape reality, who needed time away from the hustle and bustle life threw at them. The fact they were catering to overworked, tired women who needed a break from children, work, everyday responsibilities, was absolutely brilliant. Chelsea had definitely been onto something amazing.

"Do you swim?" Braxton asked, breaking into her thoughts.

"Not often. Back home I never had much time between work and . . . things."

Since the accident, actually, but he didn't need to know the details.

Juggling her parents' demanding schedule, Eric's need for trying to push forward with a wedding neither of them truly wanted, and her longing to break away, she'd not had much time for anything fun lately.

"Let's jump in," he suggested, and she knew from his tone he was smiling.

Cora stilled. "I didn't bring my suit and there's no way I'm skinny-dipping. Nice try, though."

Braxton moved away. "Swim in your dress. We can throw this blanket in my car and sit on it to get home. I'm game if you are."

"We will freeze when we get out," she claimed. "It's December."

Braxton's laugh washed over her. "It may be too cold for normal people to swim, but let's not be normal. Besides, the water will actually feel warm."

Cora hesitated. She didn't want to be afraid of water, she wasn't, actually. But she hadn't been in since she'd fallen and hit her head. The accident had ultimately given the doctors the information they needed to properly diagnose her, though nothing had been able to save her sight.

Even though the fall hadn't caused her condition, Cora was still worried. What if she got in and fear consumed her? What if she had a panic attack? What if Braxton finally saw her as vulnerable and handicapped? She'd rather die than for him to see her as damaged.

But she also refused to allow her past to consume and control her newfound freedom.

Cora took a deep breath and smiled. "I'm game."

Chapter Seven

Later, when Braxton was thinking clearer, he'd kick himself for suggesting they go for a swim. Nothing about this said "working relationship" and it was teetering on the line of friendship, nearly falling off on the side he'd promised not to cross.

"What about Heidi?" Braxton asked. "Will she want to come in?"

Cora patted her faithful companion. "She'll stay here. I'm sure she'd love to go in, but I wouldn't subject your vehicle to wet dog."

"Leather seats wipe off and I wouldn't mind a bit."

Seriously, what the hell was he saying? He washed and cleaned his car weekly, wanting it neat and tidy and perfect. But that was the effect of having a military father. Braxton prayed that sliver was all he took away from the man whom he shared genes with.

"She's fine up here," Cora stated.

When she held out her hands, Braxton grabbed hold and pulled her to her feet. Those slender fingers fit so well against his as he walked backward and eased her down the slight slope toward the water's edge.

She stiffened up as the land steepened. Her hands

tightened in his as her eyes widened. Her breath became shallower and Braxton wanted to assure her she'd be fine. No way would he let anything happen to her.

"I've got you," he murmured. "Just walk slowly."

"I know."

She almost sounded as if she were trying to convince herself. Stubborn to a fault, but he wasn't letting go and he wasn't giving her an opportunity to pull away and do this on her own. For purely selfish reasons, he wanted to experience this moment with her. He wanted to see everything from her perspective.

"Wait," she told him just as the water slid over the tops of his feet. "Maybe I should stay with Heidi and you can swim. Really. Let's do that instead."

The fear lacing her voice had him gripping her hands tighter and standing still. "You're afraid of water?"

Her eyes remained wide, unblinking. "Not afraid, I've just . . . I've not been in since my accident."

Braxton processed her words, then cursed. "Did an accident in the water cause your blindness?" Could he be more dense and selfish? Not that he knew what happened to her exactly, but why hadn't he tried to learn a little more? She'd mentioned an accident before, but he had no idea.

"No." She shook her head and continued to hold tightly to his hands. "I was swimming with friends and we were goofing off. I got a little dizzy and fell into the pool. I was fine, but during a total workup, the doctors found something that had been overlooked and ignored for too long."

Cora blinked away the moisture that filled her eyes as she chewed on her bottom lip. "I don't really want to talk about it, if you don't mind."

Damn it all. Braxton wanted to pick her up, carry her back to the dry land, and erase every bad memory and nightmare plaguing her mind right now.

"We'll go back."

"No. I want to do this." She swallowed, then offered him a light smile that did so much to his heart, he didn't even know how to describe what he was feeling. "I want to do this with you. Only you. You get me. For reasons I can't explain, I'm comfortable with you and I haven't experienced that with anyone since I lost my sight. Just . . . don't let my fear ruin this moment. Promise me?"

Promise her? Hell, he'd do anything to make her smile, to help her overcome this moment and live again with the freedom she craved.

And the fact that she'd admitted her fear . . . He knew those words cost her, but she wanted to do this so he'd damn well make sure she was comfortable. She was trusting him to lean on, trusting him to keep her safe from the water . . . from her fears.

"I won't let go," he assured her as he eased her on. "You're about to feel the water on your feet. Tell me the second you want out and I'll make it happen."

She gasped on her next step. "The water's colder than I thought it would be," she laughed. "You told me it would be warmer."

"I lied." Her instant laughter full of shock and joy warmed him. "All part of the experience."

Within moments, her dress clung against her curves as water hit their waists. He stopped, waiting for her to grow more accustomed to the temperature. Personally, he welcomed the coolness because he had a feeling when that dress became plastered to her body, his heat level would rise.

"It's going to be hard to get those jeans off now that they're wet," she commented, her tone a little shaky, and he knew she was talking through the nerves.

"Wet jeans are a bitch to remove," he agreed.

"The sun is gone now, isn't it?" she asked.

"How did you know?"

With a shrug, she explained, "The warmth isn't in the air like before. My skin doesn't feel the rays . . . if that makes sense."

Everything about her made sense. The way she explained her life so simply had him wondering what else he took for granted. Driving a car, a sunset, waving at people as he passed by on a street. She humbled him.

"Can you see okay?"

He smiled at her concern. "The lights on the back of the house are on a timer. There's enough of a glow I can see just fine."

So fine, in fact, he could see her perfect, seductive shape beneath that cotton. Braxton gritted his teeth and forced himself to remain in control. This evening was about Cora, not him, not his need for her. She was venturing out of her comfort zone, not looking for a jaded playboy with ulterior motives.

"I'm going to let go of one of your hands," he told her. "We'll stay here for a while until you want to venture out deeper."

"We can go on." She slid her hands up to his wrists and circled her fingers around him, as if she silently feared he'd let go. "I'm used to the water now."

Carefully he took one of his hands from her grasp and slid it around the dip in her waist. "I want to keep one hand on you at all times."

"I'm sure you do," she joked.

She slid into the water a bit more until he knew she

wasn't touching, but floating. He kept his grip on her, not ready to let go. Her hair fanned out around her shoulders. Braxton continued to watch as she transformed into some sort of goddess right before his eyes.

Cora eased her head back and shifted her body so she was floating on her back. She'd let go of him, giving him the control as he kept his hand on her side. He refused to relinquish his hold until she told him to. She was amazing and taking charge of this fear like a champ.

The dress had molded like a second skin against her body. The water lapped over her shape and Braxton had to shut his eyes and grit his teeth. There was only so much self-control a man was filled with and he was seriously at his breaking point.

Women threw themselves at him all the time, and after his breakup that had been just fine. He actually welcomed the distraction and the release from women who weren't looking for anything more than one meaningless night.

But Cora wasn't throwing herself at him. She was pulling him in without trying, without charming him or batting her lashes. She wasn't playing games and she wasn't asking for anything. All she'd done was given him a glimpse into her special world. She'd shown him how to take fear and kick its ass. He wanted to be as resilient as her, but he didn't know if he could.

This fascinating woman had gained his attention and interest quicker than any other woman he'd ever met . . . including his ex-fiancée.

His thoughts were pierced by her scream. Braxton jerked his gaze back around, his hands gripping her tighter now. Cora's body shifted, landing against him and sending the water sloshing around them.

"What is it?" he asked, not having a clue what had happened in the span of a few seconds.

"Something brushed against my leg."

Braxton glanced behind her and laughed. "Those ducks I told you about. Looks like one wants to be your friend."

Cora dropped her head to his shoulder as tension slid from her body. She literally relaxed right against him as she let out a sigh.

"You must think I'm an idiot," she laughed. "I was so focused on not freaking out in the water, I'd forgotten about them."

"Hey, I don't mind beautiful women clinging to me."

Cora lifted her face and her eyes widened just as her legs kicked against his to stay afloat.

"You're . . . you're not wearing pants," she accused.

"Nope. You're not either."

Her fingertips dug into his shoulders. "I'm at least dressed. Oh, no," she muttered. "Please tell me you're not naked."

Man, she was something. "Why do I feel insulted?"

"Braxton," she warned, drawing out his name.

"Fine. I'm not naked. I'm wearing my underwear."

Their legs continued to brush against each other as they worked to stay above water. He should tell her he could keep them both in place with his arms wrapped around her, but he rather liked that connection with her legs bumping his. He was a selfish guy, so what. Besides, he wanted her to continue to get used to the water and she was doing a great job. So far she'd been distracted by ducks and his near nakedness.

Stellar job, Monroe. Really nice job on helping her feel at ease.

Damn. He wanted to impress her. He wanted to help her and he wanted her to know she mattered.

"I had a date tonight."

Why the hell had he blurted that out? What was wrong with him tonight? Enter an intriguing, beautiful, *wet* woman and he couldn't control himself. He needed a filter, but it was a little late now.

Cora's eyes widened.

"I canceled because I wanted to see you," he admitted. "For some reason I can't get you out of my mind when we're not together. Trying to ignore these feelings is only backfiring because I want you even more."

Cora continued to cling to him as the water lapped gently around them. He worried he'd gone too far, but honesty was something he'd always valued.

"Maybe this swim wasn't the best idea," she whispered, her eyes on his mouth.

Braxton's entire body tightened. There was no way in hell she could see him, so she had no idea where her gaze had landed or the impact she had on him right now. But if he didn't release her soon, she'd be finding out exactly how much he was affected by their encounter.

"Actually, I think it's the best idea," he countered, still in no hurry to release her. "You're overcoming an obstacle, we had a good meal and a good laugh at your expense with the duck. I can't recall when I've had a better idea. And tonight turned out better than I'd planned."

Cora closed her eyes briefly before opening them and damn if she wasn't staring right at his mouth again.

"What are you doing to me?" she whispered. "I didn't come here for this."

He knew she was referring to Haven in general, but there was nothing he could do to change the fact she was here, in his arms, when he'd actually had plans to be with another woman tonight. Fate had intervened and placed them right where they were meant to be.

"Forget the fact I'm going to start working for you in a month," she went on. "I'm not in a place where I can let my emotions guide my actions."

"Well, that's definitely where we differ. I've let my emotions guide my actions for months now."

"I can imagine," she murmured. "Another reason this was a bad idea. Maybe we should go."

Like hell. She was running scared. Yeah, he was scared, too, but damn if he'd run from fear. He'd face this head-on . . . whatever this was going on between them. Ignoring it would only make the tension grow and he refused to allow that. He refused to let his ex continue to control his life. And he suddenly realized that's exactly what he'd been doing since she left him.

No more. This was his life and if Cora could take hers back, he could sure as hell stop feeling sorry for himself and move on. Yes, he risked getting hurt again, but wasn't Cora worth it? He had to explore whatever was happening here because not exploring it was going to drive him utterly insane.

Getting everything out in the open was the only way he lived since he'd been a nine-year-old boy. Since he'd seen his father kill his mother before taking his own life.

So, yeah, honesty was the only way he worked.

"Leaving now would be a mistake." He loosened his grip so she didn't feel so tense in the moment. "Don't let your worry and doubts make decisions for you. And whatever you do, don't let your past settle in between us."

"Us?" she questioned. "You mean friends, right?"

Braxton kept one arm wrapped around her waist

and brought his other hand up to cup her face. His thumb raked back and forth across her bottom lip.

"I have so many friends," he told her, watching her mouth part, her lids flutter closed. "I've never wanted to kiss any of my friends the way I want to kiss you right now. And I sure as hell have never wanted to ignore all the reasons why we shouldn't more than I do right now."

"It's just the moment." Her head fell back slightly as she let out a satisfied sigh, betraying her words. "You're getting caught up in the night, in the fact we're alone and it's dark."

"No, I'm getting caught up in you."

Braxton replaced his thumb with his mouth, teasing her by brushing his lips across hers. Never before had he wanted to take his time with a woman. After Anna, he'd been on autopilot. He'd find a woman, find release, and be gone. The women knew going in exactly what the game was because they were players as well.

But Cora was different. The game had changed. He either needed to relearn the rules or bow out . . . and he'd never been a quitter.

As her lips opened against his, he knew walking away wasn't an option. There was something so potent, so powerful, yet innocent about her that made him want to take his time and discover all the layers she kept hidden.

There went that snap on the last shred of self-control he'd been waiting on. It had only been a matter of time.

Her damp hands gripped his biceps and the slight tremble that vibrated against him had him holding her tighter. Whether her body shuddered from the chilled water or his touch, he didn't know, but he knew he wasn't ready to let her go . . . not quite yet.

Cora sighed against him, but just as quickly as she

melted, she pulled back. Her hands no longer gripping him, but pushing him. He loosened his hold but didn't let go because he didn't want her to get hurt.

"This isn't right," she muttered, shaking her head. "I want . . . too much."

Moving toward the shallow area, Braxton waited until their feet were touching land before he released her. "It's okay to want things, Cora. It's okay to take what you want, too."

"Not this time," she whispered. "You make me re-think my plans."

He smiled. He was the epitome of planning when it came to his work and his personal life. But everything about Cora sweeping into his life had made him want to forget details and schedules and tomorrows. He wanted now, this moment. Not just intimacy, but into a deeper level than she was letting him. When would he walk away and believe her when she said she didn't want more?

Not until he believed it. A woman didn't kiss like that, didn't talk in such a raw, honest way when she wasn't craving more. Cora was so alone, he could see it in her actions, in the way she kept holding herself back. What the hell kind of family did she come from?

Everything about her made him want to take his time, dig deeper, and forget the fact she was going to be working for his family. Had anyone taken their time to put her first? Had anyone ever tried to get Cora to open up and just be herself?

She jerked her head toward the house. "Someone's coming."

Braxton saw lights swing into the drive. He moved to block Cora from the trespassers as he continued to inch backward. Haven was such a quiet little town with low crime, he figured it was just people out being nosy.

"They're leaving," he told her as he watched the truck turn around. Once he got a good look at the vehicle, he knew exactly who it belonged to and if Zach spotted Cora here with Braxton, there would be a whole new level of attitude to his brother's teasing next time they saw each other. The last thing he needed was to be scolded over his personal life.

Braxton didn't care, but he was pretty sure he'd blocked her enough. Besides, the pond was away from the house so unless Zach was looking right at the area, he wouldn't have seen Cora. No doubt he'd seen Braxton's vehicle, though.

Yeah, there would be questions, but Braxton would handle it and leave Cora out of the discussion. She was his.

Wait . . . what? His? No, he didn't do territory and playing for keeps. All he wanted was to get her to relax, to feel comfortable and know she was welcome here and . . .

Shit. He wanted more from her than he'd been letting himself believe. He proved that the second he canceled a date.

"Who was it?" she asked, pulling him back from his wayward thoughts.

"Just someone turning around." No way was he going to tell her it was Zach. She'd be mortified and she was already doubting if she should be here.

He helped her from the edge of the water and Heidi immediately came over and sat on the bank. Cora shivered against him and he cursed himself for his impromptu swim. He'd wanted to make progress with her. In a sense he had because she'd let him take her to a place she'd ignored for years. On the other hand, he'd worried he'd pushed her too hard from too many angles.

"Stay here," he told her. "I'll go get that blanket and you can wrap up. Heidi is on your right."

"Thanks. I felt her."

Of course she did. But he wanted to tell her anyway. Braxton stomped off to his SUV, welcoming the coolness on his wet skin. Once he got her wrapped up and her teeth not chattering, he'd shed his boxers and put on his dry clothes. She could keep the blanket and be comfortable. Well, as comfortable as she could be considering the circumstances.

By the time he got back to her, she had her hair over her shoulder, wringing out the wet ends. That dress clung to every dip and curve of her body and left absolutely nothing to the imagination—and he had a damn good imagination. She folded the wet material up to her knees. The moonlight hit right on the water droplets on her bare legs and nearly had Braxton moaning. He needed to get some sort of control over his . . . well, everything. He'd only known Cora a short time and already he was falling deeper and deeper into her world.

When he wrapped the blanket around her, she jerked at his touch. "Sorry. I just thought you'd hand it to me."

"I've got it."

He didn't even want her to do something as simple as placing a blanket on her shoulders. She'd done everything for too long. It was time someone did things for her, though he'd never tell her that. Actions definitely spoke louder than words and every action Cora put out there told him she was proud, independent, and stubborn.

He'd definitely met his match. Then again, so had she.

"Listen, I can't apologize for kissing you again." She clutched the blanket tighter around her body as he went on. "Ignoring what we both want is only depriving us of something amazing. And those kisses were damn amazing."

Cora remained silent and Braxton felt like a fool standing here in his wet underwear opening himself up to her. But he'd told her he'd never lie to her and he'd meant it. Besides, trying to pretend these emotions weren't here would only cause more tension and he didn't want that in his life.

The pull here was beyond anything he could describe, beyond anything he'd ever felt before. Part of him wanted to blame his rush of emotions on the fact Cora was new, she was a challenge, but that wasn't the case. He met new women all the time and he'd never wanted to uncover more than just the outer layer . . . literally.

"Have you ever wanted to just break away from everything?" she asked softly. "Have you ever felt so crushed and molded into someone you weren't, but when you had the chance to become yourself you couldn't let anyone get in your way?"

Braxton crossed his arms over his damp chest, the chill no longer a concern. Cora was talking to him, possibly giving him a glimpse inside what made her so intriguing and unique.

"We both have pasts, Cora. I don't know what you're breaking free from, though I can guess. I understand your need. But, I refuse to let anyone take away everything I've worked for."

On a sigh, she slowly eased to the ground, wrapped

in the blanket. With her back to him, she faced the pond. Heidi, loyal as ever, lay down against her master's side.

"No matter what is happening, I can't let myself get involved." Her torn words floated back to him. "I can't lose focus of the reason why I came here, why I need to learn who I am."

Braxton took a seat beside her, careful not to get close enough to touch. Bringing his knees up, he rested his elbows on them as he looked out onto the calm water.

"I'm not asking you to be anyone or to forget why you came," he explained. "I'm just as confused and freaked out about this as you are."

Cora laughed. "I doubt that. You seem completely in charge and you have control over this situation. I don't like feeling out of control and when I'm with you . . ."

Braxton couldn't stop the smile from spreading across his face. "That's the best compliment I've ever received."

Cora shook her head and muttered, "You would take that as a compliment."

"I know you're scared—"

"I'm not scared," she cut him off, her chin lifted up in defiance. "I'm determined and you make me want more than I should."

Damn, she was something. "It's that drive you have that got my attention from the start. I know you want to keep things on a friend level, and that's fine. But I won't pretend not to want more and I won't be sorry for the fact."

"Are you always this blunt?"

"I think you know the answer to that."

Silence enveloped them and Braxton didn't want to leave this moment with her thinking he wasn't sincere. It was important for him that she understood he was just as confused and scared as her . . . though she'd never admit her downfalls because in her mind she had to always be strong and always be on top of things, especially her emotions.

"I'm going to scoot closer to you."

"Braxton . . ."

Ignoring her protest, he edged over, wrapped an arm around her shoulders, and leaned her against his side. "We're just going to sit here, like friends, and talk. Nothing more. Unless you can't control yourself and you try to kiss me, in which case I'll remind you that you don't want to do that again."

She smacked his chest as her damp head settled against his shoulder. "In your dreams."

"Every single one," he muttered.

"Think you could bring me back to swim once more before you open?" she asked. "If that's okay. I can always see if Sophie can take me sometime. I hate to ask, but I always loved the water and it's been so long—"

Braxton placed a finger over her lips. "I'll bring you. Don't be afraid to ask for something just because you aren't able to do it on your own."

"I don't like to," she murmured as he slid his hand away.

"I know, but that doesn't make you weak."

Her humorless laugh angered him. "Depends on who you ask."

The family of ducks circled by as the moonlight reflected off the water. Braxton would make a point to bring her back every night until they opened if that's what she wanted. This was the only place she'd relaxed and the time for being here alone, like this, was closing in on them.

"I don't like your family," he stated. "You don't have to say anything, but I know that's who you're running from and I know they're the reason you're so defensive."

"I'm not defensive and I'm not running."

"No? I ran like hell from my feelings when my fiancée left me. I thought I recognized the look."

She stiffened against his side. "The look?"

"The one where you don't trust easily."

"And you do?" she retorted.

Braxton squeezed her shoulder and ran his hand over the blanket up and down her slender frame. "No, I don't trust easily, but I can admit it. We're more alike than you want to realize. Neither one of us trust ourselves with what we're feeling, let alone trusting someone else."

Cora remained silent, most likely digesting his bold statement. He prided himself on honesty, but more important, he wanted her to see that while he may be leery, he wasn't afraid to take a chance when fate smacked him in the face with an opportunity.

"Tell me about your fiancée."

Her request had him gritting his teeth, ready to refuse, but if the only way to get her to open up was to do so himself, he'd lay it out there. Hell, what did he have to lose at this point?

"Anna and I dated for two years when we got engaged. She came from a family with money, but they were impressed with me because I'm a college professor. I didn't give a shit what they thought, but it was important to her to have their approval. Looking back now I should've seen the red flag waving in my face."

When Cora remained quiet, but still rested her

head on his shoulder, he continued. Once he'd started talking about this so openly, it wasn't as hard as he'd thought.

"At the time I was saving for a house. I figured we'd have Zach build it, that way we could have exactly what we wanted."

"And she was cheating on you the whole time?" Cora guessed.

"Not the whole time." Admitting he'd not been good enough was a tough pill to swallow. Male pride and all that. "I have no idea why she cheated, to be honest. I know what she said, but I just kept thinking it was my meager salary and my background."

"How old were you when you came to live with the Monroes?"

Braxton swallowed. This was not a territory he was going to get into. Rehashing his broken engagement was enough emotional angst for one night . . . for one lifetime, actually. Discussing the time before he came to live with the Monroes was more than anyone wanted to hear. Oh, she'd asked about his past, but revealing the ugly truth wasn't something she was ready for.

"I was nine." He shifted so he could fully wrap both arms around her. "What about you?"

"What about me?"

The breeze was drying her hair and every now and then a strand would lift in the air and tickle the side of his face. He smoothed down her wayward strands with one hand before holding her once again.

"I shared a bit of my baggage."

Cora shrugged beneath the blanket. "Doesn't mean I have to open mine."

No, it didn't. But a piece of Braxton ached for her

to and never before had he been so ready to discover what made up a woman. This woman.

"What color are your eyes?" she asked.

He smiled in the darkness. "Brown."

"And your hair?"

"Also brown. Basic and boring. Nothing too exciting."

Without turning her head to face him, she brought up one hand and stroked over his stubbled jaw. "Nothing boring and basic about you, Braxton Monroe. I'm just envisioning what you look like. I needed to know."

He never wanted those fingertips to stop touching him. "You have an image now?" he asked, his voice low and rough.

Her fingers slid over his mouth and Braxton stopped breathing. She. Was. Killing. Him.

"I have a beautiful image," she whispered as she tucked her hand back into the blanket. "Can we stay here? Just a little longer."

He'd stay here all night, holding her just like this, if that's what she wanted. In response, he tucked her tighter against his side and kissed the top of her head.

A part of him regretted taking this semester off from the college to help with the resort. He could use that extra out to take his mind away from all that was going on. He needed to focus on something besides his worry for the success of his late sister's dream and the new whirlwind that blew into town and left him breathless.

His lips were still tingling and he knew they wouldn't stop anytime soon.

Braxton held Cora tighter, not quite ready to let the moment go. But he didn't pursue her past any longer. If she ever wanted to open up, he just hoped she'd come to him. He hoped she'd trust him enough to let him in, to let him protect her from whatever it was she was afraid of.

And the fact he wanted to get in that deep with her was revealing. Clearly, he'd hit a stopping point in searching for something to fill that empty void in his life. Whatever the hell that meant was something he'd have to analyze later. Much later.

Chapter Eight

"You don't like them?"

The hurt in Sophie's tone had Braxton staring at Zach, waiting for his moronic brother to reassure his fiancée that the pamphlets she'd had printed—all four thousand of them—were beautiful and perfect for the image the resort wanted to portray.

"They're just . . . so pink."

Sophie rolled her eyes and snatched the glossy ad from Zach's hand. "They're geared toward women. And they're not just pink. They're champagne with a tone-on-tone pattern."

Braxton reached across Zach's kitchen table and grabbed one from the box. Indeed, they were, uh, champagne.

"I think they're just what would attract women here," Braxton stated.

Zach pushed away from the table, leaned back in his chair, and crossed his arms. "Stop sucking up. We already fed you dinner."

"If you'd think like a business owner trying to draw in women and not a grouch for once, you'd see that

Sophie hit this dead-on." Braxton turned the pamphlet toward Zach. "The picture of the house on the front in the center with the name above and hours and Web site below are simple, but it's eye-catching the way the scrolling pattern frames it all."

"And we already have the holiday fliers out, but these will be on display at the open house so people can take it with them."

Zach glared across the table. "They're fine. I'm just surprised. I wouldn't have picked pink."

"Champagne," Sophie and Braxton stated at the same time. Sophie shot him a wink and a grin.

Throwing his arms in the air, Zach stood from the table. "You two win. I'm not arguing about shades of pink. If we have guests, then that's all I care about."

Sophie's smile widened. "Actually, I already booked our first group this morning."

Braxton sat up straighter in his chair. "You did?"

With an enthusiastic nod, Sophie said, "I did. A group of ladies from Charleston are coming for a re-treat at the first of the year. They quilt or something. Anyway, one of them said they'd been searching the Savannah area and spotted our site."

"Glad I got that site up and running last week," Braxton stated.

"They booked the two guest cottages." Sophie clasped her hands together as tears pricked her eyes. "Chelsea would be so excited. I wish she was here to see all of this coming together."

Zach muttered a curse and crossed around the edge of the table to Sophie. Braxton had never seen his brother show any emotion toward anyone except Sophie and then Brock once they took him in. Braxton knew everyone had a weakness and Zach had finally found his.

"Don't cry." Zach bent down and took Sophie's hands in his scarred ones. "Chelsea would hate if you were upset, especially because of her."

With a sniff, Sophie nodded. "I know. It just hits me harder sometimes."

Yeah, Braxton knew that feeling. He'd trade off anything he had to have his sister back. She'd be giving him hell right now for being so tied up in knots over Cora, but once her teasing was over, she'd offer sound advice, hug him, and then she'd want to watch some ridiculous movie. That was their thing. The more insane and stupid the movie, the better. B-list all the way for their movie nights.

"Damn, are you going to lose it on me, too?" Zach asked.

Braxton flipped Zach a silent response.

Zach returned the gesture, then tipped his head. "Hey, what were you doing here the other night?"

"Just sitting out by the pond." Not a lie. "What were you doing?"

"I didn't remember setting the alarm system, but when I pulled in and saw your SUV, I figured you would make sure things were locked up."

Yeah, locking up the old house hadn't been on his mind. Getting Cora to open up, getting her to relax and stop fighting all the emotions she didn't want had been his top priority. Of course then his priorities had shifted when her dress had been all clingy to her curvy body and he'd had to pull up every ounce of willpower he'd ever possessed.

"When we officially open, I hope you're not going to continue to take your dates back there."

Sophie smacked Zach in the chest. "Leave him alone."

Zach raised his brows, jerking his attention toward her. "I don't want our guests to see my brother entertaining."

"You have no idea what I was doing so shut the hell up." Fine, he was entertaining, but not in the way Zach thought and it was none of his business anyway.

Before he could say anything else, Braxton was saved by the doorbell, which sent the pups into a barking frenzy, scrambling to the front door. They slid over the hardwood, bumping into one another in a mad rush to greet the visitor.

Zach came to his feet, placing a kiss on Sophie's forehead. "That's Macy. She said she'd swing by once the store closed."

Braxton picked up his dirty plate from dinner and set it in the sink. When he went back to get the others, Sophie reached for her own.

"I'll get them."

"No, you cooked. I can clean up."

Braxton actually liked coming by to eat in his old childhood home. He was glad Zach hadn't sold it months ago when he'd wanted to. Zach had worried about finances with getting the resort started, but once Liam came on board, they all tied their funds together, took out a loan, and went on their way. Sophie had just sold her home, too, so she invested that money back into the resort and moved in with Zach.

A team effort. It was as if Chelsea's hands were all over this project in getting everyone working together and forcing them to forge a deeper bond.

A decade after the wreck that left all of them scarred in one way or another, the peacemaker in Braxton was relieved that they were all starting a new life. But the circumstances around Chelsea's death were what brought them together and Braxton really wished they hadn't had to wait so long to come to terms with the past. Chelsea had wanted them all to just forgive and move on, but she'd died before she could see her wish come to fruition.

Their free-spirited sister had gone off on a ski trip with some friends and died in a freak accident when she'd hit her head after a fall down the slopes. Chelsea wouldn't have wanted to go any other way than having fun and living life to the fullest. Braxton just wished like hell she could've lived that life much longer.

Macy's laughter and cooing at the puppies filled the house and pulled him from his thoughts as he loaded the dishwasher. Soon the pups all slid in on the hard-wood floors and only two of them managed to stop in time—the others all plowed into the cabinets.

"They're getting so big," Macy exclaimed as she bent down to pet the cluster of pups that congregated around her ankles. They were bouncing all over the kitchen at the new guest. "Where's the mommy?"

"She's on the back porch," Zach stated. "We had her spayed, so she's taking a much-needed break."

Macy came to her feet and glanced around the kitchen. "Am I interrupting dinner?"

"We just finished." Sophie gathered up one of the puppies and tried to pet him, but he wiggled right back down on the floor. "We have plenty left over. Are you hungry?"

"Oh, no. Dad is cooking for me tonight. I just ran by to talk to Zach about the flooring."

"Did you get the samples you wanted?" he asked.

Braxton shut the dishwasher and hit the start button. When he turned to lean against the counter, one of the pups, Hulk if he was guessing correctly, started chewing on the lace of his sneaker.

"They're in my truck," Macy told him. "I have several. Would you just want to come out and look or do you want me to bring them in?"

Braxton reached down and plucked up the bundle of fur. Damn, he loved these dogs. He was still on the fence about taking one for his house. He was gone so much when school was in session and since he lived alone, he didn't think it was fair to the animal to be lonely all day.

"I'll come out." Zach turned to Braxton. "Can you check on Brock? He was having a hell of a time with his algebra."

Even though Braxton taught economics and history, math was his first love. "Sure thing. He up in his room?"

"Yeah. He'd rather have you help him than me. We fight."

Braxton snorted. "Imagine that. You two were cut from the same cloth, just years apart."

Macy and Sophie tried to cover their laughter, but Zach scowled at both of them. "C'mon, Macy, before I forget we're friends."

"Relax," she told him, as she followed him toward the door. "It wouldn't be a proper gathering if someone didn't get picked on."

"It's usually me," Zach grumbled. "I'm just used to Liam doing the picking."

Macy patted his shoulder and threw Sophie a smile. "We'll be right back, though I can't guarantee his mood because I have a lot of samples and I can't make up my mind."

Sophie shrugged. "I'm used to his moodiness."

"If you two are done discussing me like I can't hear

you, I'd like to look at this shit sometime today," Zach called from the living room.

Braxton shook his head. "I'm out of this. I'll be upstairs with Brock discussing girls and cars."

"Algebra. You'll be discussing algebra," Sophie corrected.

Braxton nodded. "Yeah, some of that, too."

Braxton headed down the hall, passing the new master bedroom Zach had converted so Sophie didn't have to do so many steps because of her limp. When he reached the top of the steps, he smiled. He didn't know Brock had taken his old room. Lightly tapping on the door, Braxton eased it open with his knuckles.

Across the room, Brock sat on his bed, back against the old familiar headboard. With a notebook open on his lap and the textbook at his side, Brock looked up and Braxton had to hold back a chuckle. The pleading look in the teen's eyes was a mirror image of when Braxton had been a teen.

"If it helps, I hated school, too."

Brock tossed his pencil on the notebook and sighed. "Then you're stupid because now you work there."

After crossing the spacious bedroom, Braxton sat on the edge of the bed. Spinning the textbook around to see what they were dealing with, Braxton replied, "It's a bit different being the professor and not a student."

"When will I ever use this?"

"Probably never, but that's life. We do things we don't like because in the end it's worth it. You're almost done with high school. Given any thought to college?"

Brock groaned, dropping his head back against the

headboard with a *thunk*. "I want to be done with all school."

"That's your choice," Braxton said easily, knowing Zach and Sophie would probably handle this topic differently, but he was the one here now. "You could always get a job paying minimum wage. Hard to save money for a house or a car chicks love doing that, but I suppose you could. Actually, as long as you get a job and work hard, no matter what it is, that's all that matters. Just take pride in it and anyone would be lucky to have you."

"I've actually thought about the army."

Surprised, Braxton sat back. "Really? I think that would be a great choice for you. Have you talked to Zach?"

The teen shook his head and glanced back down to his notebook. "My dad always told me a pussy like me wouldn't make it through boot camp so I haven't thought about it for a while."

Braxton wanted to get ahold of that deadbeat dad and throat-punch him . . . amongst other things. No way in hell would Brock not make it with the right support system, and with the Monroe clan all backing him, there was no way this determined teen would fail.

"If the army is something you want, then you'll make it." Braxton eased forward and patted the boy's bent knee. "Don't let your dad continue to control you. He's not around and Zach and Sophie have worked their asses off to help you. They'll support your decision."

Brock gave a half shrug. "Maybe."

The boy would learn trust, eventually. Man, weren't they a skeptical bunch? In some form or another, each one of them, and he was lumping in Cora with this, had issues with giving any control over to someone else. In trusting another person, you were, in a sense, letting them control a portion of your heart.

Braxton would work on Brock and Cora. They both needed love, and they both had problems that he technically knew nothing about. He had a feeling about both of them, but he wanted them to open up before he said anything.

"Let me see what you have down," Braxton stated, nodding to Brock's paper.

Brock shoved the notebook toward Braxton. After several minutes of checking the work, Braxton knew how to approach this frustrating topic. After an hour had passed, Brock didn't look like he was ready to give up completely.

"Understand that better now?" Braxton asked.

When Brock nodded with a half smile, Braxton knew the boy would be fine with his upcoming test.

When Braxton came to his feet and moved to the door, he turned back. "Two more things. Talk to Zach. He's more understanding than you think and he'd be all for you joining the army if that's what you want."

"What's the other thing?"

Braxton smiled. "Call me when you know your grade on that test. If you get below a ninety, you have to hang the porch swings at the new cottages."

Brock laughed. "And if I get above a ninety?"

"Then I'll do them. A little motivation for you to try your hardest. Those hangers are a bitch to get in sometimes."

"Deal."

Braxton loved the wide smile on the young boy's face. It was only months ago that he'd been a runaway, hiding in the basement of the abandoned home and discovered during the renovations.

As Braxton headed back downstairs, he felt he'd

made headway with the boy. It would be a day at a time, just like anything else worth working on. Eventually Brock would see this family was it for him. That they would have his back and support him, that they would be there for him no matter what he feared or worried about.

Braxton found himself wanting to see Cora, but he couldn't push her any more than he had. She'd come around too. He just had to be patient, let her call the shots and stay in charge of her emotions. Pushing someone like Cora would only backfire and explode in his face.

Braxton had learned patience the hard way . . . at the hands of his biological father. He could handle whatever life threw at him. He may not like it, but there was a feeling deep in his gut that told him Cora would be worth whatever he had to face and whatever obstacle he had to battle.

"You could at least hand me the damn drill instead of sitting there looking smug."

Braxton stood on his ladder and stared down to Brock, who had aced his algebra exam. This was one bet Braxton didn't mind losing. He was proud of the boy and Zach and Sophie were beyond thrilled he'd brought his D-minus up to an A-minus this school year.

Brock leaned against the newly installed post and shrugged as he popped another chip into his mouth. "Don't be a sore loser. I'm the supervisor."

"Supervisor my ass," Braxton muttered as he climbed down to get the drill from his tool bag. "You know, you may have to put down that bag and help lift the other end of the swing when I'm ready."

"If nobody else stops by I will. I was sort of holding

out that I'd only be lifting this bag of chips." He crunched on another chip as crumbs rained down all over his tee. "Zach said he'd be by. He was taking Milly to get her stitches out."

Braxton managed to get both hooks screwed into the wood above the porch, without any help from Brock. The teen continued to litter the new porch floor with crumbs, but Braxton wasn't going to say a word. The world Brock came from had been dark and ugly. If he wanted to eat chips without a care in the world, he'd more than earned that right.

"Well, looks like you and me." Braxton climbed down from the ladder and glanced toward the edge of the porch. "I'll grab this other ladder and you can get one end and I'll get the other. We'll have this baby up in no time."

Brock grumbled as he came to his feet and brushed the crumbs from his shirt. "There better be some hot chicks that come here."

Setting up the other ladder by the edge of the porch, Braxton laughed. "Well, you'll be in school and I doubt many teenagers will be coming through. But when you're older maybe you can enjoy the scenery."

Braxton grabbed the chain for the swing and waited until Brock had his end before he started up the ladder. "Count five links down. That should be the right height."

Sophie's car pulled up the drive. Braxton glanced that way, then back to Brock's work. Once the swing was set, Braxton stared at how it was positioned.

"That's still too high," he told Brock. "Let it down one link and then let's see."

Just as he settled the swing back into the hook, he heard familiar laughter that punched him straight in the gut. He hadn't seen or heard from Cora in four days—not since their escapade in the pond. He'd wanted to call her, to swing by and talk to her. He'd ached to just see her face, hear her voice. He'd been preoccupied with a former student who had texted him over a class he'd been having issues with. Braxton had tutored him a few hours and finally found out the issues at home were the root of the problem.

Braxton offered his advice, but whether the kid, who was legally an adult, wanted to take it was up to him. Braxton would check in later in the week to see how the kid was doing. But for now, he had a woman tying him up in knots.

He hadn't felt this way about anyone . . . ever. The full-on attack of unexpected emotions since Cora had stepped into his life was something he had no clue how to handle. So far he was doing a stellar job of screwing everything up.

Today she wore another of those little sundresses, this time with a cardigan and flats. Auburn hair tumbled down her back. There was so much he wanted to ask her, so much he wanted to learn about her life. She'd been so determined to be alone and do everything for herself, but how did she get groceries? How did she do her laundry? He had the most random questions that she'd find ridiculous, but the longer she was around, the more he wanted to know every single detail.

"Can you stare at that lady later?" Brock asked. "We're working here."

"That lady is our new masseuse and I wasn't admiring her."

He wasn't. He'd been fantasizing. There was a vast difference, but he still didn't want to be called on it by a teenager.

"Is that her dog?" Brock asked.

"Her Seeing Eye dog."

Braxton glanced down at the swing once more, pleased now with how it hung. Hopefully, it would last for years and years and he wouldn't have to do this again.

"She's blind?" Brock asked, not bothering to hide the shock in his tone.

"Yes and don't make a big deal about it." Defending her came natural, he didn't even have to think about it anymore. "She's amazing at what she does."

Braxton hoped Brock grasped the fact that you could do anything in life you wanted if the determination and will to work was there. Obstacles were a fact, but how you dealt with them showed true spirit and drive. It also set you apart from the rest and Cora was definitely in a class all her own.

Braxton started to step from the ladder when his foot caught. Before he knew it, the ladder tipped. As if in slow motion, his world turned and he and the ladder went crashing off the porch. The second he landed in the yard, pain radiated down his back and his left shoulder. Letting out a string of curses, Braxton rolled over and tried to get some air back into his lungs. Damn fall knocked the wind out of him and served up a heavy dose of humiliation.

"Are you okay?" Brock was crouched at his side, his brows drawn down in worry. "Don't move."

"I can move," Braxton gasped out in short breaths as he started to sit up. The pain intensified, but he pushed up onto his right elbow because he refused to stay down and appear even weaker. "Don't look so scared. I'm fine."

"Braxton," Sophie yelled as she tried to run, but her limp prevented her from picking up too much momentum. "Don't move. That was a hard fall."

"Are you all right?" Cora asked as she and Heidi neared.

Great. Just what he wanted—an audience to complete his shame. Clearly, a guy couldn't fantasize without making a fool of himself.

"I stepped wrong on the ladder," he defended, ignoring the pain as much as he could. "Not a big deal. Just let me get up and moving and I'll be fine."

Cora's face scared him more than anything. She couldn't see what happened, could only hear what the others were saying. Her skin had paled, her violet eyes were wide with fear. The only look he ever wanted to put on her face was happiness.

As soon as he got to his feet, which took a bit longer than he thought because his damn back muscles controlled way too much of his body at the moment and everything was hurting, Braxton brushed Cora's arm with his fingertips.

"I'm up and fine." He flat-out lied and hoped the pain in his voice wasn't coming through his tone. Reassuring her was his top priority right now. When he was home alone he could let the pain win, but not now, not when Cora was visibly shaken.

"You're a liar."

Brock laughed, but when Braxton shot him a look, he stopped. "This wasn't my first fall. I grew up with Ed Monroe. Construction was ingrained in us and falls and random injuries were all part of the game. I'm sore, but I'm fine."

"Leave the mess here," Sophie told him. "Zach and Brock will clean everything up."

Braxton shot Brock a smile. "Looks like you have to do more than you intended after all, hotshot."

Brock rolled his eyes, but the smile negated the

teen's actions. "Whatever, old man. Go put some ice on those joints or you'll be crying in the morning."

Braxton laughed, though he hated to admit he'd been outed by a teenager. Damn, getting older sucked. Thirty-four wasn't geriatric region, but he certainly ached more than when he'd been twenty. Maybe he'd been in the classroom too long.

"I need to get back home anyway," Braxton stated. Surely, he could get himself home, crawl into his house, and lie in misery the rest of the day. "I have a past student who is swinging by later for a textbook he wants to borrow."

"Can you drive?" Sophie asked as she crossed her arms and continued to study him.

Leaning forward, he gave her a brotherly kiss right in the middle of her drawn brows. "I promise I'm fine."

"I'll drive you home," Brock volunteered.

Braxton shook his head. "Nice try. You're on cleanup crew."

Deflated, Brock muttered something under his breath and turned to pick up the fallen ladder. Braxton shot Sophie a wink and a grin, hoping to reassure her he truly was fine. He'd walk to his SUV and drive himself despite the pain. No way in hell was he admitting it was actually getting worse.

"I'll walk you to your car," Cora told him.

Without waiting on him to agree or disagree, she gripped Heidi's collar with one hand and reached out to him with the other. Braxton shifted closer so he could offer his arm, the one that didn't hurt. Instantly inhaling her signature jasmine scent, Braxton wondered if he'd ever associate that smell with anyone or anything else other than Cora.

"Tell me the truth," she said softly once they were away from the others. "Are you hurt?"

The fact that she'd lured him away to ask only told him she cared, possibly more than she wanted to admit. If she didn't, she would've taken him at his word when he'd told Sophie he was fine. He wanted her to care, damn it. He wanted her to think of him when he wasn't around. He wanted her to be going insane with want and need the same way he was.

Getting sympathy, though, because he'd gotten hurt was definitely not the way he wanted to go about capturing her full attention.

Despite the pain, he couldn't help but mess with her.

"My arm is dangling at an awkward angle and I can't breathe."

Cora bit on her bottom lip as if she were trying not to laugh. "You're such a smart-ass. You can't be too hurt."

"Honestly, my back hurts like a bitch and my left shoulder isn't much better. Nothing a little ibuprofen won't cure once I'm home. I'll be sore tomorrow, but it could've been worse."

Sure. He could've fallen off a ladder while daydreaming about a sexy, mesmerizing, violet-eyed beauty. Oh, wait. That's exactly what happened. Nope. Couldn't have gotten much worse.

"I think you need to be seen," she told him. "Please have someone drive you to the urgent care."

Braxton ran his hand up her arm, then down. He laced his fingers with hers. "I'm fine, Cora. I would know if I need to be seen."

"Please," she begged softly. "If I could see, I'd take you. It wouldn't hurt. I mean, what if you did something internally?"

Braxton completely understood where her concern

was coming from. She was thinking back to her own fall, how they'd discovered her sight was going. But the fall hadn't caused her blindness. Still, she was emotionally scarred from what had happened and her worry was misplaced.

"Rest and ice, that's all I need right now."

When he reached his vehicle he turned to keep his back to the cottages. "What were you doing here today?"

"Sophie and I were going to work on pricing and the specials I could offer. She wants it all in the main computer so when clients check in, they can get things scheduled. She said once they see full packages, they can plan the full experience of their trip."

Braxton watched one strand of hair dance around her cheek. When he tucked it behind her cheek, she stiffened.

"You need to stop jerking when I touch you."

"I'm trying. It's just . . . hard for me." She let out a sigh and stared just over his shoulder. The worry in her eyes more evident now than moments ago. "You need to get to the urgent care, but I know I'm fighting your ego and stubborn male pride."

Braxton laughed. "You're not fighting anything and if I didn't think I was fine, I would go."

Cora chewed on her bottom lip and stared over his shoulder. "Well, I'm just glad you're okay."

She gripped Heidi's collar and started to head back toward the cottages. Watching the sway of that dress around her toned legs was absurd. The way the fabric slid over that creamy skin was going to be his undoing. When the hell did he start watching how material moved?

Since he'd taken a special liking to the body beneath the dress.

He called her name and waited until she threw him a glance over her shoulder.

"I was thinking of another swim. This time with real suits," he added quickly. "What do you say about tomorrow?"

The smile that lit up her face was brighter than any sunshine he'd seen in Haven. "I'd like that."

Then she turned and walked away and Braxton stared after her, knowing he probably looked like some wide-eyed, open-mouthed idiot, but watching Cora go was just as appealing as watching her walk toward him.

As she neared the cottage, Braxton glanced to Brock, who was throwing back a knowing grin in his direction.

Busted.

Braxton merely waved a hand and climbed into his SUV. No reason to hang around and take a verbal beating. He needed to get home and soak his back before he started crying.

Chapter Nine

"You've been home for two days. You clearly need to swallow your man pride and go get an X-ray."

Braxton rolled his eyes at Zach's comment. "Like you'd go," he retorted. "I'll be good as new tomorrow. I've lain on this damn heating pad for so long, I've lost five pounds of sweat."

"I didn't figure you'd go, but I promised Sophie I'd ask."

Braxton stared up at the ceiling, same as the day before. He was going to have a permanent mold of his body indented onto the couch when he got up. If he could get up. When he coughed, sneezed . . . hell, when he breathed his damn back started to scream in protest.

"Consider your fiancé duties done, then."

"Those are never done," Zach snorted. "Seriously, though, I want to know how the hell you got Brock to ace that test."

"He's a smart kid. He needs to work on his self-esteem more than his homework because he knows the stuff, he just automatically thinks he'll fail."

Zach muttered a curse. "I can't fault him. I know this will take time, but I wish he understood. . . ."

"I know. He will," Braxton assured his brother. Braxton knew full well that Zach wanted to make Brock's life perfect right now, but the boy had fifteen years of hell he was trying to overcome and it wouldn't happen in a few months. "He's coming along, but it's going to take time. Hell, you're still a work in progress and you're old."

"Kiss my ass." Zach sighed. "I need to go. I told Brock we would go car shopping. I'd rather shoot myself with a nail gun."

Braxton laughed. Damn, you'd think he'd remember that hurt like hell. "You're a brave man."

"No, I'm stupid, but I've told him it will be a used car. He'll put his time in on clunkers just like we did. A little more than I wanted to spend on a Christmas present, but he needs wheels."

"Good luck, bro. I'll see you tomorrow."

"I'm going to be at Macy's most of the day tomorrow, but I'll check in when I can. Hopefully, when Liam gets back in he'll take up some slack. I don't want you overdoing it and making yourself worse."

"Yes, Mommy."

Disconnecting the call on Zach's laugh, Braxton laid his cell on his bare chest. When he'd tried to put a shirt on this morning, he'd nearly been brought to his knees when pain radiated through his shoulder and down his back. There was no way he could go finish working on the resort if he couldn't even get dressed.

There was also no way he could take Cora on that promised swim. He'd called her and thankfully got her voice mail. Yeah, leaving a message was the cowardly way out, but he didn't want to have to listen to disappointment when he told her he had to postpone the swim. Not that he thought he was offering some grand event in her life and she'd be crushed, but he had a feeling she wasn't put first in too many people's lives and he didn't want her to feel brushed off. Besides, the fact she wanted to get back in the water showed just how strong and resilient she was.

Tomorrow, he vowed. He'd take her tomorrow no matter what he felt like. Damn it, he hated being laid up. He didn't recall ever being completely put out. Even when he'd helped his father and was just learning construction, Braxton hadn't injured himself quite like this. He'd had the usual hammer to the thumb, jolt of electric when he wasn't paying attention while changing out receptacles, minor things, but falling off a ladder because he'd placed his foot wrong on the rung was flat-out embarrassing. If his father were alive today he'd definitely get a good belly laugh at Braxton's expense, especially because Braxton had been eyeing a beautiful woman.

The doorbell sounded through his one-story house and Braxton cringed. Who the hell was stopping by for a visit? People didn't just drop by and visit him for no reason. Christmas carolers came out at night . . . right?

Dread settled into his stomach. If Ms. Barkley decided to stop in, as she'd done once before, he'd have to be a little more direct. He thought ignoring her calls had done the trick, but he really didn't know anyone else who would drop by unexpected.

Before he could get off the couch, his doorbell chimed again. Good grief, it would be this time tomorrow before he could make it to the door. With one hand on his lower back, he slowly made his way across the wood floors toward the door. No doubt he looked like an old man, but he also felt that way right now.

Thankfully, his front door was in the living room, so he didn't have far to go, but damn if each step didn't make those back muscles groan in protest.

Braxton flicked the lock and pulled the door open.

"Cora." Shock registered hard and fast, until he looked down to the curb to see Sophie waving from the car . . . a car that was now pulling away. "What are you doing here?" he asked, turning his attention back to his unexpected guest.

"I came to help. I know you haven't been seen, but you're still laid up here, so you're definitely hurting more than you let on." She had her defiant chin tipped up, a hold on Heidi's collar, and a large bag on her shoulder. "Um . . . can I come in?"

Braxton took a step back. "Sorry. Yes, come in."

Nothing like making her doubt herself when she'd surprised him on his doorstep. He'd never wanted a woman in his home more than now. He hadn't even considered having Cora in his house, but he liked the thought that she'd decided to come without calling. Maybe impromptu visits weren't such a bad thing after all . . . depending on the visitor.

"Wait. Let me take this bag and then help you in. There's a slight step up over the threshold here."

He removed the bag from her shoulder and set it just inside the door. Whatever she had in that tote was heavy, he hadn't expected that, nor had his back been prepared for the added weight.

"Okay." Braxton reached for her free hand. "Just a few inches up."

Gripping Heidi's collar, Cora stepped inside and immediately let go of his hand. "I've got it. Just tell me where the sofa is."

"You're already in the living room. The sofa is to your left." He carefully made his way back, turned off the heating pad, and moved it to the end table. "You're about six feet away and there's a small table beside the couch, but Heidi is between you and it, so you have a clear shot."

Cora laughed. "I appreciate that, but I want you on the couch. On your stomach, to be precise."

"Well if you want me in a horizontal position, all you had to do was ask," he joked, more from shock than anything. What was she up to? "Though I have to admit, I'm not exactly my full potential right now."

"Cute," she muttered. "Now, get into position and tell me where you put my bag."

"Right beside the door." He crossed to reach for it, but before he could bend too much, he cringed and cursed himself for his actions.

"I don't need you to get it." Cora held her hands up toward him as if to try to stop him from moving farther. "I asked you to get on the couch on your stomach. Stubborn man. This is precisely why I had Sophie drive me over. I knew you'd never let anyone help and I wasn't going to call to ask."

As he struggled to get onto his stomach on the sofa, he listened to her scold him and he still had no idea what she was doing other than steamrolling him with the help of his brother's fiancée.

Which meant Zach knew that Cora was here. Great. This would not bring about a good conversation later. Not that he couldn't handle his brother; Braxton just preferred not to where Cora was concerned. He wanted to keep Cora to himself. Selfish, yes. Did he care? No.

"I'm going to need you to take your shirt off," she told him as she slowly made her way over with her bag.

"I'm not wearing one."

"Perfect." She stopped just beside the sofa and sat

her bag down. "Is there anything in front of the couch? A table or ottoman?"

"Nothing."

Heidi took a seat next to the couch, her head nudging Braxton's hand. He smoothed his hand over her soft fur and rubbed on her ears as Cora sank down onto her knees and started feeling around inside her bag.

"Do you need something to sit on?" he asked.

"I'm fine and you're not getting up," she replied easily. "We'll make this work. I just need you to not be so stubborn for a few minutes and let me help your back."

"You had Sophie bring you so you could give me a massage?" he asked. "Honey, as much as I love your hands on me, you didn't need to go to so much trouble."

He'd let the endearment slip out on purpose. Anything to knock her off balance, to keep her guessing and wondering what he intended to do next. Braxton wanted to be on her mind, he wanted her to be in constant thought about him. No, that wasn't ego talking. With another woman maybe it would've been, but with Cora, there was something so much stronger going on here. He still wasn't sure if he wanted to get clarity on the situation or sit back and enjoy the ride.

"Don't call me 'honey' and I'm not here for the enjoyment of touching you," she sniffed. Oh, yeah, there was that underlying prim and proper upbringing he'd grown accustomed to. "I'm here to help those poor muscles you abused yesterday. I'm trying to keep you from getting worse because then you will have to go to the urgent care even if I have to drive you."

Braxton sighed. "Listen, I know this freaked you out because of your history, but nothing is wrong. I hurt like hell, and I only took today off to rest. But I'm not turning down a free rubdown."

With his hand resting on Heidi's back, Braxton waited while she pulled out various bottles. He watched her face as her hands roamed over each product. Those delicate fingers that had the power to make a man groan, that had made him a believer in the power of a simple touch. She must've found the one she was looking for because she flipped the lid and applied a generous amount to her palm. After setting the bottle aside, she rubbed her hands together before applying them to the center of his back.

"Tell me if I rub too hard."

Braxton seriously had to bite his tongue to keep a "that's what she said" from slipping out. Actually, once she started smoothing her hands in firm, fluid strokes, he couldn't form a coherent thought. Everywhere she touched seemed to instantly relax and Braxton found himself closing his eyes and letting her do her magic.

This woman was going to be a major asset at the resort. Hell, he may book appointments for himself. Exam weeks at the college were hell and he could use some downtime after semesters ended.

"Are you feeling any better?" she asked as she continued to move her hands masterfully over his back and shoulders.

"Yeah."

His voice sounded like he'd eaten sandpaper, but how the hell could a man get all rubbed down like this and not get turned on?

She used a different product, this time it felt like oil. He didn't ask what it was, he didn't need to know. Cora was here because she cared, she was here because she wanted to help, and she was here, in his home, completely outside her comfort zone.

"Thank you for coming by," he told her.

The breath of her soft laugh tickled his damp skin. "That was hard for you to say, wasn't it?"

"Not to you," he admitted, realizing just how true the statement was. "There was no way I was going for an X-ray, but I never thought of having you come and work your magic."

"Most people don't think of a masseuse for healing, but muscles can often be cured if they're pampered the right way. I wasn't going to just let you lie here in misery."

Braxton opened his eyes and stared at her. She had no idea how beautiful she looked with a lock of hair over one eye, her lip pulled between her top two teeth as she concentrated on soothing him.

"Is that what you're doing? Pampering me?"

A smile flirted around her mouth. "I'm trying."

"You're stunning."

The whispered words left his lips before he could even think through his thoughts. Her hands stilled on his back.

"I don't say that to make you uncomfortable," he went on, purposely keeping his tone soft. "Surely you're used to men complimenting you."

She picked back up her even motions. "I've been complimented, yes, but the words sound different coming from you."

He didn't comment. What could be said? She was stunning, she was breathtaking, and he wanted so much from her it scared the hell out of him. Mostly he was terrified because he couldn't pinpoint exactly what it was he wanted from her. Well, other than the obvious because he was a guy. But there was so much more and he was going to have to come to grips with that fact sooner rather than later or he'd drive himself insane.

"I was engaged." Her hands moved up to his shoulders. "Well, I was almost engaged. In the eyes of my parents and Eric, I was taken."

Finally she was opening up. Relief slid through Braxton, but he wasn't sure if he should comment or let the silence calm her enough to keep going.

"I'm just not ready to settle down," she went on. "And I definitely don't want someone my parents think is perfect simply for the fact he's the son they never had and he can take care of me."

Braxton laughed. "I've known you a week. Want me to call and tell them you can take care of yourself?"

She stared at him for a moment before her smile spread across her face. "Thank you. You get it. I was the perfect daughter for so long, then with the accident and ultimately losing my sight, they only see me as handicapped now. It's a struggle because I'm still me. I'm still the same person I was when I could see, only now I'm hurt. I hate hurting and I hate that I've let myself feel this way."

Braxton jerked sideways, cringing at the sudden movement that caused her hand to fall away. He wanted to fix these emotions, now. Every bit of hurt she had, every single insecurity, he wanted to wipe them out and wrap her in a shield of protection.

"Handicapped? Do you see yourself that way?"

She perched her hands on the edge of the cushion, right next to his side. "I don't know," she told him, her tone a bit defeated. "It's just . . . never mind. No reason to dredge this topic up. It is what it is. I've learned people will think and say what they want. Not all of it is kind, but I can't control that. It's been nearly three years, but it still seems like yesterday and I wonder if I'll ever stop adjusting to this new life."

She had so many doubts, so many insecurities that she tried to keep hidden. And from the veiled conversations about her parents, he knew she had little to no support from them. Braxton wanted five minutes with her parents. He wanted to tell them what an amazing daughter they had, how loyal and loving and perfect she was regardless of her vision.

On a sigh, she moved her hands to her lap and tipped her head to the side. "How's your back and shoulder feeling now?"

Slowly he eased into a sitting position, surprised how he wasn't groaning or praying for strength. He rolled his shoulders and expected that familiar pain to radiate down his back, but it didn't.

"I'm still sore, but that intense pain isn't there anymore." He continued to move with caution, but he was so damn glad to be moving this well at all, he couldn't stop working out those sore muscles. "How the hell did you do that?"

Cora felt for the bottles at her side and placed them back in her bag. "It's what I was trained for."

"You were also trained as an accountant," he reminded her.

"Don't remind me. I get bored just thinking of how my life could be right now."

Braxton reached for her busy hands and took the bottles from her, setting them on the floor by her side. "I know my opinion doesn't matter in the grand scheme of things, but I want you to know how amazed I am by you. Every single day you show me something new about the world you live in."

A world he was sinking deeper into.

"I'm sorry you're hurting," he told her, tipping her chin up when she tried to hide her face. "I'm sorry people in your life don't see the special person you are. Tell me you don't believe that you are flawed. Please, tell me you know how valuable you are to everyone whose life you enter."

Cora opened her mouth, then closed it and shook her head. Heidi had curled up next to Cora, but as soon as Cora shifted her body, the dog immediately jumped to her feet. Cora patted her head, calming down the obedient dog, who went back to a curled-up position by the sofa.

"I don't want to talk about this," she told him, feeling around her for the bottles and quickly shoving them back in her bag.

Braxton glanced at the clock, shocked to see an hour had passed. Dark clouds gathered outside, making the evening seem darker than what it really should be at this time of day. He didn't know what Cora's plans were now that she was done, but he wasn't in any hurry to see her go and he definitely wasn't letting her out of here while all this turmoil surrounded them.

Leaving her to battle her issues alone wasn't an option. She'd come here to help him, he damn well would see that she was comforted, too. Her comfort would just be of the emotional variety, but still just as important.

Steady rain started beating against the windows on the side of the house. Braxton loved this lazy type of weather and he had a feeling Cora never took time to appreciate the simple things in life. Whatever she came from was a world of rushed, fast-paced living and trying to fit inside a perfect box.

Braxton wanted to be the one to obliterate that box.

"Is Sophie coming back to get you?" he asked.

Cora felt for the sofa and eased up onto the cushion beside him. "I told her I'd call her when we were done."

Perfect.

"I'm going to take your hand and you're going to trust me."

Tipping her head to the side, her hair falling over her shoulder, Cora pursed her lips. "Is that a request or demand?"

Braxton stood, took her hands in his, and pulled her to her feet, ignoring the ache in his muscles. Her abrupt movement caught her off balance and she tumbled against his chest. The pain in his back was worth enduring. Having Cora plastered to his front definitely kept his mind off his injury.

When she made no move to step back, he gripped her shoulders and slid his cheek over her silky hair for just a moment before he took her hand and cautiously moved toward the entryway.

"What are we doing?" she asked as he led her from the room. "Do I need Heidi?"

"You don't need her, but she's always welcome to come."

"You're heading toward the door." She reached down and took Heidi's collar. "It's raining."

He chuckled as he opened the front door. "It's getting ready to storm and we're going to enjoy it."

"By doing what?" she repeated.

Braxton moved to the porch and steered her to the left. "By doing nothing."

Gently guiding her to the swing, Braxton held it still as she took a seat. He snapped his fingers until Heidi came to him and he gestured for her to have a seat at enough of a distance to avoid getting hit by the swaying swing.

"There," he sighed, taking a seat beside her. "We'll listen to the rain."

"And then what?"

Braxton shook his head and laughed. "There's no more. Damn, I thought I was a stickler for schedules."

"Maybe being on break has spoiled you and now your life is just one big open slot. Maybe you don't know how to fill your time so you're choosing to do nothing."

He reached over, slid his hand over hers, and squeezed. "Or maybe I'm choosing to do exactly what I want, which is more important than anything. Maybe I want to sit on my porch with a beautiful woman and watch the rain bounce off my rail."

Cora pulled her knee up onto the seat between them as she turned to face him. Her hand still in his, she offered a smile. "Tell me what you see."

She'd had the same request at the pond. He wanted to be able to show her the world through his eyes, a world she'd never see again. And, he feared, a world no one cared to show her.

He watched as the sidewalk in front of his house started to develop puddles. The slightest dips in the concrete soon became mini wading pools for birds. He loved a good, hard rain. Could sit on this porch swing for hours and just listen to it fall down, almost as if washing away the worries and cares of the world. These cooler evenings and nights were the most relaxing times. Winter in Georgia was actually rather nice. He never wanted to live where they had piles of snow and slick ice. He'd take the Southern temps any day.

"The sky is darker than usual right now. Almost as if there's just one, big gray cloud hovering over Haven."

He glanced around, trying to figure out exactly what to share with her. Everything around him he took for granted. Rain, flowers, grass, trees, cars. Every single thing he saw day in and day out was just mundane, but to her it was everything.

"My sister planted some shrubbery along the edge of my porch," he told her. "She claimed my bachelor pad needed some curb appeal and I let her go at it. I have no clue what the hell she called it, but it's nice."

He stared at the white blossoms on the bushes, wondering if Chelsea would be proud of him for keeping it alive for another season.

"Drops of rain are settling into the petals," he added. "Almost like teardrops, I guess. They land, then they slide away."

Cora's head dropped to his shoulder. "Keep talking," she murmured. "Your words are pretty."

Braxton swallowed. He'd never been told his words were pretty. He'd never taken the time to think about pretty words before, but with Cora he found he wanted to. Whatever made her happy, made her smile, he wanted to be part of.

"The drops are hitting the railing around the porch. They splatter and every now and then occasionally hit my arm."

"Close your eyes," she told him.

Tipping his head down toward hers, he asked, "Close them?"

"Please."

Wondering what she had in mind, he closed his eyes. "All right. They're closed."

"Now tell me what you see."

Shocked at her request, Braxton shook his head. "I can't see."

Her hand squeezed in his. "You can. Just think about it."

Concentrating, Braxton tried to pull in anything from his other senses. The difficult exercise he was struggling with was her everyday life and he totally understood why she wanted him to do this. She was giving him a glimpse into her world. A glimpse he'd been wanting and the fact she was exposing herself in such a unique way humbled him. He would do this for her, and for himself.

He inhaled and instantly caught something. "Sweet. I smell something sweet."

"It's the flowers. What else?"

"My skin feels damp, not just from where the droplets are hitting, but everywhere. We have more humidity than normal."

When she remained quiet, he reached further into his senses. How the hell did she do this? He just wanted to open his eyes and see. A simple task he took for granted. Sight was such a powerful sense, one she'd been robbed of. His admiration for her kept rising. But she was so much more than a blind woman. He admired her for her determination to reclaim her life, for her drive to keep going when giving up would be so easy. She captured the spirit of every single thing he didn't know he was looking for.

"The rain is picking up," he went on. "It's harder now than it was, but still steady."

A drop of moisture landed on his arm and it wasn't from the rain. Braxton shifted in the swing, wrapping his arm around Cora as she nestled deeper into his side.

"Why the tears?" he asked, reaching with his other hand to swipe away the dampness.

"It's nothing. Really. I just get emotional sometimes."

Stroking his thumb over her bare arm, he chuckled. "Honey, I haven't known you very long, but I can say you're not one to get emotional. You're pretty strong and determined not to let your feelings show."

"Being strong is my only option."

Braxton didn't like the underlying vulnerability in her tone, he didn't like how defeated, how tired she sounded. He tipped up her chin and stared down into those violet eyes that he'd found so mesmerizing from day one. She pulled him in and had no clue she'd done so. Women flashed cleavage at him, licked their lips suggestively, batted their lashes and passed their number to him with promises in their eyes.

But none of that packed the punch quite as intense as a look from Cora with unshed tears as she bared her soul.

"Has anyone ever tried to see the world through your eyes in the past three years?" he asked.

"You."

He stroked a finger over her wet cheek. Pushing her into humiliation wasn't his goal, so he let the subject drop. Something much more important was happening here. Something beyond chemistry and even a little deeper than intimacy, but the label couldn't be made. He'd never been in this territory before and he'd never wanted to get so deep with a woman. But here he was, in a playing field he knew nothing about with a woman who pushed away each time he took a step closer.

But she wasn't pushing now. She was actually leaning on him, literally and figuratively. He wanted her to smile, though. He needed to see her smile, to know he caused it because wherever she went in her mind just now wasn't a happy place. When she was with him, he was going to demand happy.

Damn it. When had he turned into the man who wanted to care again? When had he turned into the guy ready to put his feelings, possibly his heart, on the line again?

Was he ready for that?

Braxton sighed and shook off the thoughts. He couldn't analyze anything right now, not when Cora was touching him. His mind went to her, but later, when he was alone, he could decipher what all of his mixed thoughts meant.

"Take your shoes off," he told her.

She lifted her head from the crook of his arm. "What?"

"You heard me." He leaned down and slid off her dainty black slip-ons. "I have the best idea."

"What else do I need to take off?" she chuckled.

Braxton came to his feet, which prompted Heidi to stand at attention and move closer to her master. "If you want to take that dress off, don't let me stop you."

"I think I'll keep it on," she stated, reaching over to pat Heidi's head. "So where are we going with no shoes and where clothing is optional?"

Braxton took her hand and brought her to her feet. "You may want Heidi to stay on the porch."

Cora jerked back. "We're going out in the rain?"

"Don't look so shocked. It's water."

Before she could protest fully, he tugged her to the edge of the porch. "Remember the two steps here," he cautioned, and held on to her hand as she carefully inched one foot down at a time.

"Ready to have fun?" he asked.

"I'm already scared by the tone of your voice."

The rain had already soaked them and they'd been in it for ten seconds. Braxton reached out, smoothed the hair from her face, and eased her toward the sidewalk in front of his house. With the street having very few houses, the lots were wide and neighbors were fairly spread out. Even if they'd been close and people could see, he wouldn't care. This was all for Cora.

The second her foot hit a puddle, she gasped, then smiled. "Are we dancing in the rain?" she asked.

"We're stomping in the rain," he yelled over the roaring downpour.

They were absolutely soaked. Cora laughed as she lifted her face to the sheets. With her arms wide, her hands up toward the sky, Braxton had never seen a more beautiful sight.

Stepping forward, he slid his arms around her waist and waited until she dropped her arm and tipped her face back down to his.

"Dancing was a great idea, though," he told her as he began to move.

He had no clue how to dance, had never had a reason to know. But right now, he didn't care if he made a fool of himself, he wanted to hold this woman in his arms and move to the rhythmic music the rain provided.

"You've never done this, have you?" she asked, her smile still spread wide across her face as the rain trickled down her pink cheeks.

"Never."

She held his hand tighter, threaded her fingers through the hair on the nape of his neck. "Let me lead. I've been schooled on dancing."

"The control is all yours."

He didn't mind one bit relinquishing the power to

her. As they gently spun in uniform circles, Braxton quickly picked up the footsteps. He threw a glance to the porch where Heidi obediently sat beneath the shelter of the roof, no doubt wondering what on earth was going on.

Braxton couldn't help but wonder himself. Any other woman he would've already been trying to peel that wet dress off and explore all that was beneath. But with Cora he knew she was different, she was special. He didn't give a damn that she would be working for him. That was the least of his worries. What kept weighing heavy on his mind was how fast and far he'd fallen. He'd sworn when Anna had betrayed him that he'd never let a woman get close enough to hurt him again. Yet here he was aching to be with Cora, needing to spend more time with her, wanting to uncover so much more about her.

He didn't know how long they swayed, he didn't care. Her body moved against his, eventually she relaxed even more and laid her head against his chest, their hands tucked between their shoulders. As much as Braxton wanted her on a physical level, he wanted her to know that whatever was happening between them meant so much more than that.

Braxton stilled his movements, causing her to stop and raise her gaze to his. Droplets settled on her lips, her lashes, they streaked down her porcelain skin. Braxton lowered his lips to kiss away the moisture that fell onto her cheeks, her nose, and finally her lips.

She opened beneath his touch, sighed into him, and returned that control he'd given her moments ago. Braxton plunged his hands into her wet hair and tipped her head just enough to give him more access. Cora was a craving he didn't know if he'd ever grow tired of.

She was in his system and he couldn't imagine how he'd be months from now. Cora wasn't just some girl passing through. She wasn't like the other women he found himself entertaining lately. She was here for the long haul and he had to decide what to do about that.

Braxton kept his grip on her, not ready to completely let go, but he lifted his head and watched as her lids fluttered open. She blinked away the moisture.

"I've never been dancing in the rain," she told him, then quickly laughed. "I've never played in a puddle in the rain, either."

He stroked his thumbs across her jawline. "What about being kissed in the rain?"

"Definitely not."

Everything in him was thrilled to hear he'd been a first for her. She continued to surprise him with just how adaptable she was. Everything about her screamed money, another common thread between Cora and Anna. He didn't know how Cora would react to being pulled out into the rain to just have fun, but she'd loved it.

Braxton slicked back the soaked tendrils from her forehead. "Maybe we should go dry off inside. Those clouds are getting darker. Storm is coming."

He took her hand and led her to the porch. Once they were beneath the roof, Braxton shook the water from his hair and noticed Cora shivering.

"Come on in and I'll grab you a blanket."

"I'll get your floors all wet," she protested.

Braxton opened the front door, gesturing for Heidi to come. "They're wood and I'll wipe them up. You need dry clothes and a towel."

Cora laughed as she cautiously moved forward. "Why is it when I'm with you I'm always needing a towel or a change of clothes?"

With his hand on the small of her back, Braxton led her down the hall toward the bathroom. "It's safe to say you always need to be prepared around me."

"I don't even think that's possible," she muttered.

Cora's hand felt along the wall and he knew she was learning the layout of his home. Another aspect that warmed him. He'd not brought another woman here since Anna. He hadn't wanted to, but having Cora here seemed . . .

He really didn't want to put a label on how much he liked having her here. He didn't want to put himself in that vulnerable position again. Unfortunately, here he was and all he could do at this point was hold on for the ride.

Chapter Ten

Cora inhaled once, then twice. She'd dried off in the bathroom and Braxton had brought her a change of clothes . . . clothes that smelled amazingly masculine and very much like Braxton's familiar cologne. Once she'd put on an extremely large T-shirt and a pair of sweatpants she'd had to roll numerous times at the waist, she gave him her wet things so he could throw them in the dryer.

She took longer than necessary in the bathroom because she seriously needed a minute to compose herself. How did she process all of this at once? The rain, the dancing, the playfulness?

And that kiss. That sweet, slow, eyes-rolling-back-in-her-head kiss. The man was so potent whether he was trying to seduce her with pretty words, the full-on attack kisses, or the sensual touches that left her wondering what the hell she'd gotten herself into.

Heidi settled against Cora's right leg as Cora leaned her palms onto the edge of the counter and pulled in a deep breath. She'd made use of the towel and had done what she could with her hair, but whatever it looked like now was out of her control. Her mother would most likely be mortified, but her mother wasn't here and the man outside that bathroom door most likely didn't care.

She couldn't stifle the laugh as it bubbled up. The difference between Eric and Braxton were so extreme, yet she didn't know why the comparison kept creeping into her mind. She didn't want to compare them. Didn't want to think how dull her life had been when she'd been in Atlanta and how alive she felt since coming to Haven. She didn't want to dwell on the fact that Eric wouldn't be caught dead in the rain without an umbrella because his Ferragamo loafers and Louis Vuitton raincoat would get wet or the part in his hair would be messed.

And she refused to allow herself to think of the difference in the way the two men kissed her, touched her. Eric kissed her in that stiff, let's-get-this-over-with way. But Braxton . . . kissing Braxton was an experience that couldn't be summed up in one thought or a few adverbs.

"Well, girl. We can't hide in here forever."

Cora reached down and held on to Heidi's collar. She'd counted the steps into the bathroom, so she recounted them back to the door. Feeling around, she found the knob and turned, stepping back as the door swung in.

"Everything okay?"

Cora jumped at the nearness of Braxton's voice.

"Sorry," he added. "I was just coming to check on you. Those clothes are huge, but they're all I had."

Part of her was glad to hear he didn't have a spare outfit from ladies he'd brought home. "They're fine," she told him with a smile. "They're dry and warm, so that's all I care about."

"Would you like me to take you home?" he asked.

"You're more than welcome to stay. The storm is getting bad, so if you want to go, we should leave now."

Cora leaned against the doorjamb and contemplated her options. If she left, she could be home where she was familiar with things and, unlike most people, she didn't care if the electric went out. She'd be fine and probably just listen to an audiobook on her fully charged device.

On the other hand, if she stayed . . .

There were too many possibilities to even comprehend and the ball was seriously in Braxton's court.

"I can hear you thinking." There went that low, sexy voice again. "Seriously, Cora. No pressure either way. I expect nothing from you if you stay."

"That's a shame," she muttered.

Braxton's laugh filled the hallway. "Don't tease me, woman. Why don't you just hang out here? If the weather gets worse, I have a spare bedroom."

Cora lifted her brows. "And you fully expect me to use that?"

"I said I had one, I didn't say you could use it. My room is also available."

Cora knew he stood close, so she reached out and swatted, but her aim was a tad off and she ended up swiping across a very impressive set of abs. What college professor was built like stone?

"How about dinner? Why don't we work on that?"

Braxton gave her damp hair a tug before taking hold of her elbow. "Come on. Maybe if I whip up my famous hot dogs with potato chips, you'll sleep with me."

Cora nearly choked from instant laughter. "Your ego ever get you into trouble?" she asked.

"My ego and I are a team and we tend to get what we want."

She counted off the steps in her head, not at all surprised at how fast she'd adjusted to his home. "Is that right? Well, Mr. Get-What-I-Want, don't hold your breath on that sleeping arrangement. I have a feeling the storm will pass and I'll be home in my own—"

A roar of thunder so fierce, the windows of his house shook, cutting her off.

"You were saying?" he asked, no doubt smiling because he figured she wasn't going anywhere.

"I would almost bet you made a deal with the devil himself for this storm," she told him as Heidi blocked her from hitting something.

"Have a seat. And no, I didn't make any deals, but I would've."

Confused, Cora felt in front of her. "This chair wasn't here earlier. I counted my steps."

"I moved it so you wouldn't have as far to go."

Speechless at his thoughtfulness, Cora turned toward the left in the direction of his voice. When she reached her hand up to touch his face, his hand closed over hers in midair.

"You didn't have to do that." She couldn't stop her smile because . . . well, no one had ever wanted to try to adapt to her world. For the past three years, she'd been adapting to everyone else's. "I'd already memorized the layout of the living room."

Braxton sighed as he squeezed her hand. "I didn't move anything else. Sorry."

"Don't. Don't apologize for being you, for trying."

He placed a kiss on the palm of her hand before letting go. With a slight nudge, he urged her to sit. "Then I'll apologize for the meal I'm about to make."

Cora laughed and settled back against the cushy chair, leather if she was guessing right. "You can bring me a bowl of cereal and I'll be fine with it. I'll be ecstatic if you have the kind with the knockoff marsh-mallows that are crunchy."

"You like junk food? Why didn't you say so? My kitchen is stocked with junk. Liam is the chef in this family. I'm happy when my microwave mac 'n cheese doesn't burn."

Heidi settled right on top of Cora's foot, but she didn't mind. Cora had become used to the heavy dog and actually loved the familiarity when she was in un-familiar territory. Too bad Cora didn't have some sort of security blanket for her mental territory because all of this with Braxton was completely new ground she was covering.

Braxton ended up making them turkey sandwiches and he had some fruit to go with it. The simplest of meals, but one of the best she'd had in a long time. Come to think of it, sharing meals with Braxton had become something of a common thing lately.

"I've been waiting on that."

Cora curled her legs beneath her on Braxton's leather sofa. "What?"

"The electric finally went. The lightning is crazy out there."

"Maybe you should've taken me home after all."

The couch dipped at her side and Braxton's arm slid behind her back. "Not a chance. I like you right here in my house, on my couch. Wearing my clothes."

There was something so sexual about his tone, Cora had to force herself not to tremble. But her body be-trayed her and shivered anyway.

Braxton shifted her shoulders back against his chest

and Cora swiveled her legs around to stretch out on the cushions.

"I don't know that I've ever had such a relaxing evening." She sighed as she settled into his embrace. "You make trying to resist you more difficult, though your friend skills are amazing. I haven't had this much fun in years."

She didn't have to say why, they both knew the reason.

"Tell me about your family. About this fiancé."

A groan slipped out. "I'd rather not spoil this evening."

His thumb stroked along her shoulder and Cora knew she was drowning fast. How could she keep her old life and her new one separate? She wanted to be this Cora, the one who fulfilled her own dreams and goals, not those of her parents.

"I'm sorry my fall scared you, but I'm not sorry you're here."

Cora jerked around slightly. "Your shoulder. I didn't even think with the way I was leaning on you."

Braxton eased her back against his chest. "I want you close. I have an amazing masseuse who came by and helped work out most of the stiffness."

Easing back down, Cora sighed. "I'm sorry I overreacted when you fell, but I had flashbacks. I'll probably always think the worst when there's an accident."

"Don't apologize for caring or for your emotions. Trust me, if Sophie or Zach thought I needed to be seen, they would've tied me to the car and taken me."

"I know I've only been here a short time, but I love being part of a family who is so close." Cora toyed with the hem of the tee he'd given her to wear. "I left just to get away, to see if I could manage on my own and I am. But I've found so much more than I thought I would."

"Am I part of that newfound adventure you're glad you found?"

His voice rumbled in his chest, vibrating against her back, and Cora tipped her head up in his direction. "You are. As much as I didn't want to meet a man who gave me any feelings whatsoever, you dropped into my life."

Braxton laughed. "You don't have to sound so upset. Besides, we're friends. Right?"

Friends. Sure. That's what she wanted.

But she felt as if she were cheating herself out of something that could be absolutely fabulous.

"Maybe there's more here than friends," she muttered. "Those kisses were more than I'd ever share with any friend."

Braxton's hand slid up along her jawline, his thumb stroked her bottom lip. "What are you saying?"

Before she could think better of it, she licked her lips, accidentally swiping the tip of her tongue across his thumb. What was she saying? That she wanted to sleep with her boss? That she wanted to attempt a relationship?

Cora blinked and pulled away as she shook her head. "Nothing. I'm just . . . ignore me. I'm getting caught in the moment and not thinking clearly."

"Oh, no." The sofa cushion dipped as Braxton shifted and grabbed her shoulders. "You're not brushing this aside again. You're worried because you work for me, right? Forget that for now. I know you feel this connection to me, the same way I feel it for you. Damn it, Cora, why do you keep doing this push-pull thing with me?"

Taking a deep breath, she closed her eyes and let her head drop on the exhale. "Because I'm terrified of what I feel when I'm with you," she whispered, hating this exposed vulnerability. "I don't like being out of control."

His fingertip slid beneath her chin as he raised her face. Silence enveloped them, her heart beat fast, and she was almost afraid to know what he was thinking.

"I wish I could see your face." She'd already confessed so much, why not keep going? "Your eyes, really. I wonder what I'd see if I could look at them right now."

Braxton's thumb came up to caress her bottom lip. "You'd see a man who's dying to kiss his friend."

Those raw, honest words hit her right in the heart. She didn't want her heart involved in any of this. Too late.

"I'm pretty sure we've crossed that friend line," she murmured. "When did that happen?"

Braxton let out a soft chuckle. "A while ago. I've just been waiting on you to catch up."

His hand eased up to cup the side of her face. Instinctively she turned toward his powerful touch. "I didn't want to catch up," she admitted.

"I know."

His lips hovered just over hers. She could feel his warm breath, the featherlight touch, and she tipped her forehead to rest against his.

"This is a mistake."

"Won't be the last one I make," he admitted a second before he covered her mouth.

Cora gripped his shoulders, telling herself she should pull away, but the woman in her who was achy and needy couldn't get close enough. Denying herself any longer wasn't an option. The man wanted her. He'd been patient, he'd been giving, and he'd been totally selfless. Yes, she'd only met him a short time ago, but every feeling he pulled from her was new, exciting, and she couldn't just ignore that.

Braxton shifted, changing the angle of the kiss as one of his hands settled on her side. She arched into his touch, wanting him to be bold, to make a move and take control of this moment.

For once in her life she wanted to completely hand over the reins and let someone else have all the power. Cora knew without a doubt that Braxton's taking charge would leave her both breathless and satisfied.

When his hand slid beneath the hem of the shirt, she stilled. Was she seriously going to let this happen? Was she going to get intimate with her boss on his couch during a storm? She didn't want to be a cliché and she definitely didn't want him to think that—

"Relax." His whispered word cut off her thoughts. "I can hear you thinking and you're throwing my game off."

Cora laughed. "I'm not a player you're used to."

His lips grazed back and forth over hers. "That's for damn sure. I've never wanted a woman like this, Cora. Those aren't just words. I'm serious. You've torn me up since you first had your hands on me."

"I've been pretty torn up too since that day."

Without asking, he eased up the T-shirt and whisked it over her head, leaving her bare from the waist up. She shivered at his lack of touch because she knew without a doubt that he was taking in the sight.

"I wish the lights hadn't gone out," he muttered. "I'd give anything to see all of you."

Cora reached for him. "Then we'll have to explore each other in the dark. You'll learn my body the same way I'll learn yours."

He caught her hand and kissed her palm. Those talented lips traveled to her wrist, the inside of her arm, and kept going. "I plan on taking my time getting to know your body, Cora. I've lain awake at night wondering, fantasizing. I have a need for you that runs deep."

She closed her eyes. She didn't want the words, she couldn't afford to let them sink in, to give her false hope. This . . . whatever this was, couldn't go anywhere. She was in such limbo emotionally and with the mess she'd left with her family. She couldn't drag him into her life and she knew he had his own baggage to deal with.

"Don't think, Cora." His fingertips tickled over her bare skin just beneath her breast. "Just feel."

At this point she had no choice but to feel. Even as light as his touch was, there wasn't a nerve that hadn't sizzled the second he'd found his way under the shirt.

His hands traveled over her. A second later his lips landed on her collarbone and that mouth cruised over her heated skin as his fingertips explored.

Cora reached out, finding his bare shoulders. Clutching that taut muscle, she arched into his touch, silently seeking more of anything he was willing to give. His touch was dizzying, consuming, addicting.

When his mouth closed over her breast, Cora bit down on her lip to keep from crying out. Braxton shifted closer, urging her back. When his broad shoulders lined up with hers, Cora wrapped her arms around him and let him guide her down. The cushion dipped beside her head just as he winced and muttered a curse.

Then she remembered he'd been hurt.

"Is it your back or shoulder?" she asked, gently gliding her hands over his back.

"Just a twinge." His words were said through gritted teeth and he was lying.

Cora pressed her hands against his chest and pushed him back up. "Why don't you lie down and let me . . ."

"Let you what?" His husky question sent shivers through her. "Have your wicked way with me?"

Cora smiled. "Maybe that's been my plan all along."

Snaking an arm around her waist, Braxton pulled her flush against his body and settled back onto his side of the wide sofa. "I'm more than okay with that plan."

She knew there were reasons this was a bad idea—hadn't she just reminded herself of that a few minutes ago? But with each passing moment, with each touch, she was forgetting them. Braxton's seductive tone dripped with intimacy and the way he held her as if she were going to go anywhere made her realize he was worried she actually would.

And now that she had the control, she had no idea what to do with it.

"I have a confession," she whispered, settling her hands over his extremely impressive pecs.

He stilled beneath her. "I'm not sure I'm ready for a confession."

"I'm not that . . . experienced."

"You're a virgin?"

Shaking her head, Cora let out a sigh. "No. I've done this before. It was okay, not explosive like I thought it would be. But with you, it already feels different and I guess I'm just worried I'll screw this up for you."

Braxton's hands slid up her bare back, sending chills racing over her skin. "Did you just request explosive? Because that is one area I can guarantee to deliver."

Cora bit down on her bottom lip as Braxton continued to glide those roughened hands over her. "Maybe I'm not ready for this."

He gripped her hips, pressed his forehead to hers, and held her still for a moment before replying, "Baby, you're ready. Your body is more than ready, your mind is trying to tell you this is a bad idea, but continuing to ignore this is the bad idea."

"I know what I want. I just need you to tell me if I do something wrong."

He kissed her softly as his thumbs hooked into the folded waistband of the oversize pants she wore. "Everything about you is right."

"But—"

He completely covered her mouth, forcing her hips into his. She wanted explosive? Those lips of his could set her on fire.

A piercing ring cut into the moment and Cora froze.

"Ignore it," he muttered against her mouth, still working at getting her pants down. "Everything we need is right here."

But the phone kept ringing. When it stopped, Cora breathed a sigh of relief, until it started up again.

"Damn it," he muttered, easing her aside so he could sit up. "That's mine."

Cora felt around on the sofa, looking for the shirt that had been carelessly tossed aside. She heard Braxton answer, but she desperately wanted to find something to cover herself with. All she came up with was a throw pillow.

Better than nothing.

"Damn it. I'll be right there."

Braxton came to his feet and sighed. "Brock was in a car accident," he explained. "That was Sophie. I need to go."

Cora clutched the pillow to her chest. "Go. I'll be fine here with Heidi."

Braxton shuffled over the floor and a moment later he was grabbing her hand. "Here's the shirt. I don't like leaving you here alone."

Fisting the shirt and holding the pillow tight to her chest, she offered a light smile. "I'll be fine. I'm used to being alone."

"That's the problem," he muttered. "I don't know how long I'll be. Do you want me to—"

"Braxton. Go. I promise, I'm fine. Your family needs you."

His fingertip trailed over her jaw as he slid his lips across hers. "What about you, Cora? Do you need me?"

Honesty. He valued honesty and while she hadn't let him in on the biggest aspect of her life, she could let him in on this part.

"I'm beginning to think I do."

With one last gentle kiss, Braxton left her alone in his house. Alone with her thoughts while still tasting him on her lips was not a good combination. She wanted to tell him who she was, but at the same time, she didn't want to be that person anymore. She may be running, okay, yes, she was running. But she loved this newfound freedom and she wanted to embrace it for as long as she possibly could.

Chapter Eleven

"Stop hovering. I'm fine."

Sophie smoothed Brock's hair back from the bandage on his head. Now that they were home from the hospital and starting to crash from the adrenaline high, Sophie was still right at Brock's side, Zach was still scowling, and the puppies were . . . oblivious to the turmoil since they were running through the house chasing each other and sliding across the wood floor.

"You scared the hell out of us," Zach stated. "If we want to hover, we damn well will."

"It's just a concussion and a few stitches," Brock grumbled, staring down at his hands.

Braxton stood off to the side in the living room of his childhood home. As somewhat of an outsider, he completely understood why Zach and Sophie were so worried. Aside from the fact Brock was their son now, both Zach and Sophie were no doubt reliving that tragic night so many years ago that altered their lives and sent Zach to prison for a year.

The muscle in Zach's jaw kept ticking as he stood there with his hands propped on his hips. Sophie couldn't seem to stop touching Brock and Brock looked as if he wanted to be left alone.

"Brock, why don't you head on to your room?"

Both Zach and Sophie jerked their attention to Braxton. He merely stared right back because everyone needed a break, especially the poor teen who was going to pay the price for the fears of his new parents if Braxton didn't intervene.

After a heavy dose of awkward silence, Brock threw a glance to Sophie and Zach before coming to his feet and quietly walking out of the room.

The second he was gone, Zach whirled on Braxton.

"Shut up." Braxton held up his hands. "Just calm down for a minute and think before you speak."

"I don't need to think and I don't want you coming in here trying to keep the peace. If I want to get upset, I sure as hell have been given that right."

"Getting upset is understandable—"

"Thanks for the permission," Zach snarled.

"But being an ass to a kid who's already shaken up is not okay," Braxton went on. "We all know why you're so emotional over this, but think of this from his standpoint. He just got his license, he was trying to come home when the storm hit and he hydroplaned. He wasn't speeding, he wasn't texting and driving, he was paying attention and had an accident. It could've happened to any of us."

Sophie came to her feet and put her hand on Zach's arm. "Sit down," she told him. "You look like you're ready to hit something."

Braxton figured of the options in this room, he was the only contender.

Zach let Sophie ease him down onto the couch. Raking his hands through his unruly hair, he blew out a breath. "My damn hands are still shaking. I've only been this terrified one other time in my life, when I couldn't get Sophie and Liam out of that truck."

Sophie rested her forehead against his shoulder, reaching down to grip his scarred hands. "He's fine. The doctor said the concussion was very mild and the cut on his head will be fine when the stitches come out. It could've been worse."

Braxton knew that was the crux of the entire situation. It could've been worse.

"I don't like this part of parenting," Zach grumbled. "Damn it. Can't he just stay in his room where he's safe?"

Braxton laughed and pushed off the doorway he'd been leaning against for the past several minutes. "Imagine how Mom and Dad felt about you if you're worried about Brock. Brock's a good kid. You were—"

"Rebellious?" Sophie chimed in.

"I was going to say impossible."

Zach shot him a glare. "I wasn't impossible or rebellious. Strong-willed. We'll go with that."

Braxton stared out the window to the steady rain. The storm had passed through, leaving random tree limbs littering yards and roads. More than likely a few shingles from roofs would be found lying around. The wind had been a bitch and the thunder and lightning hadn't been much better. He wanted to get back to Cora, but he needed to make sure everything here was squared away because he didn't want to leave when there was so much turmoil filling the house.

"Brock needs you to be understanding right now," Braxton went on. "Be angry and scared all you want, but keep in mind he's angry and scared too. That was his new car he just put a good dent in and shattered the window."

Sophie smoothed her hair back from her face and sent him a smile. "Thanks for coming. I hope I didn't interrupt anything when I called."

Braxton bit the inside of his cheek. "No. Nothing at all."

Zach sat straight up and glanced between the two. "Oh, damn. I forgot Sophie dropped Cora off at your house. What the hell, man? Can you keep it in your pants with our new employees?"

Braxton wasn't going to get into this with Zach and he sure as hell wasn't going to hash it out while his brother was still coming down from an emotional setback.

"Cora was helping with my soreness."

Okay, even to Braxton that sounded lame and pathetic and like a total lie. But she had helped his soreness. And when he'd whipped her shirt off and kissed her creamy skin he'd nearly forgotten all about his aches until his damn back had decided to catch.

"You can't even lie," Zach stated, shaking his head. "Don't screw this up for us. Or for Chelsea."

Braxton took a step forward, but Sophie jumped to her feet. "Don't," she stated, holding up her hands. "Thank you for coming, but right now we all need to be in our separate corners."

Fisting his hands at his side, Braxton stared down to his brother. "Don't ever throw Chelsea in my face again. Next time I won't let Sophie stop me from putting my fist in your face."

Slowly, Zach rose, his eyes never leaving Braxton. He reached for Sophie and shifted her aside.

"Zach," she muttered, worry lacing her tone.

Zach said nothing, but the silent exchange was more than words could say. Braxton clenched his teeth. Tensions were too high to say something he couldn't take back. But damn it if he was going to allow his brother to start homing in on his territory and knocking how he spent his time . . . or who he spent it with.

"I'll let myself out." Braxton turned to Sophie. "Call me if you need anything. I'll check on Brock tomorrow."

Without waiting for a reply, not that he thought he'd get one, Braxton turned and headed out. Brock was going to be fine, the crazy storm had passed, and Cora was home waiting on him.

Home. Just using that term in the same sentence with Cora was . . . hell, he didn't even know how he wanted to describe it.

Holding his head down against the evening rain, Braxton raced to his SUV in the drive. Something changed in their relationship tonight, something he hadn't had time to fully ponder, but knowing Cora, she'd thought of nothing else since he left, which meant she also most likely has talked herself out of letting anything like that happen again.

But Braxton was determined. He wanted her now more than ever and he was ready to deal with whatever she would throw at him once he got home. For the first time in a long time, Braxton was warming to the idea of a relationship and one that lasted for more than one night.

Cora disconnected the call and sighed. Every call with her mother was absolutely draining. She would've ignored the special ringtone indicating her mother was on the other end, but she had already done that for the past day and she needed the distraction. Cora knew she was desperate when she was using her mother as an outlet.

Barbara Buchanan was still requesting her daughter's presence at the annual New Year ball. Cora used to live for those annual events. When she'd been younger, with a detailed career and life laid out before her, she'd actually embraced every aspect of dressing up, schmoozing the attendees, and discussing shop while sipping champagne and eating decadent chocolates, of course. But now, none of that held any appeal.

Still, she felt a tug of guilt. She was an only child, she had an entire empire at her disposal, and she had to make a decision at some point.

Easing back onto the couch cushion, Cora couldn't stop her mind from traveling back to only a few hours ago when she'd been lying in this exact spot with the weight of a passionate man settled on top of her.

Her body still tingled and hummed from the experience. Hadn't she told herself she couldn't let this happen? Yeah, apparently she wasn't taking her own advice because now that she'd had a sample of Braxton Monroe, she couldn't un-sample him. Now more than ever she wanted to ignore every single reason she shouldn't do something and just take what she wanted. Wasn't that the whole reason for setting out on her own? To have her own life and do what pleased her?

This fine Southern man most definitely pleased her.

The sound of a car door brought her out of her thoughts. Heidi came to her feet, her tail swishing against Cora's leg.

"It's okay, girl."

Heavy footsteps on the porch followed by a key in the lock had her pulling in a deep breath. Between wondering what had happened to Brock and worrying if the awkward tension would settle between Braxton and her, Cora was a jumbled mess. Hence the acceptance of her mother's call.

When the door opened and closed, Cora shifted on the couch to face his direction.

"Sorry I was gone so long." She heard two clunks by the door and assumed he'd taken his shoes off. "Brock was at the hospital, then the police took a report, and then Zach and I . . . never mind. I hope you weren't too bored."

"I told you I'd be fine," she assured him. "How's Brock?"

The cushion beside her dipped and Braxton let out a heavy sigh. "He's got a mild concussion, four stitches in his forehead, which will make for a nice scar for him to show to chicks, and his car is in need of some major repairs."

Cora laughed. "Your nephew has a gash on his head and you're thinking ahead to him getting chicks?"

Braxton's fingertips slid against her shoulder, brushing her hair aside. This time, she didn't jump. His touch was becoming something she not only had gotten used to, but something she'd also craved.

"He'll be fine," he assured her with a smile to his voice. "I guess I hadn't thought of Brock as my nephew, but he is. Blood isn't always about biology."

"Your family is much stronger than any DNA. Trust me."

Silence settled between them as Heidi circled at Cora's feet and lay down. Cora wasn't sure what to do or say next. Braxton's fingertips toyed with the ends of her hair and he may as well have been touching her entire body for the sizzling effect he had on her.

The sexual tension hadn't disappeared one bit. If anything it was supercharged now because they both knew full well how potent they'd been . . . and they'd barely gotten started.

"What now?" she asked.

"What do you want?"

Thankfully, he didn't ask her to spell it out, he totally got it. With each accidental brush of his rough fingertips against her jaw or neck, Cora had to fight herself from begging him to whip her shirt off and pick up where they left off.

"I thought for sure you would've sat here and talked yourself out of this," he told her. "I was ready to come in and battle with you over how amazing we could be. I had a speech rehearsed and everything."

Cora laughed. "A sex speech?"

"Wanna hear it?" he asked with a soft laugh.

"I think I'll pass."

Braxton's other hand settled on her thigh as he gave a gentle squeeze. "Are you hungry? I was gone for a while."

Cora shrugged. "I hadn't even thought about food, to be honest. I was worried about Brock, thinking about what was going on between us, and then my mother called—"

"What did she want?"

His question was a simple one, too bad the answer was more complex than she wanted to get into. Cora covered his hand with her own and wondered just how much of her life she should reveal. He valued honesty and she valued her freedom.

"She wants me to come home, same as any other call. I wish she understood my need to be away, to break free from the life she wants me to live."

"It can't be that bad, can it?"

Braxton shifted, turning her to nestle into the crook of his arm. Cora threw her feet up on the couch and tried to relax, not an easy feat when discussing her mother.

"My life is a bit complicated," she explained slowly. "My family is wealthy. We actually own a large company."

The hard body behind her stilled.

"From the time I was born I was molded into the next CEO," she went on, suddenly wanting to share a piece of herself. Above all, he had to understand her independent need. "I didn't know any different, to be honest. My parents missed the majority of my school events due to work and I never thought twice about it."

She knew he was listening and the fact he wasn't interrupting was a blessing. She wanted to go at her own pace, reveal pieces at a time. Whatever was happening physically between them was moving so fast, she needed to keep in control of something.

"My parents wanted me to marry Eric. He started working for the company about six years ago and he clicked perfectly with my parents."

"And you?" Braxton asked, his tone soft as his hand ran over her shoulder.

"At first, yes. I mean, I was all business, just like them. Nothing came between my work and me. Eric and I started dating and I think everyone just thought we'd get married and take over the company. But I started having dizzy spells, black dots would randomly hinder my sight. I saw doctors, but nothing much was thought of it. My parents brushed it aside, too, and I honestly thought maybe I was just working too hard and not sleeping enough."

How wrong she'd been. But wishing to go back in time and change things wouldn't actually make that happen.

"When I got a dizzy spell and fell into the pool, the doctor who saw me was a specialist because my parents insisted on the best." As if they settled for anything else any other time. "After talking with him and going through some tests, he diagnosed me with macular degeneration. It's a slow disease that will rob you of your sight if not caught early enough."

Braxton wrapped his arms around her shoulders. "You don't have to tell me all of this. I don't want you uncomfortable."

Reaching up, Cora curled her fingers around his wrist. "I know. I need you to know why I'm here, what brought me to Haven, and that I may be running, but my reasons are justified."

"You don't have to defend yourself to me or anyone else," he told her. "But I'll listen if you feel better."

"After the accident when we knew my sight was limited, I saw my control slipping." Cora swallowed. This was the hardest part, actually. "I was fine, but they were already treating me as if I was broken, vulnerable, and unable to take care of myself. I started seeing my life in a whole new light. I wanted different things, I wanted out of that mold I'd been shaped into."

Cora tipped her head back onto Braxton's shoulder and closed her eyes. "Eric pressed marriage, saying someone needed to care for me once I went blind permanently. No way in hell would I marry someone just so he could take care of me, but I know Eric was worried about his place in the company. With me pulling away, my parents were worried, and he was worried. If we weren't married, he didn't know if he'd still have a high position in the company once my parents retired."

"This guy is an ass."

Cora laughed. "A bit, but I shouldn't have let things go on the way they had. I shouldn't have let him think there was a chance because I never wanted to marry, especially after my accident and I knew what I was facing."

"And they still don't know where you are?" Braxton asked.

"I'm not ready to tell them," she admitted. "I know

it's cruel, they're my parents, but in all honesty, they're more concerned about their company than my well-being. I don't want to be a burden to anyone. That's why I had to leave. I couldn't handle it."

That familiar burning in her throat and eyes built up and she cursed herself for the tears that threatened. She didn't want to cry, didn't want to let this have such power over her.

"I could hear them whispering about me," she went on, swallowing the lump in her throat. "I could hear them talking and already making plans for who they could hire to come in and help me while they were all at work. They didn't ask what I wanted, they didn't even think to consider my needs. Everything was about them and their needs."

Braxton's hold on her tightened as he placed a kiss on top of her head. "You made a bold move coming here alone. How did you get here if they don't know where you are?"

"I had one of my coworkers from the salon bring me. I had already scoped homes out and had been in contact with Sophie, so I knew I'd be fine once I broke free. Besides, I have Heidi and she's seriously the best thing that's happened to me in the past three years."

A slight release of pressure lifted from her shoulders now that she'd told him a bit about why she was here. She needed him to understand her position, but at the same time she wasn't quite ready to reveal who she was. Money changed people and she'd already picked up on the fact Braxton wasn't too keen on padded bank accounts. Whatever his ex had done to him, she'd really damaged a portion inside of an incredible man.

"I don't want to get in on family issues," he stated as he eased his hold on her. "But I wouldn't shut them out. I know you want your independence, but I'm sure they're worried about you."

Perhaps in their own way they were, but she'd lived her life for them for the past twenty-four years and it was time to live her way.

"You're the peacemaker," she muttered. "I heard Zach say it, but I've seen it. You're doing it now."

His silence spoke volumes. Something had happened to instill such a strong trait in him.

"Care to tell me what has you so determined to keep everyone happy and all waters around you calm?"

He moved lightning fast and lifted her up and over to straddle his lap. The man was strong, that was for sure.

"When I've got a beautiful woman in my house, wearing my clothes, and I can still taste her on my lips, the last thing I want to talk about is my past."

Braxton cupped the back of her head and brought their mouths together, no less explosive than hours ago when he'd done the same thing.

Cora held on to his shoulders, warmth radiated through her body. When Braxton framed her face with his strong hands and lifted his mouth slightly, Cora nearly whimpered.

"Stay," he muttered against her mouth. "Stay with me and I'll take you home in the morning."

Okay, spending the night was a whole other level of intimacy. Cora hadn't expected the question, hadn't expected him to even want her to stay.

"I haven't had a woman here since my breakup a year ago," he told her as if sensing her internal battle. "Your call, but I want you in my bed. It can be for now or all night."

Cora closed her eyes as her body continued to hum against his. "I'll stay."

In another unexpected move, he lifted her up and carried her. With her legs locked around his waist, her arms looped around his neck, Cora laid her head to the side and relished the fact she was being pampered by a man who obviously wanted more with her than a quick romp.

The last thing she expected to find when coming to Haven was a man who made her feel anything, really. She had never experienced such fierce emotions, she'd never ached for more and needed a man's touch more than she needed her next breath.

But Braxton pulled passion out of her she hadn't even known she possessed.

She'd lost all sense of direction in her state of euphoria and anticipation. Suddenly she was tipping and her back hit the plush mattress. When she started to rise up on her elbows, Braxton gently placed his hands on her shoulders.

"Don't move. Let me."

Let him what?

A tug on her shirt had her easing up slightly and in an instant the material was whipped over her head. His thumbs hooked into the folded waistband and slid the pants down her legs. She'd not put anything on under his clothes for two reasons: For one they'd been wet from the downpour, but for another she craved just that sliver of intimacy.

Now that she was bared to him, she was thankful for the electric being off due to the storm. She wasn't too self-conscious, but she was a woman and well . . . okay, fine. She might have worried what he thought.

"You're already tensing up on me," he whispered. "I'm going to have to work harder at relaxing you."

"If I relax any more I'm going to melt into a puddle."

Braxton gripped her foot and started massaging.

Then he moved to the other foot and moments later he was gliding those talented hands up her legs.

"You're going to put me out of a job before I can even start," she moaned. "You're very good at this."

"I'm memorizing every inch of your body."

Instant. Chills.

The way he spoke to her in that raw, sexy tone had her trembling beneath his touch. When he skimmed right over the spot she ached for him the most, Cora groaned.

"Easy," he laughed. "I'm taking my time with you."

"Can you take your time later? Now I'm kind of in a hurry."

He slid his hands over her stomach and up to cup her breasts. "I like that you're already planning a next time."

"If you don't get this show on the road, there won't be an encore."

When his mouth replaced one of his hands, Cora arched off the bed and gripped the comforter. She pulled her knees up on either side of Braxton's body as he laid his weight on her.

"You're overdressed," she panted.

Suddenly he was off of her and a rustle of clothing had her smiling. Perhaps Mr. Take His Time was in a hurry after all.

When she heard the unmistakable crinkling of a wrapper, she smiled. "That's more like it."

"Damn it. My hands are shaking," he half laughed.

Cora sat up and reached for him. When she hit his thighs, she slowly moved up to grip his hands. "There," she murmured. "Let me help."

He was indeed shaking beneath her, but that only proved just how monumental this moment was for both of them. Cora was humbled and excited that he was so nervous. At least she wasn't alone.

She glided her palms up his arms and curled her hands around his shoulders. "I'm scared too, if that helps. For reasons I can't think about, this matters more than I wanted it to."

Braxton's lips nipped at hers. "You've mattered since I met you."

With that declaration, he eased her back down and settled between her legs. Cora thought she'd mentally prepared herself for the emotions that would flood her once they came together, but when Braxton joined their bodies, Cora had to shut her eyes to hold back the tears.

"Am I hurting you?" he asked, his voice husky, full of desire.

Cora shook her head and bit her lip. She couldn't speak, didn't want to ruin this moment with words. Everything about being here with him was so much more than she'd thought it would be. The intensity, the slow, easy passion they shared consumed her and pulled out sensations she'd never felt before.

Only this man had the ability to do that.

Cora lifted her knees and tilted her hips as he started to move. Part of her wanted him to hurry, to fulfill both their needs. But the other part of her, the woman who relished in all of these newfound emotions, wanted Braxton to take his time, to make this last so she didn't have to face reality and analyze what all of this meant.

Braxton caressed his lips over hers as he continued to move. Cora opened for him, needing to feel even more of a connection. She wrapped her arms around his shoulders at the same time she encircled his waist with her legs.

He tore his lips from hers to trail his mouth down the heated skin of her neck and across her shoulder. "Feels so good," he muttered.

Cora threaded her fingers through his hair as her body started to rise. Wave after wave slid through her entire body until she was bowing up, tightening around him, and crying out his name.

Braxton whispered something as he trailed kisses along her neck. Before she could fully come back to reality and grasp what he was saying, his entire body trembled against hers. She held on to him as his release took over. Beneath her palms, the muscles in his back tightened, strained. He chanted her name over and over, and Cora knew what they'd just shared was something far beyond what they'd anticipated, far beyond sex.

Intimacy was too mild a word. The bond they'd forged was deep, it was strong, and now they had to figure out where to go from here.

Braxton settled against her side, tucking her against his warm, solid frame. "Sleep," he murmured as he kissed the top of her head. "I'm not letting you go."

Cora swallowed and closed her eyes. He may not want to let her go, but once he found out who she was, would that be a total game changer?

"I'm glad the electric was off," she muttered. "Only fair that if I can't see you, you can't see me."

His fingertips trailed over her side, leaving goose bumps in his path. "The lights came back on before we started. I saw every amazing inch of you."

Cora froze. "What?"

He kissed her softly. "I've never seen a sexier sight than your body, your face when you think I can't see you. Nothing about you could turn me off. Absolutely nothing."

Cora wasn't so sure of that, but she was still reeling from the fact he'd seen her. Truly seen her. Even when she'd been with Eric she'd demanded lights off. But Braxton made her feel beautiful, cherished, and . . . dare she say, loved?

Too tired and scared to delve into that territory, Cora rested against his side and welcomed sleep. Whatever newfound emotions she had to face would have to wait. Right now all she wanted to do was rest in the arms of a man who was everything she'd ever wanted and hadn't known she was missing.

Chapter Twelve

"Our chef quit."

Braxton had barely taken a step inside the back door of the resort when Zach dropped the bomb.

"Quit? How can she quit when she hasn't technically started?"

Zach shrugged as he hung the last pot on the hook above the massive center island. "Her boyfriend wanted to take off and drive out West for the next three months and she's going with him."

Braxton shook his head and closed the door behind him. The irony of a free-spirited employee for their free-spirited sister's resort just taking off was . . . well it would be laughable if they had a plan B.

"The open house is next week and Christmas is in two weeks. We open for business the next day," Braxton stated.

Zach glared across the room. "Thank you. I had no idea the time line."

"Don't be a smart-ass. What are we going to do?"

"Not we." Zach was shaking his head, pointing to Braxton. "You. You're going to ask Liam to fill in until we find someone more permanent."

"Shit," he muttered, wiping a hand down his face. He should've stayed in bed with Cora. He was happy there. The world ceased to exist when he'd been between the sheets curled around her lush body.

"He's actually coming in this afternoon, so you can talk to him in person."

"I don't want to talk to him at all because I can tell you he will say no."

Zach snarled. "Don't give him an option."

"Afraid to do it yourself?"

"I'm afraid if Liam and I don't see eye to eye and fists start flying, my fiancée will kill me."

"You're afraid of Sophie?"

Braxton laughed as he ran his hand along the new quartz countertop. So many people gravitated toward granite, but the quartz was a favorite material of Zach's and since he was the lead carpenter on the project, Braxton really didn't care. Quartz also fit a bit better into their tight renovation budget.

"If you ever settle down and find the one, you'll be terrified of pissing her off," Zach defended. "Trust me."

The one. He'd thought he had that once. Now that he'd shared the night with Cora, Braxton knew without a doubt that anything he'd felt for Anna wasn't even close to what he felt for Cora. He was falling hard and fast. Part of him couldn't believe he'd only known her two weeks, but could he really put a time on how long he should take to have strong feelings for a woman? He'd known Anna for years and look how disastrous that turned out.

Speaking of Anna, he'd had a missed call from her when he'd woken this morning. What the hell could she possibly want? Didn't his lack of returning calls compute with her?

Zach slammed his hand on the countertop. "Dude. Are you with me?"

Blinking, Braxton nodded. "Yeah, yeah. What were you saying?"

Dark brows drawn in, Zach studied Braxton. "Oh, shit," he muttered as he narrowed his eyes. "Don't even tell me you're getting all wrapped up in our new masseuse."

"Fine." Braxton shrugged. "I won't tell you."

"Man, we lost the chef. We can't afford to lose another employee."

Braxton sighed. He really didn't want to get into a pissing match with his brother. "Listen, Cora isn't going anywhere and whatever is going on between us is none of your business."

"It sure as hell is my business when you can't keep your pants on with one of my workers."

Braxton didn't even try to control his anger. His fist connected with Zach's jaw, sending Zach's head whipping back.

"Keep your damn mouth shut," Braxton warned. "Cora is not your concern."

The back door slammed. "Such a warm welcome. I just love coming home."

Braxton turned at the sound of Liam's sarcastic tone . . . and that's where he went wrong. Zach seized the opportunity and plowed his fist into Braxton's gut. Doubled over, trying to take in much-needed air, Braxton braced his hand on the countertop.

"What could you two possibly be fighting about?" Liam asked, his tone worn and tired.

"Ask your brother, who is currently screwing the new masseuse."

Braxton lifted his arm, fist raised. Liam snaked his

arm around Braxton's stomach and jerked him back. "Easy, killer. I've never seen you this worked up."

Rage bubbled inside Braxton and he realized there was only one other woman in his life he'd ever wanted to defend so fiercely . . . his mother.

"Zach has something to tell you about the chef."

Zach narrowed his eyes, one of which was starting to swell. Braxton couldn't help but smile in return. He shrugged out of Liam's hold. "I'm fine. I'm not going to kill him unless he says something else about Cora."

As if to be safe, Liam stepped between the two. "Cora? We'll get back to that later. What's this about the chef?"

Zach continued to stare at Braxton. "She quit."

Silence filled the kitchen and Braxton waited for another fight to break out. When he risked glancing at Liam, his brother was simply shaking his head.

"No. Don't ask me, don't even look my way."

"We have no one else and the open house is next week. We open the week after," Zach reminded him. "It's only temporary."

"Temporary? It will still interfere with my very *not-temporary* job in Atlanta."

Now that he was able to pull in a full, deep breath, Braxton propped his hands on his hips and jumped on the begging wagon. "Listen, we all have had to sacrifice here, but we're so close to fulfilling Chelsea's dream. I took off a semester, surely you can take a month off. I'm sure we can find someone by then and if we get someone earlier, then you are free to go."

"A month?" Liam lowered his head and sighed. "This is the busiest time of the year. I don't even know if I can take off an entire month."

Zach slapped Liam on the back. "Now that it's settled, you can talk some sense into Braxton."

"Nothing is settled," Liam growled, and eased out from under Zach's clutch. "And whatever Braxton is doing or not doing with Cora is none of our concern. If she quits because of him, then you can kill him and I'll help you bury the body."

The support was beyond comforting. "Why don't we focus on getting this place ready for the open house next week? Liam is going to have to come up with a menu or work off the one the other chef was going to use."

"I'll make my own damn menu," Liam grumbled.

A cell chirped and Zach reached into his pocket, pulled out his phone, and quickly read the screen. With a groan, he dropped the phone back into the pocket of his worn jeans.

"I need to meet Sophie at the tree lot and pick up the trees and wreaths. She's going to have this place looking like the North Pole if I don't keep her under control."

Leaning against the center island, Braxton crossed his arms over his chest. "Let her do whatever she wants. She knows a hell of a lot more about decorating than you do. Besides, women love all that and isn't catering to them the whole point?"

Zach raked a hand through his messy hair and glanced around the polished kitchen. "This going to work for you, Liam?"

Surveying the area, Liam walked around the island, checked out the double wall ovens, the industrial stove, the fridge camouflaged as more cabinets, and finally turned back around. "I'll work on the menu tonight and run everything by Sophie."

"I need to get Cora's room finished," Braxton chimed in. "I'll be bringing over her equipment today and the items we ordered should be in tomorrow."

Liam tipped his head, the scar on the side of his cheek facing away as always. "You going to screw this up with her and the resort?"

Braxton leveled his brother's gaze. "No. Are we going to have a problem? Because get it all out of your system now. I plan on seeing Cora now and after we open."

"Is she aware of this?" Zach asked, stepping around to stand by Liam. Ironic his two brothers who were always at odds looked as if they were teaming up against him.

"If you don't have anything else to discuss, I'm going to go pick up that equipment."

"You can dodge the question, but you better make sure your head is on straight with this girl," Zach warned.

Braxton gave a mock salute and turned to walk out the back door.

"How's the back today?" Zach asked.

Braxton threw a glance over his shoulder. "Better. I'll be back."

He wasn't about to get into the fact Cora had massaged him into a state of near nonexistent pain. Seriously, they'd have to consider advertising that little aspect because Cora had some amazingly talented hands and had performed some miracle on his battered muscles.

Yeah, best to leave all of that out.

Before he could escape out the back door, Macy stepped up and started to knock. He waved her on in and moved aside.

"Hey," she greeted, then glanced around the room and nearly froze in place when her eyes landed on Liam. "Am I interrupting? I didn't know you were home."

Liam lifted a shoulder in reply and turned away,

walking out of the room. What the hell was going on with these two?

When Braxton glanced back to Macy, he caught a quick flash of . . . regret? She quickly masked it with a smile as she turned to Zach. "Dad took over work for the day and I thought I'd swing by and see if there was anything I could do to help."

"You want to meet Sophie at the tree farm and save me from hauling twenty trees?"

Braxton snorted. "She's not buying twenty."

"Fine. Twelve trees and fifteen wreaths. It's going to take a while to haul that." Zach shook his head and cussed beneath his breath. "I sure as hell hope nobody is allergic to pine."

Macy crossed the space, placed her hand on Zach's shoulder, and gave him a slight pat. "I'll meet her there. We'll have a girl-bonding moment where we discuss men and how frustrating your species is."

Braxton didn't miss the hint of anger lacing her tone. Even her megawatt smile couldn't hide the fact Macy was upset with someone . . . most likely the man who just stalked off into the other room.

"If you're having trouble with a man, please don't bring Sophie in on it," Zach begged. "She likes me. I'd like to keep it that way."

Macy adjusted the cuff on the folded sleeve on her plaid shirt. "I have a date later, so maybe we'll focus on that."

A cabinet door slammed, causing each of them to turn. Liam had come back into the kitchen, but Braxton hadn't heard him. Clearly, he wasn't too keen on the idea of Macy on a date with another man.

Finally. After years of trying to hide, trying to shut the world out and ignore those around him, Liam was showing some emotions.

"Text Sophie and tell her I'm on the way with my truck," Macy stated, but her eyes remained on Liam's broad back. "We'll be back shortly."

Liam muttered something under his breath and marched from the room once again.

Zach reached for Macy before she could exit. "Something going on with you and Liam?"

Braxton had never seen Macy anything but chipper and happy. But a sad smile tipped the corners of her mouth. "Nothing at all."

Zach released her arm when she turned. Once the back door closed behind her, Braxton glanced to Zach and simply shrugged. Liam chose that moment to come back in, most likely because he'd heard the door and knew it was safe.

Bracing his palms on the center island, Zach closed his eyes and seemed to be counting beneath his breath. When he opened, he stared across the space to Braxton, then to Liam.

"If you two don't get this shit taken care of before the open house, I'm going to have to kill both of you and then I'll be really pissed because the last thing I want to do is run this women's resort alone."

"I don't have anything to take care of," Braxton defended easily. "Whatever is going on with Liam and Macy, though . . ."

"Nothing is going on." The thunder in his voice implied differently. "Drop it and mind your own damn business."

Braxton shook his head and headed out the back door. Regardless of what was or wasn't going on with Liam and Macy, maybe this was good for him. Perhaps he'd be back in the game of life. He was showing more feelings, anger and rage, but hey, that was progress. He kept too much bottled inside.

As Braxton slid in behind the wheel of his SUV, he wondered about the secret Cora was keeping. Whatever it was, he hoped she trusted him enough to let him in. And, he realized, in Cora's world is where he wanted to be.

But if he was allowed access to hers, did that mean she'd have full access to his? Because the world he came from wasn't all sunshine and puppy dogs. Braxton wasn't sure if he was ready to let anyone in on that ugliness . . . let alone the woman he was falling for.

Braxton was just about to knock on the back door of Cora's house when a piercing scream from the inside had him jiggling the knob only to find it locked. He didn't think twice as he gave a swift kick at just the right spot and had the door springing open.

A small flame licked the sides of a pan on the stove and Cora stood back, clutching her arm.

Braxton surveyed the area quickly before jerking the pan off the stove, tossing it and the contents into the sink, and turning off the burner.

His weapon in slapping out the tiny flame was a half-burned towel with dark, jagged edges sitting next to the stove. Finally, once the fire was out, he tossed the towel into the sink, too, and turned to Cora.

Her skin had lost all color and her wide, unblinking eyes stared in his direction.

Slowly he crossed to her, trying to see the damage to the arm she still clutched against her body.

"Let me see," he told her softly. "Did you get burned?"

She nodded, biting down on her lip as her chin quivered. Braxton took hold of her fingers and extended her arm where an ugly red-and-purple burn had marred her forearm.

"Let's get some cold water on this." He gently eased her over to the sink. "I've got you."

He turned on the water and flinched just as she did when the cold made contact with her skin. "Sorry, baby. I know it hurts."

Once he was satisfied with the amount of coolness to the burn, he turned off the water and wrapped an arm around her waist. "Why don't you go sit on the couch and I'll find something else to put on that."

She said nothing as he led her to the living room, Heidi obediently at their side. As soon as she collapsed onto the couch, Cora tipped her head down and attempted to hide the fact she was crying, but her shaking shoulders and unsteady breath tipped him off. Braxton knelt down in front of her.

"I know it hurts," he told her, stroking her good arm with his thumb. "I'm going to get something to help take that edge off."

"No," she whispered. Braxton studied her, watching as she tried to compose herself. "It's not the pain. I just . . . what if they were right?"

Using the pad of his thumb, Braxton swiped her damp cheeks and smoothed her hair away from her face. "Who was right about what?"

"Maybe I shouldn't live alone." Her defeated tone crushed him. "Damn it, I don't want to be dependent, but I can't even make a stupid grilled cheese."

No way was he letting her beat herself up over this. "It was an accident," he told her, squeezing her hand. "The towel was too close to the burner. It could've happened to me or anyone else."

Her wet eyes stared straight ahead, directly at him. "But it didn't. Now all I've done is prove that living alone is harder than I thought. What if you hadn't been here? What if I'd stepped away for a moment?

The entire wall could've gone up in flames and all because I'm running away and being stubborn."

Braxton eased up onto the couch beside her and pulled her into his arms. "You're stubborn, yes, but you're also human. Accidents are going to happen. Even if I'd been here, that towel could've still caught fire."

But maybe it wouldn't have and she wouldn't be hurt. Damn it, he didn't want her injured, and he sure as hell didn't want her to doubt her ability to live a normal life without a keeper. He'd never seen her defeated, he'd never experienced a lack of confidence.

"I'm just having a bad day." She pushed away from him and pulled in a deep breath. "I talked with my mother this morning and we actually had a good talk, but—"

"You're feeling guilty," he finished, noting the tone in her voice.

Cora nodded. "I've done so well through the years of ignoring her jabs, but she thinks I've just deserted them. Understandably, she's worried about the future of her business. I get it, I really do. I just wish she would try to grasp where I'm coming from too."

"Why don't you invite her to the open house next week?" he asked, a little shocked the idea came to him so quickly. "Have both of your parents see where you'll be working, show them your house and how well you're—"

She was shaking her head. "Absolutely not. I don't want my parents here. I don't want them to meet . . ."

Her words died between them, but it was obvious she didn't want her parents to meet him. A sense of déjà vu swept through him as he shifted away.

"I didn't mean that the way it sounded," she muttered, toying with the hem of her cardigan.

"Sounds like you're ashamed of what we have, of

me." Braxton closed his eyes and forced himself to fight the hurt threatening to consume him. "After last night I thought we'd grown closer."

"We have," she insisted, glancing toward him. "My parents are complicated people and I just don't want them here. You have to trust me. I have my reasons."

He didn't want to compare Cora to Anna, but the similarities were too blatant. The red flags were waving in his face and he shoved them aside. He didn't want to see them, he didn't want to believe that she was embarrassed of him, of what they shared.

"I know that all of this with us is new, but I need to know where we stand. Was last night just a one-time thing? Because that's not how I went into this."

Cora worried her bottom lip with her teeth and reached her hand out, searching for him. Braxton met her halfway and laced their fingers together.

"It wasn't just one time," she told him softly. "This does mean more, but my parents aren't part of whatever is happening here. Please, understand that I need time to adjust to this new life. I wasn't expecting to find such a great job, let alone a guy who makes me feel . . ."

Braxton smiled and tugged her against his chest. "Makes you feel what?" he whispered against her lips.

"Achy."

Sliding his mouth over hers, he trapped her hands between their bodies and set out to prove just how achy he could make her feel. Last night wasn't a one-and-done thing. When he'd dropped her off at home this morning, he hadn't wanted to let her go. Waking up with Cora at his side was different and unexpectedly . . . perfect.

But she wasn't ready to hear that and he wasn't quite ready to say it out loud.

He nipped at her lips before pulling back. When her tongue slipped out to slide across her bottom lip, it was all Braxton could do to stay focused.

"Let me get something for that burn." He smoothed her hair away from her face as he came to his feet. "Then I need to load up the equipment and get it back to the resort."

"I'll come with you," she told him.

"You sure?"

Nodding, Cora smiled. "Despite what you think, I like what's going on with us. Forget my parents, forget all the reasons this is bad timing, and let's just see where things go. Can we do that?"

Even though Braxton wanted to know more, he wanted her to lay out for him the reasons she was so adamant about keeping her parents at a distance, he also had a need to keep Cora in his life. For now, he'd play things her way, but soon they were going to have to talk, because if he was going to invest his heart again, he wanted the full truth.

Cora tried to hide the yawn, but when Braxton chuckled, she knew she'd been caught.

"Sorry," she muttered behind her hand. "It's been a long day and I didn't get much sleep last night."

Braxton's low groan had her realizing what she'd just said. "I didn't mean—"

His hand covered her thigh. "I know what you meant and I'm not apologizing."

Cora reached back to grab her seat belt, but instantly Braxton was across her and pulling it into place.

"I can get it."

"I'm aware of that, but I'm using this as an excuse to cop a feel." His warm breath tickled her cheek as his hand slowly grazed across her chest. "Unless you'd rather I not touch you."

Had the temperature gone up? Cora's entire body heated at those low, seductive words. Her belt clicked into place, the sound cutting through the tension.

"I have a surprise for you." His lips slid across her jawline.

Cora tipped her head to the side, needing more, silently begging him to continue. "What's that?" she whispered, hoping it had something to do with less clothes and a bedroom . . . or at least not the passenger seat of his SUV.

"I can't tell you, but it's not far." His hand slid up beneath the hem of her shirt, his thumb stroked over her heated skin. "But this will have to wait until later. I just wanted to touch you in private."

They'd spent the last two hours working on her room in the resort. Zach had come and gone, Sophie and Macy were busy putting up trees, which may be the reason Zach had gone because he was getting his head bit off by the other two women when he kept trying to tell them there were too many decorations.

Braxton had been a total professional and Cora appreciated the fact he wasn't flaunting this fresh relationship in front of his family. She couldn't deal with that step quite yet. All of this happened so fast, yet she couldn't stop herself from getting caught up in the roller-coaster ride. She was starting to crave Braxton more and more.

"I want you to stay with me tonight," he told her. "Tomorrow is Saturday and we have nothing to do."

"Braxton—"

His lips covered hers, halting her protest. But when his tongue eased her mouth open and he took the kiss from sensual to curl-your-toes sexy, she completely forgot what she was about to protest. When a man kissed with this much passion, he wanted more.

Cora placed her hand on his chest and eased back. "I can't think rationally when you're kissing me."

"Perfect." The smugness to his voice had her laughing. "I hope I keep your mind muddled."

When he brought the engine to life, Cora was still reeling from his touch. Her entire body tingled and she couldn't deny she'd never felt as alive as she did with Braxton. He was special, he was too good to be true, and she held out a very big secret from him.

"I need to tell you something," she blurted out before she could think better of it.

"You sound serious."

Cora swallowed the lump in her throat. "I-I'm . . ." This was harder than she thought.

Braxton's hand covered hers. "Whatever you want to tell me can wait until you're ready. Yes, I want to know everything about you, but not at the expense of your nerves. When you're with me I don't want you to worry about anything."

Cora sighed. She should press on, but fear gripped her and she took the easy way out. "Tell me what this surprise is."

"Not a chance."

"Tell me you didn't get me a Christmas present. I don't think we're at the present stage."

Braxton's laughter filled the vehicle. "I can honestly say I didn't spend a dime. But I'm curious about these stages. What stage are we in? The great-sex part?"

Cora felt her face heat as she clasped her hands in her lap. "I don't have definite stages," she defended. "And I certainly wasn't planning on the great sex, but buying gifts isn't something I think we're ready for."

"Baby, if I want to get you a Christmas present, you can sure as hell believe I will."

When he called her "baby," something shifted inside her. Each time he threw out an endearment, which wasn't often, something clicked in her heart that she couldn't identify. Okay, she could, but she wasn't ready for that.

Clearly, there was quite a bit she wasn't ready for where Braxton was concerned. He deserved more. He deserved a woman who could get on the same page as him. Worry settled deep within her. Where were they going with this relationship? Would they turn into something more or was a heartbreaking end in their future?

"We're here," he announced, cutting into her thoughts.

Cora blinked and turned toward him. "Where's here?"

"You'll see. Don't move. Let me come around to you."

He was aware that she didn't want help, but she wasn't going to say anything, not when he sounded so pleased with himself. Besides, she couldn't recall the last time anyone had surprised her with anything at all.

She unfastened her belt just as her door opened. "Take my hands," he said, taking hold of her. "Just follow me."

"Heidi—"

"I'm getting her to put in the other car. Trust me."

The other car? What was he doing?

He led her a few short steps away. "The door is open." He placed her hand on the inside of the driver's door, she could tell by the angle at which it was open. "Go ahead and get in."

Cora froze. "What?"

"You're going to drive. Don't worry, I'll be in the passenger seat."

Instantly her eyes burned as tears clogged her throat. "Are you making fun of me? Where the hell are we?"

Braxton's strong hands framed her face. "I would never make fun of you. I'm giving you a bit of your freedom back. I heard that sad tone in your voice when you mentioned the things you haven't done since you lost your sight and it gutted me. I just want to give back, Cora. That's all."

Damn it. Now her tears did spill over and Braxton promptly swiped them away. "I can't believe you thought to do this," she whispered. "I've never had anyone . . ."

Words failed her as she closed her eyes. Braxton's soft lips settled against her forehead as he muttered, "I'm finding I'd do anything to see you happy."

Oh, man. How could she fight this battle with herself? How could she keep denying the fact she was falling for this man? He'd proven over and over again that she mattered more than on a physical level. He was the most giving person she'd ever met.

"Where are we?" she asked again, once she trusted her voice.

"At the edge of a wide, open field. One of my students has a farm and this field isn't occupied by any livestock. I called him earlier today and he was more than happy to let us use it." He swiped her damp cheeks and tipped her chin up. "So get in the driver's seat and take me for a ride. You've got seventy-five acres to do what you want."

Cora turned toward the car and reached out to find the steering wheel. Braxton didn't help her, he didn't attempt to get her belt or anything. Once she was in, she reached back for the handle and closed the door. The back door opened and closed and Heidi's head was instantly at Cora's right side. The passenger door opened and Braxton blew out a breath as he settled in the seat.

"There's not a tree or fence around. I made sure to pull in the middle gate, so let loose."

Cora couldn't contain her smile as she felt the steering column for the keys. She pressed her foot on the break and brought the engine to life. Gripping the wheel, she simply sat there for a minute, unable to believe this was happening.

"Take your time," he told her. "I've got nowhere else to be but with you."

Cora bit her lip to keep it from trembling. He got it. He got her. Braxton knew she wanted to savor this moment, to cherish her sliver of freedom . . . a freedom he'd understood was so important to her.

"I'll thank you for this properly later," she promised.

"If you keep talking like that, this ride will be cut short."

With her right hand, she felt around for the gear shift and found it in the center console. Such simple things as gliding the gear from park to drive were a thrill.

Easing off the break, she started forward, clutching the wheel. Her foot barely touched the gas as they crept along, the bumpy field shaking the vehicle.

"You can give it more gas. We're in an old Jeep that belongs on the farm. They use it out here. You can't hurt a thing."

Maybe not, but she was still getting her feet wet with being the driver. "Can we put the windows down?" she asked.

"I'll do one better. Stop the Jeep and I'll put the top down."

Cora stopped the car and waited while Braxton

removed the top. Once he was settled back inside, she decided to let loose.

Instantly the wind whipped her hair around, the uneven ground jarred her entire body, and she felt as if she were flying. This was by far one of the greatest moments of her entire life. She actually tasted freedom and it was all thanks to Braxton.

He never said a word, but she could feel him at her side. He'd made these arrangements only to see her smile and keep her happy. Everything about Braxton Monroe filled her with more joy than she ever knew possible.

"Can I turn?" she asked.

"Do what you want," he yelled over the wind. "Nothing is around us."

She slowed down enough to turn the wheel and once she started, she just kept making circles. Then she started zigzagging. This was like being a kid at an amusement park on one of those silly car rides for children. There was nothing to worry about and fun was the top priority.

Cora didn't know how long she drove, but she could feel the air turning a bit cool, so she knew the sun was starting to set.

"Where are the lights on this thing?" she asked, slowing down.

"I can still see just fine," he told her. "The sun hasn't faded completely yet. Are you planning on driving all night?"

His question was asked on a chuckle and Cora shrugged. "Maybe I am. Maybe I'm thinking about driving until it gets pitch-black and then having my wicked way with you."

Braxton growled. "You're pushing me and you're

going to have to pay the consequences if you keep taunting me."

"I hope so," she retorted, feeling a bit more sass than usual. He brought out the absolute best side of her, the real side of Corinne Buchanan.

"You drove so long, Heidi is passed out in the backseat," Braxton told her.

"She's earned her naps. She's adjusted so well to being here and I've had her working hard on learning the path at the resort."

"There should be a lever on your left side," he told her. "Check the end of it and see if it turns for the lights."

Cora felt for the lever and turned the end as instructed. "That do it?" she asked.

"We're good. Drive as long as you want. We have plenty of gas."

A sliver of guilt slid through her. "Are you bored out of your mind watching me drive aimlessly?"

"I watched you sleep last night. I tried to sleep, but you were so breathtaking lying there that I couldn't take my eyes away. I wasn't bored then and I'm not bored now."

Cora brought the Jeep to a stop but continued to grip the steering wheel as his words washed over her.

"For the past year of my life I've been restless and out of control," he went on, his voice softer now. "I've been searching for something to fill this void after Chelsea's death and then when my engagement ended. Being with you feels like nothing I've ever experienced and I can't explain it. So never doubt that I want to be with you. I'm not bored. I'm happier than I've been in a long time."

Too many emotions ran through her at his raw confession. He'd not come out and said the words, but she knew his feelings were running deeper than she'd been prepared for . . . which gave her a little relief considering her feelings were a bit out of control. She couldn't keep up with how fast her emotions were running away from her, so Cora opted to go along for the ride. Literally and figuratively.

Putting the car in park, she killed the engine and unsnapped her belt.

"What are you—"

In an instant, she hiked up her maxiskirt, fumbled over the console and straddled Braxton's lap. "I thought I'd show my thanks now. Is that a problem?"

For a half second he said nothing, did nothing, then those big, powerful hands of his gripped her hips. "The only problem is you're wearing too many clothes."

He took the bunched material and jerked it higher around her waist. Cora tipped her hips toward his and let her head fall back as his hand traveled up her bare thigh to her center.

Cora reached out to hold on to his shoulders as he caressed her. The man could pleasure her so fast with very little effort, which just proved how potent he was when it came to knowing her body, her needs.

She trailed her fingertips down his taut abs, then reached for the button on his jeans. She lifted slightly on her knees for better access. When his hands covered hers, she froze.

"I'll get it," he told her, his voice husky. "You've got me too worked up."

"I haven't done anything yet."

"You're sexy as hell just sitting there and your little pants are just about to kill me."

Had she panted? Hmmm, probably. Braxton and his talented hands were most definitely pant-worthy, that was for sure.

"I don't have any protection," she stated, realizing now was the worst time to have this revelation.

"I didn't plan on this out here, so I don't either. But I swear I'm clean. I've been reckless, but I haven't been stupid."

Cora slid her hands up under his shirt, needing to feel those rippled muscles beneath her palms. "I'm on birth control and I know I'm clean. I've only been with one other person and I've had a physical since."

Braxton's lips nipped at hers. "Then what are we waiting on?" he murmured. "I'm ready to be thanked properly."

Cora laughed as she adjusted her body against his. Slowly she joined them, closing her eyes and giving in to the desires flooding through her. Braxton's hands gripped her hips and held her still.

"Not yet," he whispered. "Don't move. I just want to feel you."

Cora's head tipped forward, meeting his. Their breath mingled, the tension seemed to crackle between them, and Cora thought for sure she would die of want. He wanted to feel her? Could he be sexier? He knew the right words to make the biggest impact on her and he wasn't even trying.

Cora rotated her hips. "I need . . ."

In a flash, he shoved her shirt up and whipped it off her. He was tugging the cups down on her bra at the same time he started to move. All at once he seemed to be touching her, kissing her everywhere, and all Cora could do was clutch those strong shoulders and let him.

His mouth worked over her chest, his hands dipped at her waist as he ran them back down to her hips.

"This what you needed?" he asked.

"Yes," she whispered, unable to use any energy to even form a full sentence.

Those lips moved on up her neck, over her chin, and finally claimed her mouth. Cora kissed him with every bit of passion she had in her. She wanted him to know she wasn't holding back, not anymore. Everything she had to give was his.

Every part of her body started to hum as wave after wave swept through her. He continued to kiss her, swallowing her cries and taking in her release.

Braxton covered her thigh with one hand, the other grabbed her hair and tipped her head to the side as he deepened the kiss. His entire body stiffened as he continued his assault on her mouth. Cora was still trembling from her own climax as Braxton started his, but she wanted to keep this bond, wanted to keep this connection. She couldn't touch him enough.

As his body settled beneath hers, his lips softened until he was placing short, sensual kisses over her lips, then across her jaw and back to the sensitive spot beneath her ear.

"You're becoming more," he whispered. "This is just the beginning."

Cora lay against his chest, trying to pull in enough air to just keep breathing. Nothing could've ever prepared her for what just took place. Nothing could've prepared her for those honest words just delivered to her, and nothing could've prepared her for falling in love with a man she'd only known a short time.

No. Nothing in her polished, well-cultured life had prepared her for Braxton Monroe.

Chapter Thirteen

"It's not tacky, it's festive."

Braxton rolled his eyes and ignored the bickering between Zach and Sophie from the other room. Those two would not survive this decorating. The open house was in two days and they still were discussing tree and wreath placement. Braxton really wished Zach would just shut up. The man wasn't going to win this fight, but for once, Braxton wasn't going to get involved.

Braxton worked on washing and drying the new glasses and plates. Macy had some connections with her hardware store and had ordered from a housewares wholesaler at a ridiculously low price.

"When will he ever learn to shut the hell up?" Liam asked from behind.

Braxton dunked another glass in the suds. "He won't, but Sophie's a good match for him since she gives it right back."

"He deserves it." Liam rolled out more red fondant across the wide island. "Now that he's occupied, want to tell me about Cora?"

Braxton froze, his hand gripping the glass. "You

want to talk about Macy?" he asked, throwing a glance over his shoulder.

Liam grunted and remained silent.

"That's what I thought," Braxton muttered.

They worked in silence for a few more minutes before Liam spoke again. "You really think this is going to take off?"

Braxton rinsed the final crystal glass and dried his hands. "Yeah, I do." He turned, resting back against the counter. "Sophie said she's got nearly every room and the cottages booked all the way through for the next month and several bookings in February and March. I think we'll be fine."

Liam nodded. The muscle ticked in his jaw, just below where his scar ended. With careful precision, he sliced the tiny knife through the fondant. "I got fired."

"What?" Braxton pushed off the counter and closed the distance between them. "What the hell, Liam?"

With a shrug, he continued to meticulously cut miniscule circles out of the thick icing. "I asked for a couple months off, I even offered without pay, and they said this wasn't the time to be taking off with the busy holiday season. We had a few choice words and they told me if I wanted to come here, then not to go back. So, here I am working on fondant holly wreath decorations for the open house wondering if I just committed career suicide."

Braxton listened to his brother speak. He didn't raise his voice, didn't show any emotion as he maddeningly concentrated on the slice of the knife.

"How are you so calm?" Braxton asked. "You loved working there."

"I'll have to love working here." Liam finally straightened and met Braxton's eyes. "Looks like you won't have to be in such a hurry to find another chef."

Braxton knew this was hard for Liam to handle, knew the last thing his brother wanted to do was move back home. Braxton actually hurt for Liam. For the past decade Liam had made a life for himself away from Haven, only coming home when needed. After the accident he'd wanted to get away, to ignore the pain and the memories that came along with this little town.

But maybe it was time for him to come home and heal. Maybe this was the path in life Liam was supposed to go down. And maybe Chelsea was somewhere smiling down on them, loving that all of her brothers were finally going to be in the same town, working on the resort she'd always dreamed of.

"What are you going to do with your condo?"

"My lease is up at the end of the year." Liam glanced down to the pile of red circles and went back to cutting more. "I'll look for a place here for now, but I don't plan on staying."

"You can stay with me."

"Not a good idea."

Crossing his arms over his chest, Braxton leaned against the island. "And why is that?"

With a snort, Liam shook his head.

"What? Just say it."

On a sigh, Liam laid down his knife and braced his palms on the counter before focusing on Braxton. "Whatever you and Cora have going on, I don't want to be in the middle of."

"I didn't plan on inviting you into our relationship."

Liam narrowed his eyes. "You know what I mean."

"I'm trying to help and you're being stubborn."

"Stupid, stubborn man." Sophie stormed through the kitchen and slammed her hands on the island. "What does he know about decorations?"

She glanced back and forth between Liam and Braxton as if they'd actually answer her. Hell no. Braxton knew when to keep his mouth shut when it came to women and fits of rage. He'd lived with Chelsea long enough to know sometimes it's best to just weather through the storm. Women's moods changed fast enough, he'd hold out for the next one.

"You have a wreath hanging on the mirror in the entryway," Zach defended as he came into the kitchen. His mess of hair was even more disheveled than usual.

"Because it's pretty." Sophie whirled around and glared at him. "If you don't like how I'm doing things, then leave. Chelsea would've—"

Her last words died off in a sob, and Sophie turned her back on Zach and covered her face with her hands.

"Well, shit." Braxton rounded the island, but stopped short when Zach jerked his gaze in his direction.

Liam fisted his hands on the counter and stared at Zach, who rubbed a hand down his face before reaching out to grip Sophie's shoulders. He turned her around and held her, patting her back and whispering something Braxton couldn't hear.

Stupid jerk. Emotions were high, everyone was stressed, and by next week they were supposed to be at their top performing level with smiles on their faces. The first time those doors opened to the public, they knew there better be perfection staring back at them or this dream of Chelsea's would fade and all of their work would be in vain.

"Keep the wreaths," Zach stated, still holding Sophie. "I'll go get more. We'll put them over every window outside and I'll keep Braxton off the ladder this time. I swear we can put up any decoration you want, but please stop crying."

Braxton exchanged a look with Liam. Only Sophie could pull out such emotions and compassion from Zach. She'd always been the one for him, it just took him a tragic accident and a decade to get his head on straight and wake up to what was in front of him.

Sophie sniffed as she eased back and curled her hands into Zach's T-shirt. "Sorry. I just want it all to be perfect. I want Chelsea to be proud and I want this place to be packed just like she envisioned."

"It will be," Zach assured her. "With all of us taking charge, there's no way this place will fail."

Sophie swiped at her eyes and straightened her shoulders. "I'm going to go call Macy. She ordered some extra wire and hangers for me and I need to see if they came in."

When Sophie left the room, Zach blew out a breath and stared up at the ceiling.

"I'll be sticking around longer than we first thought," Liam stated. "I was fired."

Zach turned toward his brother and stared.

Braxton snorted. "Why don't you kick him while he's down? You delivered that about as softly as a two-by-four to the head."

Liam shrugged. "No way to sugarcoat the truth."

Zach laughed, not a this-is-hilarious type of laugh, more like an if-I-don't-laugh-I'll-explode-and-hit-things type of laugh. "Well, sorry you lost your job, but we could use you here and actually, that's one less thing we have to worry about."

Braxton didn't know why he thought Zach might show a bit of compassion, but clearly he had used it all up on Sophie.

"What the hell is all of that?" Zach asked, pointing to the red circles and the clump of leftover fondant.

"Balls for the holly wreath decorations for the cupcakes."

"You have to make this up that far in advance?"

"When you're wanting a few hundred cupcakes all festive and shit, yeah. It'll be fine in the freezer."

Zach braced his hands on the edge of the counter and dropped his head between his shoulders. He was worn out and the fatigue was finally taking its toll. They were all stressed and worried and flat-out irritable at times, but the end of this road was in sight and they were about to start a journey that would prove just how strong their bond and loyalty truly was.

"I'm sorry you lost your job because of this," Sophie said with a sniff as she swiped at her damp cheeks. "But for purely selfish reasons, I'm glad you're going to be here."

Liam turned to the fridge and pulled out another tub of fondant, this one green. "It's not permanent, but I'll kick things off until we can find a permanent replacement."

Sophie took a step, but winced, and Zach quickly wrapped his arm around her waist. "I'm fine," she assured him. "Just turned wrong."

"Reschedule that showing," he told her.

Shaking her head, Sophie replied, "This is the third time they've looked at this house. I'm hoping they're ready to make an offer. I don't need to walk through like I have before, so I'll be just fine."

Zach looked like he wanted to argue, but Sophie put her hand over his mouth. "You're not going to win this argument, so don't start it. I need to head out so I can freshen up my makeup. I should be home by six."

She didn't even give him a chance to say anything else as she kissed him and headed toward the front of the house.

"Is it just your default to argue with people?" Liam asked, focusing now on rolling out the green icing.

Braxton sighed. "Yes, he argues by default just like you poke the bear and get him angrier. You two need to cool it and concentrate on the open house and the business. We each have our roles and we need to stick with it. If we start agitating each other it will only hurt us."

Zach narrowed his eyes. "Why the hell are you in charge?"

"I'm not in charge, I'm just the only one thinking straight right now."

"I'm thinking just fine," Liam replied. "I'm thinking how I want you two to get the hell out of my kitchen so I can work in peace and quiet."

Zach reached into his pocket and pulled out his keys. "You don't have to ask me twice. I'm heading over to Macy's to see how the work came along today."

"When will her house be done?" Braxton asked, noticing how Liam was trying his hardest to look like he was working, but his hand had all but stilled.

"We're hoping within the next two weeks."

"She deserves a new house," Braxton replied. "She's worked her ass off since school and gave up everything to stay here for her dad."

Zach nodded in agreement. "I'm trying to get her in before Christmas, but she may be moving that day."

"Need my help with anything?" Braxton asked.

Shaking his head, Zach headed toward the back door. "Nah. You'd fall off the ladder and then sue me."

Braxton rolled his eyes. "I wouldn't fall off the damn ladder."

"If you two are done, some of us are actually working," Liam growled.

Zach reached for the door. "You gonna stab me with your little knife?"

"Don't tempt me." Liam glanced to Braxton. "You leaving?"

With a laugh, Braxton nodded. "Yeah. I'm going. You seem happiest when you're baking and I don't want to be the reason these cupcakes don't turn out. Sophie would kill all of us."

Braxton followed Zach out the back door. Before Braxton could reach his SUV, Zach turned and held up a hand to stop him.

"I need to get this off my chest."

Braxton blew out a breath and crossed his arms. "Cora."

Nodding, Zach shifted his stance wider. "How serious are you?"

So serious he could still feel her when she wasn't with him. "Pretty serious."

Zach adjusted his hat and stared out toward the pond for a minute before looking back. "You were serious about Anna."

The words could've been a jab, but the tone in Zach's voice was too soft, too caring . . . a rare thing for Zach to be concerned, so Braxton didn't reply with sarcasm.

"Anna was nothing compared to this."

Zach's eyes widened as he took a step back. "Okay, then. I didn't expect you to be that deep with her."

"Yeah. I didn't expect it either." Braxton rubbed the back of his neck. "She's different and I have no clue what's going to happen, but I won't let it cause a problem with the resort."

"I know you won't," Zach replied. "Just make sure you don't get your heart handed back to you like last time. I don't want to see you go through that again."

Braxton smiled. "It's like you really care."

"Hell," Zach muttered, throwing his hands up in the air. "I knew you couldn't go two minutes without being snarky. Yes, I care, just because I'm not all hugs and smiles all the damn time. Now get out of here."

Braxton gave his brother the one-arm man hug and slapped his back. "Love you, too."

He was still smiling when he slid behind the wheel of his car, but the smile died when his phone rang and Anna's number lit up the screen.

Placing the phone in the console, he ignored the ring, same as the other times. Anna was in his past and whatever she wanted now was no concern of his. He had a future he was looking forward to and a woman who filled him with such happiness and a sense of perfection, he never wanted to look back. So he wouldn't.

He didn't even think twice as he drove to the tree farm. It was time to see that smile of Cora's once again.

Cora jumped when she heard heavy boots on the porch. Heidi let out a sharp bark, swishing her tail against Cora's leg. She wasn't expecting Braxton, but she didn't know anyone else who'd show up on her doorstep.

When he knocked, Cora pushed away from the computer and padded barefoot to the door.

"It's me," he called. "I have a surprise."

Laughing, she flicked the lock and pulled open the door, his last "surprise" banging against the window panel. The wreath was actually so sweet and she still smiled when she thought of him picking it out for her.

"Another surprise?" she asked.

"Can you hold the door open? And have Heidi stand

back, I don't want to step on her. I can't see very well in front of me."

Confused, Cora pulled the door open wider. "What on earth are you doing?"

She snapped her fingers for Heidi to come to her side. Instantly, Cora heard rustling, Braxton's light grunt, and then the scent of fresh pine assaulted her.

"You got me a tree?" When his shoulder brushed across her chest, Cora tried to inch back more to make room for the man and the tree. "How big is it?"

"The fattest one I could find," he stated, sounding a bit winded. "Damn, that thing was heavy. I'm going to prop it in the corner and grab everything."

As he brushed by her again, he stopped, grabbed her face, and kissed her hard before releasing her. "Keep that door open. I have a few more trips to make."

Cora wasn't quite sure what had gotten into Braxton, but he was in a mood. A surprise tree, a kiss like he'd just come home from work and they were sharing a house. She couldn't help but smile. No matter the fact they'd known each other a short time; something about Braxton's take-charge attitude with a side of sweet compassion had her wondering if this was going to be so much more than she bargained for. She wanted to reach for this relationship with both hands, she wanted to hold it inside her heart where the outside world couldn't damage it.

By the time Braxton finished, he'd made three trips and she had no idea what on earth he'd brought in.

"I'm sorry, I just completely overtook your house. Let me help you to a safe spot because I've got stuff all over."

She reached out her hand but squealed when he picked her up and carried her. "I can—"

"Walk. I know. But I want to hold you and I've missed you."

Okay, when he said things like that how could she be stubborn?

"So what all did you bring besides the tree?" she asked as he eased her down onto the couch. "Did you smuggle in little elves to help, too?"

That rich laugh of his slid over her. "No, but I may have gone overboard with decorations."

"You bought decorations?"

"A few. I never put up a tree since I live alone, so I had no idea what it would take to cover this thing. I tried to do the math for the size and do a ratio with the lights and bulbs, but . . ."

Now Cora laughed as the mental picture of Braxton in the Christmas aisle filled her head. No doubt he'd stood there looking all sexy and confused and a bit nerdy in that drop-dead gorgeous kind of way. Her heart filled with so much for him, but she wasn't ready to label her emotions. It was too soon . . . or so she kept telling herself.

She'd known Eric nearly her entire life, as their parents had run in the same circles, and logically to them, Eric and Cora should automatically mesh together.

But she'd known Braxton for such a short time, and the bond they had was already so strong and unlike anything she'd experienced before. Which just went to prove that time meant nothing and character meant everything.

"Let me get the tree set up in the bucket with some water and once all that is done you and I will decorate it."

Cora reached her hands out. "Come here." Instantly he took hold, gripping her hands in his rough ones.

"You keep doing all these things for me and I have no idea how to thank you or even return the favor."

He released her hands and the warmth from his body settled over hers as he leaned into her. The cushion on either side of her head dipped as he caged her in.

"I have several ideas on how you can return the favor," he muttered against her lips.

Cora reached up to touch his face but landed on the side of his neck. "I'm serious."

"I was too."

He slid his lips over hers, so slowly and so . . . promising, she sincerely hoped he planned to deliver on that veiled promise later.

When he eased back, Cora was more than ready to forget the tree.

"I'm not doing any of this to get something in return," he told her. "All I want is to see you happy."

He'd put her happiness in the forefront of this relationship and never expected anything for it. He was so selfless, so giving. Guilt washed over her. She needed to tell him who she was, she needed to be up front and honest. She wanted more with Braxton, wanted to see where this led, and they couldn't do any of that if she was keeping a secret from him.

But she didn't want to ruin this surprise he'd worked so hard for. One more day. She only wanted one more day of being Cora, not Corinne.

"Right . . . there."

Braxton's back muscles strained as he held Cora up so she could place the angel on the top of the tree. She'd only needed a bit of guidance as she'd felt along the branches in front of her.

His back and shoulder were so much better, but lifting her so high was starting to remind him he still wasn't in perfect condition. Still, he didn't care and he wasn't about to say a word. He loved this moment with her, loved these memories they were making.

"How does it look?" she asked as he eased her back down to the wood floor.

"You did great."

"Oh, please. You bought everything."

Braxton may have put a hurting on his credit card, but he'd do it again without question to see the happiness in her eyes. He hadn't seen that bright light before. When he'd first met her she was guarded, hesitant, but the more they grew together, the more he was seeing a relaxed side, a side abandoned by cares and worries. Whatever had plagued her since she arrived in Haven seemed to be fading into the background. Or she was just adjusting so well, she wasn't concerned with her old life.

Regardless of the reasons, Braxton was thrilled to know that he had a hand in helping her with the new life she'd wanted to find.

"I feel like we should have hot cocoa or something now," she told him.

"My mother used to make me cocoa." The words were out of his mouth before he even thought about holding them in. "She was amazing."

"I didn't mean to bring up memories," she told him.

Now that the past was creeping up, he found he wanted her to know. He wanted to take that risk and bare himself to her. If he was going to put everything on the line, he needed to expose himself in a way he never had before.

"I told you my mother was killed." Braxton fisted his

hands and tried to hold it together and keep those images from his mind. "My father was abusive—"

"Oh, Braxton."

"No," he said, shaking his head, though she couldn't see him. "I need to get this out. I want you to know, I need you to understand what I came from."

Reaching out, he took her hands and led her toward the sofa. The worry lines between her brows increased as she tightened her hold on his hands.

"You don't have to explain anything to me, Braxton. I don't want you to revisit a time that hurts you."

"Everything happening between us matters too much to me to keep secrets." He licked his lips and pulled in a deep breath. "Because you mean something to me, I care about you and I want you to be part of my life. And, I need to give you the opportunity to see what you're getting involved with."

"If you're implying you're like your father, I won't believe it. You'd never hurt anyone."

Braxton let out a soft laugh. "Maybe not, but I could've easily gone that route. My life before the Monroes was up and down at best. The highs were high and the lows were . . . a nightmare."

Cora's hand slid from his and traveled up his arm, over his shoulder, and cupped his cheek. "You overcame your past. That's what makes you so special."

The warmth of her touch combined with her comforting words filled him with the courage he needed to continue.

"My dad was a strict military man. He wanted things done a certain way at a certain time and there was no room for error. He was toughest on my mother. I know now that he suffered from PTSD. That damn disease destroyed my family and turned my father into a monster."

Braxton wasn't going to go into how he was abused,

how even the slightest things would set off his father. Going there was irrelevant and there was no need to make Cora feel sorry for him. That was definitely not the angle he was after.

"My mother would explain how he wasn't like that before he'd been deployed, but when he'd come home he was a changed man." His beautiful mother, always seeing the good in people, always wanting to make things right. "She stayed with him, in hopes she could fix him, that loving him through the illness would show him that she wasn't abandoning him."

"Your mother sounds like a strong woman."

Braxton swallowed the lump in his throat. "She was perfect."

Memories of her taking him to the park, teaching him how to swim, taking him to the movies all washed over him. She'd done everything in her power to give him a wonderful childhood, but he'd seen how hard she worked trying to compensate for being both loving mother and doting father.

"You can stop right there," Cora told him, stroking his jaw with her delicate fingers. "I can imagine how the story ends."

He reached up, took her hand in his, and settled them in his lap. "One night my father couldn't find his lighter. I had used it to light the candles on my mother's birthday cake. I was only nine, but Mom helped me because she knew I wanted to be big. I didn't put the lighter back, so when he went to find it later, he got enraged."

Cora's soft breathing, her very presence was everything he needed to stay strong, to face the demon that still haunted him.

"He grabbed my shoulders and shook me." Braxton could still feel those strong hands gripping his slender frame. "My mom grabbed his arm and tried to tell him she'd find the lighter, but he turned on her and slapped her across the face. When she fell, I ran into my room and locked the door."

A decision he'd regret until the day he died.

"My dad tore through the house, stomping and yelling. I heard my mom crying and decided I couldn't hide, not when she needed me." He pulled in a deep breath, the hardest part yet to come. "When I came out, my dad had a gun and was waving it around. He always had one on him because he was paranoid even inside our own house. He didn't see me at the top of the stairs and my mom was frantically still searching for that damn lighter."

Braxton blinked back the burn in his eyes. Tears wouldn't change the ending. "At that point he was just angry because that was his default emotion. He kept waving that gun and when my mom came up behind him with his lighter, he turned and fired."

Closing his eyes, Braxton willed the pain to go away, and fought to finish. He'd come this far.

"When he saw what he'd done, he crumpled to the floor and held her. For a few seconds, I caught a glimpse of the man my mother swore he was. In those few moments, he held on to her and told her how much he loved her, how sorry he was. And I know he was sincere. It took killing her to snap him back. But the second he picked up his gun, I knew. I just knew in my gut what he was going to do. I was still frozen at the top of the stairs, he never looked my way."

Braxton choked out the last words. Cora framed his face, swiping his tears with her thumbs. He bit his quivering lip, hating that he couldn't keep up his strength.

"I'm sorry," he whispered. "I didn't mean to ruin the evening, but I had to tell you. I didn't want my past between us because it did shape the man I am today and I wanted you to know everything about me."

She threaded her fingers back through his hair and tugged until he rested his forehead against hers. "Nothing you tell me could change my feelings. If anything, I'm even more in awe of the struggles you've faced and how you've overcome each of them."

Relief flooded through him. Needing the contact, Braxton slid his hands around her waist and held on. "I need to tell you something else."

"Anything."

He lifted his head, wanting to look into those beautiful violet eyes. "I'm pretty sure I'm falling in love with you."

Cora stilled, her breath caught as her mouth parted. "You-you don't mean that. It's too soon."

He smiled despite her reaction that stemmed from fear. "Is it? Because I can't put a time frame on feelings. If you're honest, you feel the same."

She blinked a few times, her lips pursing together. "Really? You and that ego are full of it again. You have no idea how I feel."

The pulse at the base of her neck quickened, her cheeks pinkened. Braxton closed the space between them and hovered his mouth just over hers.

"I know how you look at me, I know how you're guarded, but when we're together you let loose and you have this look of contentment."

Her lids fluttered down as he stroked his lips back and forth across hers. "And I know you have feelings because I can tell when you touch me. You aren't just trying to take in my physical appearance, you're actually seeing me, all of me, and now you've seen my darkest side. You're still here, you're not afraid."

Braxton trailed his fingertip down the column of

her throat. Her head tipped back and rolled to the side as a soft sigh escaped her lips.

"Tell me you don't feel everything when I touch you," he whispered. "Tell me we aren't on the same page."

"Fine," she groaned. "You win."

Arching her back, she bit her lip as he continued to stroke his fingers over her skin. "Say it," he demanded.

Cora sat straight up, gripped his wrists, and looked directly at him. He knew she couldn't see him, but she literally stared right into his eyes.

"I'm falling for you, too. I didn't want to, I even told myself I wasn't, but you consume all of my thoughts and this new world I have started building. I need you, Braxton."

Every bit of his tension, every single thing wrong in his past suddenly vanished for a moment. All that mattered was right now, this second and how Cora was opening herself just as much as he was. The fact they were both exposed and vulnerable only proved how deep they were forging their bond.

He knew her admitting her need didn't have anything to do with right now and intimacy, but everything to do with life. And he needed her in his life, too. Needed her in a way that left his heart wide open for the risk of being crushed, but he didn't care. Cora was worth . . . everything.

Braxton came to his feet and scooped her up into his arms. "I need you, too," he told her as he carried her down the hall, toward her bedroom. "I'm staying tonight."

Her hand caressed his jawline as she rested her head on his shoulder. "I wasn't going to let you go."

Chapter Fourteen

Tangled in sheets with her head resting on Braxton's shoulder was exactly where she wanted to be. The way he'd opened up to her last night had shaken her and completely caught her off guard. Thinking about all of these feelings was so much different from getting them out in the open. Once they were said, they couldn't be *un*said.

Would she take the words back, though? Cora closed her eyes and sighed with content. No. The timing may be bad, the upheaval that was her life certainly would cause issues sooner rather than later, but she didn't for one second regret being honest with Braxton.

And her revealing her heart had nothing to do with the gut-wrenching story of his childhood and everything to do with the strong man who trusted her enough to open his life in such a way.

Braxton's arm tightened around her, drawing her even closer to his side. She had no clue as to the time, no clue if the sun was coming in through the windows or if it was pitch-black outside. She didn't care. Time didn't matter at this moment, not when her body was still humming after last night.

The man couldn't be more perfect. He brought her a freaking tree. And ornaments. And lights.

What man thought to bring a woman Christmas decorations? A blind woman at that? She couldn't see what they'd done, but to know that her home was festive for the holidays had seriously warmed her heart. He'd wanted to make her feel more at home, had wanted to share the tradition with her of putting up a tree. Somehow that seemed more intimate than lying here naked with him.

After last night, with Braxton projecting every single thing about his life, she knew she needed to tell him every part of hers. It was only fair and he deserved a woman who was completely honest. He hadn't had that in the past and she didn't want to be just another woman who betrayed his trust.

He shifted in the bed, the coarse hair on his legs tickling hers. When he rolled to his side and wrapped his other arm around her, Cora inhaled the sexy, masculine scent she'd come to associate with Braxton.

"Why are you awake?" he muttered against the top of her head.

"I'm enjoying the moment."

"You enjoyed it last night," he told her. "Now you should be resting up."

No, she needed to rehearse her speech in her head so she could tell him the truth. But the end result would be the same and there was no easy path to get there.

"What time is it?"

He shifted a bit, then moved back to nestle deeper into the pillow with her. "Five. Way too early to be talking."

Yeah, well, there wouldn't be a good time. Cora slipped her hand beneath the sheet and rested her palm over his taut abs. The man was absolutely amazing and the fact he cared so deeply because of such a tragedy only made her want to be with him even more. She only hoped it was possible after she explained who she was.

Not that keeping her life a secret was a big deal, but he prided himself on honesty and he'd been burned before because of money. Would he see that she was so much more than a company worth millions?

"We're not going back to sleep, are we?"

Cora laughed. "I haven't been asleep."

He smoothed her hair away from her face and ran his hand down her bare shoulder. "Tell me what's on your mind because clearly I didn't do a good enough job of keeping you distracted."

Cora pulled in a deep breath. "I don't want any secrets between us, but I also don't want to tell you where I came from before I settled here."

"You can tell me anything," he assured her, still stroking her shoulder.

"My family is . . . wealthy."

He snorted a laugh. "I know. You have class and poise written all over you, but you still have fun and relax when your true side comes out."

"I want you to remember that." It was imperative that he keep that image of her in his mind. "I have a large company that is my responsibility. It's a responsibility I don't want, but one that isn't easy to just pass on to someone else."

Well, legally she could pass it on, but at what price? What would signing over her shares and the title of CEO do to the already strained relationship? Just because she didn't see eye to eye on things with her parents didn't mean she wanted to be completely cut out of their lives. But she worried they might never see things on the same level no matter what she decided to do.

"How large a company are we talking?" he asked.

Cora sat up, gripped the sheet to her chest, and kept her back to him. "Buchanan Chocolates."

Silence settled into the room and she'd never known how deafening the void of noise could be. She closed her eyes, cringing at the unknown reaction yet to come. She'd said it, she'd gotten this out in the open, and now she had to wait and see how Braxton would deal.

"What the hell are you doing here?"

His slow question didn't shock her and she knew he wasn't referring to here in bed with him.

"I can imagine how this looks to an outsider, but I didn't want to be stuck in that life another minute." She sounded like a spoiled brat even to herself. "After I lost my sight, I realized how much my parents were counting on me, then I saw how they struggled with my blindness, but not from a parental standpoint. They were worried about the company and how it would continue on after them. They kept pushing Eric and me together, kept saying how if we married I'd have someone to take care of me, someone to help run the company."

Braxton remained still behind her, he hadn't moved one bit. She kept waiting, wanting to feel his reassuring hand on her back.

"I didn't want to marry or be taken care of," she went on. "I had my degree in accounting, but that was also at my parents' request. I wanted to do something for me so I got my massage therapy license. After that I started working part-time in the spa in Atlanta. My clients had no idea about my family status, the name Buchanan is too common."

Restless, Cora shoved the sheet aside and reached for the robe she kept on the bedside chair. She couldn't sit here another second waiting for him to say something or reach for her. After pulling her robe around her, she came to her feet and jerked the ties together.

"I don't expect you to understand and I'm sure you'll have questions, but I need you to know that I didn't plan on finding you, I didn't expect to fall for someone because I've never had the idea that I would ever find anyone. And all of this has snowballed and I just wanted to live in the moment and be with you."

She carefully moved toward the window seat and sank down onto the cushion. The sheets rustled and she held her breath.

"This is why you didn't want to invite your parents to the open house?" he asked. "You didn't want them to see this new life, to meet me. It's all clicking into place now."

The bed creaked slightly and Cora knew he was up. Fear gripped her. "No, you're looking at this from the wrong angle."

"Really?" he mocked. "How can it be wrong when plain as day you made a fool out of me and this relationship? Damn it, Cora, I let you keep this secret even when I knew it was big. I knew you weren't ready to share and I respected your decision to take your time."

She heard him jerk his jeans on, the rasp of the zipper slicing right through the tension. Cora came to her feet.

"Are you seriously leaving?"

"If I stayed what would happen?" he asked. "I don't even know how to respond to this. Leaving is the best choice for both of us."

"I'd think if you stayed we could talk."

He moved across the hardwood floor, more rustling

of clothes, the *thud* of shoes. Each noise made her heart clench more.

"What do you want to discuss, Cora? The fact that you could've told us up front who you were? The fact that you're a millionaire, yet you want to work for us? Were you serious about staying? Was this just a spur-of-the-moment decision to get back at Mommy and Daddy? Because this is my damn life and you can't just play with people's feelings like this."

"I would've stayed," she defended. "I wasn't playing with your emotions and I wasn't going to leave the resort in a bind. I bought this house, didn't I? That should tell you this wasn't some fleeting phase."

Silence once again filled the room. She wanted to crawl back into the bed, have him wrap his arm around her and tell her that he understood why she made the decisions she did. She wanted to have that reassurance that she hadn't killed this bond between them, but she feared she'd done exactly that.

"I'm not quitting," she whispered. "I still want to work for you."

His mocking laughter had her cringing once again. "Well, you're in luck, seeing as how we have no one else and the open house is less than a week away."

Cora wrapped her arms around her middle, trying to keep any more hurt from seeping in. "Will I hear from you before then?"

"I wouldn't count on it."

Heavy footsteps sounded out into the hall, the front door opened and closed, leaving Cora alone and wondering how this could be fixed. For the first time in her life she had actually found a sense of happiness, a sense of belonging, and a place she wanted to call home. But home had nothing to do with her new house and everything to do with the man she'd just driven away.

Three days had passed and Cora was in no better mood than when Braxton walked out. Sleep had become her enemy, leaving her alone with her thoughts. She'd done way too much online shopping, but it was Christmas and she figured she deserved to give some gifts to herself. Unfortunately, retail therapy wasn't working either.

She'd just finished washing her plate and putting it into the cabinet when her doorbell rang. Instantly she smiled, but then reality hit. Braxton wouldn't be back. She'd pushed him too far and she couldn't blame him for being angry.

So who could be dropping by?

Heidi obediently brushed against her side as she felt her way down the hall and toward the foyer. With her hand stretched out in front of her, she closed her fingers around the dead bolt.

"Who is it?" she called.

"It's Sophie and Macy. Can we come in for a minute?"

Sophie and Macy? Cora wasn't necessarily in the mood for company and she hadn't met Macy before, but she'd heard mention of the local hardware store owner.

With a sigh, she flicked the lock and opened the door. It would be rude to turn them away and, honestly, she was getting sick of herself at this point.

"We come bearing gifts," Sophie stated. "And I'm sorry I didn't call, but this is sort of a last-minute girl gathering. We hope you don't mind we're using your house."

Two sets of feet moved on into the foyer so Cora closed the door and forced a smile. "I'm in a crappy mood and I'm out of junk food, so I can't guarantee the ambiance for this party."

Sophie laughed. "Bad mood? We're in the right place, Macy."

"I'm Cora." Cora held out her hand, hoping Macy would take it so she didn't look like a fool. "We haven't met before."

Macy shook her hand. "I'm sorry for barging in on you. Sophie was on her way to your house when I called her. I needed to vent and she said she was coming over here because you and Braxton were having problems, so she picked me up and here we are."

"I didn't say they were having problems," Sophie defended.

Macy laughed. "Fine. Your exact words were 'Braxton is acting like an ass and Cora hasn't been around for a few days. I want to figure out what's going on.' Did that sum it up?"

Cora crossed her arms, intrigued at the banter between the ladies and the fact they were talking about her as if she were their old friend. Small towns. Gotta love them.

"Pretty much," Sophie stated. "I'm sorry, Cora, but I can't handle seeing Braxton like this and I figure if he's miserable, then you probably are, too, and I know you still haven't made many friends in town and I like to think we're friends—"

Cora held up her hand. "We're friends and I'm actually glad you guys are here. I need some serious girl time."

"Good because we have rocky road ice cream," Macy proclaimed, a smile in her voice.

"It's like an early Christmas present." Cora gestured

toward the back of the house. "Head on back to the kitchen and we'll get some bowls. Ice cream is exactly what I need."

As they gathered in the kitchen, Cora pulled out the bowls and spoons. Sophie scooped up the servings and they all sat around her small kitchen table.

"Cora, do you want to start?" Sophie asked.

"Not really. I'd rather just plant my face in this bowl of ice cream."

She also wanted to know how Braxton was acting. He was obviously hurting if he was being a jerk. And if he was hurting, why didn't he talk to her so they could work this out?

"I'll go first," Macy chimed in. "I'll keep it short and simple. I've been interested in a guy for a while—"

"Liam," Sophie interrupted. "Don't be so veiled about it. Carry on."

A spoon clanged against the side of a bowl and Cora dug in for another bite herself. So Macy had a thing for the quiet, mysterious Monroe brother. Interesting. Those men were something, that was for sure. And right now, Sophie seemed to be the only one who was happy with one of the frustrating men—granted she'd had to struggle through a decade of heartache to get to this point. Cora didn't think she had the energy to fight that long.

"He refuses to give me the time of day," Macy went on, not denying the fact she had a thing for Liam. "So I go on with my life, because I'm not sitting around and waiting for him to wake up. So this guy I've dated a couple times lately ends up being a total control freak. We were set to go out tonight and when he showed up to get me, he told me to change. Told me, not asked. Of course, if he'd asked I still would've said no."

"Why did he want you to change?" Cora asked around a bite of gooey marshmallow.

"He claimed other guys would look at me because my top was too revealing."

"Men look at boobs through a turtleneck," Sophie replied. "They see a woman, they zero in on boobs. It doesn't matter what you wear."

"Yeah, well, I told him I didn't feel like going out tonight and that I didn't think it would work out."

Cora scraped her spoon around her bowl, sad to find she'd already eaten the last bite. "I'm going to need more ice cream before I get into my mess."

"I'll get it," Sophie said as she scooted her chair against the wood floor. "So, Macy, now that you're done with this guy, are you going to make a play for Liam?"

"I've tried to talk to him, tried to flirt even, but he just pushes me away. He doesn't even act like we're friends sometimes."

The pain in Macy's voice hurt Cora. It was clear this woman had feelings for Liam, but why was he keeping her at a distance?

"I'm new here, so I don't know all of the logistics here, but did you and Liam date in the past? I mean, if he's purposely keeping you at a distance, it sounds like he has feelings but he doesn't want them. Does that make sense?"

Macy laughed. "Oh, does it ever make sense. We never dated. I was interested in him in school, but I was so tied up with softball and then I got a scholarship and went away to college. When he was in the accident with Zach and Sophie, that was about the time I had to come home because my mom died unexpectedly."

Cora's bowl clanged on the table in front of her. "Double serving this time," Sophie whispered.

"After my mom's death, I stayed and helped Dad with the store. I tried to visit Liam, but he didn't want to see me and then he moved to Atlanta. Over the past several years he rarely came home, until Chelsea's death and the renovating of the estate."

"He's going to be here for a while," Sophie added. "He's going to be the chef at Bella Vous since ours quit."

"What?" Macy's question came out as a gasp. "He's staying? But, he's avoided this town for so long and . . . oh, no."

"What?" Cora asked.

A loud sigh filled the room. "He texted me about renting the room above the hardware store. I didn't know it would be for him, but if he's coming back, then I guess that's who it would be for."

"Looks like you may get that opportunity after all," Sophie said softly, a smile and a little naughty to her tone.

"I can't even think about him being that close to me. He'll ignore me and that will only hurt more. Damn it. I'm going to need a double serving, too, Soph."

"Coming right up."

"I can't discuss Liam anymore. You want to go, Cora, or should we just finish off this carton of ice cream and discuss something neutral like the weather or the holidays?"

Cora attempted a smile, but she just wasn't feeling happy. "Honestly, if Braxton is angry or not acting right it's completely my fault. I kept something from him, but it was personal. I didn't expect to be so swept away by him. Everything happened so fast and I just went along for the ride."

"You don't have to tell us what it is," Sophie stated, setting back down at the table. "But I'm sure you know he was lied to by his ex-fiancée, right?"

Cora nodded, the lump of guilt growing thicker in her throat. "Yeah, he told me all about her. Which is why I know I hurt him. But I had my reasons and he doesn't believe they were completely innocent."

"If you want to tell us what happened, it won't leave this room," Macy promised. "But if it's too personal, then we understand."

Cora chewed her ice cream and contemplated how to even begin her story. There was so much that happened in such a short time, she was still spinning. She gave them the shortened version of her life before she came to Haven, then went on to explain her need for freedom, to break away from the corporate world and the lifestyle molded just for her. She expressed her concerns about getting involved with Braxton, but the man was impossible to resist.

"So, you're seriously an heiress to a chocolate company?" Macy asked. "You are honestly the coolest person I know."

"I find that only slightly offensive," Sophie chimed in. "But since that is pretty damn cool, I'm going to agree."

Cora shook her head and pushed her bowl away. "I promise, that life isn't eating chocolate and sipping wine all day. It's hard work and your life revolves around business meetings, traveling, marketing, spreadsheets, quarterly reports. The boring list is absolutely endless."

"So when you lost your sight, your parents thought you needed a keeper?" Macy asked.

"Pretty much. I wasn't in love with Eric to begin with, we were more compatible in the boardroom and looked good on paper. But after the accident, when we knew blindness was inevitable, all of a sudden Eric wanted a ring on my finger and so did my parents. That's when I realized I'd been living for them all along and everything in my life was theirs. I had nothing of my own. Not one aspect of my life was happy because I hadn't chosen a thing."

Silence filled the room and Cora wasn't sure what the other ladies were thinking.

"I really hope I didn't come across as a spoiled brat," she went on, suddenly nervous. "I know I have everything at my disposal, but money truly can't buy happiness. I don't even care about the money, not with what all comes with it."

"I'm still processing all of this," Sophie said. "It's hard to like you when you have all the money and chocolate a woman could ever want, but I love you so I'm trying to see your struggle."

Cora laughed, she couldn't help it. "Thanks, I think."

"I admire you," Macy said. "I gave up everything I wanted for my family, but I wouldn't change it. You've put your entire life on hold for your family and you're finally going after what you want. I think you're making the right move."

For some reason Macy's words comforted Cora. She hadn't realized how much she wanted someone to see her point of view, how much she wanted someone to understand that this wasn't an easy decision for her.

"Has Braxton . . . you know, has he said anything?"

Could she sound any more like a high school girl trying to find the dirt on her ex? But she couldn't resist asking, she was human. She was brokenhearted and sick that she'd hurt someone she cared so deeply for . . . someone she'd come to love.

"I almost hate to tell you, but he hasn't said anything." Sophie delivered the words with regret in her voice and almost a sadness. "He's been quiet, keeping to himself more than I've seen from him."

Cora swallowed, hating the question she was about to ask, but she couldn't resist. "Was he like this after his breakup with Anna?"

"He was angry," Sophie replied. "He was flat-out mad and suddenly he was acting completely unlike himself. He started drinking, nothing major but definitely more than the norm. Then he'd go missing for a day or two at a time. We figured out he was . . . um . . ."

Cora offered a smile. "I know what he was doing. He told me what happened after Anna."

Heidi's fur brushed against the side of Cora's leg. Cora reached down to pat her faithful friend, loving how the dog sensed the emotional pain.

"That time he was angry because he felt like he'd been played for a fool," Sophie added. "But this time he's like an injured animal slinking away to lick his wounds."

Cora closed her eyes and blew out a breath. "Is all the ice cream gone?"

"Yeah. We pounded that carton in about ten minutes."

Flattening her hands on the table, Cora pushed away. "Then let's go have a movie marathon. You guys up for it?"

Silence and then she realized how that had sounded.

"I still enjoy movies," she laughed. "I just listen to them. And if they're ones I've already seen, then I already know what's happening."

"Are you sure?" Macy asked. "I feel like we steamrolled right into your house."

"Please, I was getting so sick of hearing myself whine and my Christmas shopping is done so I've been online shopping for myself. I need a break from me."

When an arm slid around her shoulders, Cora jumped.

"Sorry," Sophie said, still hugging her from the side. "I just wanted to tell you that Braxton will come around. He just needs some time to process how special you are and how you didn't mean to deceive him. He was just blindsided, that's all."

Cora nodded, willing the burn in her throat to go away. She didn't deserve to cry, not when she'd done this to herself.

"Let's go watch something ridiculous and funny," she said.

"Sounds good." Macy's chair scooted against the floor. "So, would you happen to have any chocolate around here anywhere?"

"Macy," Sophie scolded at the same time Cora groaned.

"What? It's a legitimate question."

Cora shook her head. "No, sorry. I've had my fill for a while. I have potato chips and popcorn. Will any of that work? Oh, and I have wine."

"Yes," Macy replied.

"Yes to which one?"

"All of it," Macy laughed. "Bring it all. Let's binge on crap food and funny movies."

"I'm game," Cora replied, suddenly thrilled that these two crashed her pity party.

"What about you, Sophie?" Macy asked. "You're in

a disgustingly happy relationship. You able to stick around?"

"I can always use some girl time," Sophie replied. "I think Brock and Zach are having some male-bonding time tonight anyway. Zach's been trying to kiss and make up to Brock since the car accident when he over-reacted."

"Then let's grab the necessities and head into the living room," Cora suggested. "I have nothing to do tomorrow. Stay as late as you like."

Maybe then her house wouldn't feel so lonely. Braxton had only been in it a handful of times, but she still hated being here without him now. He'd filled every room. When she smelled the tree she instantly thought of his kindness, when she went into her bedroom . . . well, that was impossible not to picture him there.

He was everywhere. Now she just had to figure out how to fix the damage she'd done. She hadn't come this far in her journey to give up the one amazing thing that had happened to her.

Chapter Fifteen

Braxton sipped his drink and half listened to Zach. The open house was set to start in an hour and everything was in place. Christmas trees were lit up in every room, fresh garland was wrapped around the thick banister curving up the steps, wreaths were on every single window, and a few even hung on mirrors on the inside. Classy white candles on pewter candlesticks adorned the mantel in the main living area. There wasn't a stationary item that didn't have a decoration of some sort. But instead of being tacky, the place looked like something from a magazine. Sophie had seriously outdone herself and Zach owed her a huge apology for doubting her and giving her a hard time. If all of this had been left up to Liam, Zach, and Braxton, they may have thrown a tree in the living area and called it a day.

The food, though, was definitely something that was going to be a huge hit. Liam wouldn't settle for anything less than the best. He was currently setting out an insane assortment of finger foods and pastries. Everything was magical and perfect and exactly how Chelsea would've wanted it.

But Braxton couldn't take his eyes off Cora, who had entered the room exactly three minutes ago. For the last three minutes Zach had sounded like the teacher from *The Peanuts*.

"And then I won the lottery."

Braxton jerked around. "What the hell?"

Zach almost cracked a smile. "I've been saying shit since you spotted Cora and the lottery got your attention. I also told you I had a sex change, so apparently that isn't as exciting for you."

Braxton took another sip of his bourbon. "You're an ass. What do you want?"

"For you to go talk to her or quit sulking. We have a lot riding on this and the last thing people need to see when coming in the door is your pissy face."

Braxton downed the rest of the bourbon, welcoming the burn. "I'll talk to her when I'm ready and it's none of your concern. Don't you have a fiancée to annoy?"

"I like her," Zach stated with a shrug. "Even if she did make me wear a suit. I'd rather annoy you."

Across the room Cora moved gracefully, elegantly. That upbringing of hers was embedded so deep within her. She was a damn millionaire, yet here she was wanting to work as a masseuse and live on her own, out from under the thumb of her controlling parents.

Braxton wished like hell he knew what to do with all of these emotions. When Anna had cheated on him and informed him she was calling off the engagement, Braxton had hated how he'd been played and how foolish he looked being the second guy in her life. He'd vowed from that moment on to never be a fool again.

Yet here he stood, staring at the one woman whom he actually loved, the woman he couldn't get out of his mind. She'd wedged herself so deep, he knew she would be part of him forever.

But she hadn't trusted him enough to say who she was initially. There had been ample time to come clean. Had she been embarrassed by him? Had she thought her parents wouldn't approve? Just because she wanted to start a new life didn't mean she wouldn't revert back to her old one. She may want to work now, but what about six months from now, a year? Would she find it so easy to be out on her own, away from the only life she'd known?

"Either talk to her or get outside for some air and cool off before guests arrive." Zach snatched the empty glass from Braxton's hand. "Do it now or Liam and I will kick your ass."

"You and Liam teaming up together? Not likely."

Zach muttered and walked away, but Braxton's eyes were still on Cora. The fitted sapphire-blue dress was stunning. With her long, auburn hair tumbling down her back, Braxton fisted his hands at his side and tried to rein in his emotions. His control had been utterly shredded and he had no clue how to piece it all back together.

All he knew right this minute was that he couldn't keep his hands off her another second. With his sight set on her, he marched across the room. She was talking with the new beautician, laughing and totally oblivious to his presence, which pissed him off. How could she be so happy when he was so . . . not?

And how selfish did that make him that he wanted her to be unhappy simply because he was? Damn it, this love thing seriously screwed with all common sense.

"Excuse me," he interrupted. He patted Heidi on the head and shot a smile at the newest staff member who had only been hired last week. "Would you excuse us for a moment?"

Haley nodded and returned his smile. "Of course."

Apparently, she wasn't picking up on the tension as she turned on her heel and walked away.

Cora blinked in his direction, her knuckles tightening on Heidi's collar. "Braxton."

He reached for her arm, careful not to grip too tight. "Come with me."

When he started to move away, he was met with resistance.

"I'm fine here," she told him, stubborn chin lifted in defiance.

"I want to talk before people arrive and I want privacy."

Turning her head slightly, Cora sniffed. "Well, you could've stopped by my house any day in the last week since you left. Plenty of privacy there."

Raking a hand through his hair and keeping his hold on her, Braxton blew out a breath and attempted to count backward from twenty . . . he made it to nineteen. Why did this have to be so damn complicated? Couldn't he want a woman who was passive, smiled and nodded, went along with everything he said, and was completely honest? No, he'd chosen the woman who had the ability to crush him in ways he'd never known possible and he wanted more.

"We're talking now. You want to do it where everyone can hear?"

The muscle clenched in her jaw and he knew she was biting back her words. "Fine."

He led her from the room, ignoring the glances from Zach and Sophie. Whatever they thought was none of his concern and he honestly didn't give a damn. All he wanted was to . . . hell, he didn't know. He knew he wanted to be with her, touch her, taste her. It had been too damn long. The time gap between them had seemed like an eternity and for once in many months, he didn't even think of another woman. There was nobody else. Yes, she'd lied to him. Yes, he was furious. But damn if he didn't still want her. There was no shutting off that emotion or desire. If anything, the absence only made him ache more.

"Where are we going?" she asked as they traveled through the hallway.

He didn't say a word as he led her into her own room where she'd be working. Once inside, he pulled the double doors closed. The *click* of the lock sliding home seemed to echo through the room.

Heidi obediently sat next to Cora. Releasing the collar, Cora crossed her arms and tipped her head to the side. "Now you want to talk? I've waited for you to cool off for days and you choose now to—"

He hadn't even realized he'd closed the space between them, but he cut her off with his lips. A gasp escaped her as her hands came to clutch his shoulders. She willingly opened for him and Braxton knew nothing but this second, this woman. He didn't care what was going on outside these doors, didn't care that a party was getting ready to happen. All he cared about was the fact that Cora wasn't pushing him away.

Braxton slid his hands around her waist, pulling her flush against his body. She felt so damn good. He'd missed this familiarity, he'd missed her.

Cora pushed against his chest. "What are you doing?"

"I have no idea." Honesty, he lived by that damn rule. "I thought I could avoid you, I thought I could stay away and keep my head on straight, but when you walked in tonight all of my intentions were shot to hell and I realized how much I need to touch you."

Cora shook her head. "I can't keep up with you."

He tightened his grip on her waist and nipped at her lips. "I don't want to analyze this."

Carefully her hands traveled over his shoulders, up into his hair. "I'm a fool for letting my emotions lead me, but I've missed you."

Relief flooded through him. He didn't give her another second to say anything or to fully think this through. He didn't give a damn what waited outside those doors.

Braxton wrapped one arm around her waist and plunged his other hand through her hair, tipping her head to claim her mouth once again. With a soft groan she opened, arching into him as if she'd craved this just as much as he had.

He'd never missed a woman like this. Despite his confusion, he still wanted her. Yes, she'd withheld information from him, but at the same time, this whirlwind relationship took them both by surprise.

Braxton gathered the skirt of her dress in his hand and yanked it up to her waist. Gliding his hand over her silky panties had him fighting for control.

"What about the party?" she muttered as her lips slid along his jawline.

"We're having our own private one."

He roamed his fingertip along the edge of the satin, teasing her and torturing himself in the process. Those breathless pants of hers were driving him insane. When she eased her legs apart, he wasted no time in taking what he wanted.

Cora's forehead fell to his shoulder, her hands clutched at his biceps. Her hips worked against his hand and Braxton couldn't believe he'd gone days without touching her. They needed to talk now that he had some time, but right now, all he wanted to do was give her pleasure and secure that bond they'd started forming weeks ago.

"Braxton."

Yeah, he knew. Her fingertips dug into his arms, her warm breath came out fast and harsh against his neck. This is what he'd missed. Her coming undone, her completely at his command. When she shattered, Braxton tipped his head to the side, kissing her on the sensitive spot just below her ear.

She'd barely stopped trembling against him when someone pounded on the locked door. Cora jumped back, forcing Braxton to pull away. Heidi, who'd obviously been resting off to the side, shot to her feet as well, wagging her tail as she stared at the door.

"Guests are arriving. Wrap it up."

Zach, a man with tact and sensitivity.

Braxton adjusted Cora's clothes as she brushed her hair away from her face. Her eyes were wide, face flushed as she rested a hand over her chest.

"I can't believe we did that," she whispered. "Wait, I didn't do anything, except . . ."

Braxton smiled. "You did what I wanted you to do. Now we need to get out there before Zach comes back."

"What about you?" she whispered, smoothing her hands down the front of her dress.

Yeah, he was a bit uncomfortable, but anything more would have to wait. "You go on out. I just need a minute to think of overweight men in Speedos. Wait, just saying it is helping."

Cora laughed, which is exactly what he wanted. Too much tension had wrapped around them and tonight was supposed to be fun and enjoyable. They had a mission and nothing could get in his way of seeing Chelsea's dream through. Okay, he'd gotten a bit sidetracked by

Cora, but he was back on course . . . until after the open house.

"We need to talk," he told her. "I'll take you home after the open house."

Cora crossed her arms, her stare landing on his chest. "Are you saying that so we can finish what we started here or are you seriously wanting to talk?"

"Both."

She nodded slightly and patted her side. Instantly Heidi stood by her. "We'll talk first."

Without waiting on him, she moved cautiously toward the door. Her palm hit the wood, sliding down until she found the lock. With a soft *snick*, she opened the door and closed it, leaving him to figure out just what the hell he was going to say when he got to her house.

On one hand he wanted her to apologize for keeping such a big part of herself from him. On the other hand, he figured he should be the one to apologize since he left her house and didn't speak to her for several days.

Still, she had to understand that dropping a bomb like that wasn't going to go over easy with him. He'd trusted her from the start and he knew she had trust issues, he got it, but he didn't see the reason for the secret for so long.

Honestly, he could get past this as long as he knew without a doubt that she wasn't ashamed of him, that she wasn't keeping her other life at arm's length because she was afraid to let him into that world. Because, damn it, he wanted in that world of hers more than he ever thought. These past few days had seriously given him some time to think, pout a little, brood a bit more, and think again.

"Damn it." Zach strode through the door. "Now is not the time."

Braxton blew out a breath and strode toward the open door. "Not now, Zach."

"I told you to talk to her, not screw her." Zach stepped in Braxton's path, blocking the door. "You can't go out there and stare at her all night. Keep your head on straight."

Braxton narrowed his eyes at his brother. "I can handle it. Get out of my way."

"When I think you're ready to face people without a scowl I will."

Braxton gritted his teeth and forced himself to calm down. As much as he wanted to have a deep, meaningful conversation with Cora, it would have to wait. She agreed to let him take her home, now all he had to do was make it through these next three hours of smiling, mingling, and talking spa shit all while pretending his life was all puppy dogs and rainbows.

"I'm fine," Braxton assured Zach.

Zach studied him, but Braxton held his ground. No way was he going to act as if he couldn't handle the turmoil in his life.

"There you are." Liam came up behind Zach. "I was hoping to catch you away from the people who are already arriving."

Braxton didn't like the tone Liam was using, nor did he like the sympathetic way he was only looking at him.

"What's wrong?" Braxton asked.

"Anna's here. She's asking for you."

Damn it. Now was not the time to have a confrontation with his ex. He'd avoided her at all costs after she humiliated him and ignoring her recent texts and calls hadn't deterred her any, apparently.

"Want me to handle it?" Liam asked.

"I'll handle her," Zach chimed in.

Braxton held up a hand. "I can deal with my own issues. Where is she?"

"She's waiting on the patio," Liam stated. "Do you want to talk somewhere private in case she decides to make a scene?"

The last thing he wanted was to be alone with her, but he also had no idea what she wanted or if she would cause drama. He wasn't in the mood to talk to her at all, but maybe if he finally did then she would leave him alone.

"Tell her to come in here." Braxton rubbed his hand over the back of his neck and willed for more patience to magically appear. "I'll wait."

"Are you sure this is a good idea?" Zach asked.

"Might as well get this over with."

Liam nodded and walked away. Zach simply stared and shook his head before he finally turned and headed toward the foyer and the sitting room, where voices and laughter seemed to be growing. This was good. Braxton wanted all of this interest to lead to bigger, better things for the resort.

Braxton turned and paced deeper into the room. He'd have to get this unfortunate chat over with because guests were going to want to look around and the last thing he wanted was to be spotted in this room with Anna. Haven's gossip mill would explode before he could even attempt to defend himself.

The door closed and Braxton whirled around to see Anna leaning against the door, her eyes locked onto him. He'd not seen her in person for months; thankfully, he'd been able to avoid her in public. Her hair was shorter now, near her chin in some trendy style that suited her. The fitted dress hugging her every curve was no doubt some designer brand she so loved. There was no denying what a beautiful woman Anna was, but standing here right now, he felt nothing. He didn't even feel anger. A sure sign he was completely over her and he had Cora to thank for that.

"Anna." He figured he'd have to break the ice since she still remained in place. "What did you want?"

She flinched at his harsh tone, but he was immune to her. He wanted this over with and he wasn't in the mood for games.

"I've been calling you," she told him. "You never even replied to my texts."

Braxton crossed his arms, feeling no need to reply when she was stating something they both knew.

Pushing off the door, Anna slowly made her way toward him. "I know I hurt you," she started. "But I want a chance to get back what we had, we were—"

Braxton held up both hands. He'd suspected something like this when she'd been relentless in her attempts at getting in touch with him. "No. Don't even finish that sentence. There are no second chances here, Anna. Yes, you hurt me, but I'm over it and I've moved on. So have you."

Tears welled up in her bright blue eyes. "Rand and I are over. I made a mistake with him and tried to find a life I thought I wanted."

Braxton would've given anything to have heard these words months ago when he'd lashed out and had opted to shut down emotionally. When he'd been using one-night stands as a balm for his wounds, he would've given it all up for Anna. Looking back now, he didn't even know why he thought what they had was love. They were compatible in bed, they laughed and enjoyed each other's company, but she was always a step above him . . . in her mind anyway. She'd always wanted bigger and better of everything.

"I'm sorry you made a mistake," Braxton replied, finding he was sorry. The only emotion he had right now for Anna was pity. "But trying to rekindle anything we had would only lead to a whole host of other mistakes."

"You know we were good together." She took a step forward, closing the distance between them and placing her hand over his chest. "Give us a chance, Brax."

He cringed at the familiar nickname she'd used. Hearing it now only reminded him of a time he truly didn't want to revisit.

"Anna, this night is about Chelsea and this resort." He took a step back, causing her hand to fall away. "We have nothing left to discuss unless you want to book a visit and if so, that's Sophie's area."

Those tears that filled her eyes moments ago were blinked away, instantly replaced by anger. "You're turning me down?"

"You turned me down, I'm only following through with the best decision you ever made. I've finally found what I've been looking for and I should honestly be thanking you."

An unladylike growl escaped her. "Is it that blind woman I heard about? I know you've been around town with her. Rand told me all about your new employee."

Hell no. He was not getting into a discussion about Cora with Anna. Absolutely not. Cora was off-limits.

"If we're done here." He gestured for her to head toward the door.

"We're done," she spouted. "I don't know why I ever thought we could get back together. Clearly you're not the man I thought you were."

"I'm nothing like the man I was when I was with you," he easily agreed. "If you'll excuse me, I have guests to see."

Anna spun on her heel and marched from the room. Braxton propped his hands on the masseuse table and dropped his head between his shoulders. He needed some air, he needed a drink. He needed to be alone with Cora and get their ordeal straightened out because he desperately wanted to be with her. Now more than ever. After seeing Anna in person, talking with her, Braxton realized whatever they had was dead. Cora seriously filled his heart and he planned on telling her later. No more waiting, no more dancing around the topic. He was going to tell Cora how much he loved her and if she'd have him, he wanted to meet her family, to see where this relationship would go.

"Everything okay?"

Braxton lifted his head, nodding to Liam, who stood in the doorway. "Fine. Just taking a second."

"The way Anna stormed out of here I'm assuming she didn't like what you had to say."

Laughing, Braxton pushed off the cushioned table. "Not really. Is there a good crowd out there?"

"Pretty good." Liam's mouth tipped into a smile. "Chelsea would've loved this."

"Yeah, she would've. I know she's somewhere laughing her ass off at the three of us."

Zach came up behind Liam, Sophie at his side. "Everything okay?" Sophie asked.

Braxton nodded. "Everything is fine. Let's get out of here and make Chelsea proud."

Braxton followed his family out into the wide open two-story foyer. There were people walking around with wineglasses, several were already holding the "champagne" pamphlets and a couple of ladies were oohing and aahing over the pencil sketches. Sophie's sketches were definitely appealing. Simple, clean, and classy artwork. Chelsea would've loved having her best friend's sketches hanging on the walls.

As the evening progressed, Braxton was surprised at how many people came through the doors and how long they lingered. The interest was evident; now if all of that interest turned into bookings and happy clients, they'd be golden.

Soon the spacious home started feeling cramped, but on the cozy side. With all the ladies holding their half-empty wineglasses, chatting, laughing, and checking out every aspect of the resort, Braxton knew they'd done something spectacular. He'd give absolutely anything for his sister to be able to see her dream come true. She would have loved how her brothers came together and actually pulled this off.

He overheard some of the new employees discussing the historical aspect of the home and the utter geek in him smiled. The house was pretty damn cool.

But as he mingled, answered questions, and greeted guests, he realized he hadn't seen Cora for a while. Braxton excused himself from a group of elderly ladies and searched the room. When he spotted Sophie, he made his way through the crowd.

"Have you seen Cora?" Braxton asked once he reached Sophie.

"Not for a while. I brought her here, but I was hoping you'd be taking her home."

Sophie's smile was that of a nosy sister. "I already planned on it. If you'll excuse me."

He barely made it a few feet before he was stopped by another group of ladies asking about the history of the home, wanting to know more about Chelsea's vision and how soon they could book a weekend getaway. Braxton spent at least thirty minutes with them and by the time they'd walked away, he was pretty sure they'd be booking the cottages. Sophie had set up a small station at the old secretary in the parlor to take reservations for those who didn't want to wait and book online or call later. Braxton steered the women toward that area and left them in Sophie's hands.

As he passed through the foyer and headed back through the house, he still didn't see Cora. The patio area was lit up with various sizes of evergreens. Sophie had put clear lights on anything that would stand still. She wanted the perfect Christmas ambiance and she'd nailed the decorating perfectly, much better than he or his brothers would've done.

Where the hell was Cora? He'd gone over nearly the entire house and hadn't seen a sign of her anywhere. A niggle of worry started to take root. Had she gotten overwhelmed and gone for a walk? Did something happen that scared her?

Braxton didn't know what happened, if anything, but he wasn't going to stop until he found her and made sure she was okay. It wasn't like her to just disappear.

Cora opened the bathroom door and ran smack into someone. Gripping Heidi's collar, Cora stepped back. "Excuse me."

"No, I don't think I will."

The harsh female tone shocked Cora. "Pardon?"

A fingertip pushed Cora back another step. "Don't use the innocent act. I know what you're trying to do to Braxton, getting him to play on your handicap, but we are going to work things out. You're nothing but a distraction."

Anna.

"If you and Braxton have things to work out, then you need to talk to him, not me."

"Oh, you're the stumbling block," Anna laughed. "He has a soft heart and you're using that to try to keep him. It won't work."

Heidi let out a low growl. Cora tightened her grip on Heidi and eased her back. Heidi wouldn't bite or hurt anyone unless there was a real danger, but clearly the wise dog didn't like this visitor.

"I'm not using anything and he's not a piece of property," Cora retorted. "Whatever issues you have, they don't involve me."

"They do when you're in my way," Anna said from what sounded like between clenched teeth. "I'm giving you fair warning that I always get what I want and Braxton and I had planned a future together. I made a mistake, but he's forgiving. Our bond is something you'll never have."

Cora swallowed. She didn't want to be in the middle of this and she highly doubted Braxton was taking his ex back . . . not after all they'd shared and considering what just took place in the massage room.

"You may have had a little fling," Anna went on, her voice low now. "But his heart is with me."

Why wasn't anyone coming to use the restroom? Surely to goodness someone would pass by and offer some sort of diversion so Cora could escape this awkward situation. She didn't want to fight, this wasn't her battle. Anna clearly had issues that Cora wanted no part of.

"Oh," Anna whispered. "I just spent a little time

with Braxton in what I believe will be your work space. I hope you're not bothered by that visual image next time you go in."

Jealousy speared Cora's heart. No. She didn't believe it.

"You're lying."

"Ask him," Anna stated, smugness lacing her tone. "Ask if I was in there with him. He won't lie."

Cora didn't want to be here another second. She needed to get out now.

"You know how reckless he became after me," Anna added. "I'm sure he's shared that with you. Once a player, always a player. I'm the only woman he stayed with for any amount of time. You think you're special? You're just another distraction."

No. No. Cora wanted to shake her head, but she refused to show any weakness toward this woman.

"I'm sorry," another voice chimed in. "My daughter needs to use the restroom. Is this one open?"

Cora pasted on a smile and squared her shoulders. "Absolutely. I was just leaving."

With that, she pushed forward, ignoring Heidi's warning that she was about to run into something, or someone. Cora heard Anna grunt just as Cora's shoulder knocked hers. If Anna didn't want to move, fine, but Cora was more than finished here.

The threat of tears angered her. She wouldn't have a breakdown here of all places. She just wanted to get home, but how could she?

Braxton. Just his name hurt because she didn't want to believe he'd done anything with Anna, but she'd sounded so convincing and she'd made a point to drive home the fact he'd been a restless wanderer for the past several months. "A player," she'd called him.

Had he played her? Had she been that naïve and swept into his charm that she'd missed the real Braxton? She didn't think so, but Anna had succeeded in planting that seed of doubt.

Cora maneuvered down the hallway toward the kitchen. Maybe if she just went out back and got some air—

"Hey." Brock's worried tone hit her as his hand slid over her arm. "You okay?"

Cora bit down on her quivering lip. All it took was that one caring touch and she was near the point of losing it. "No," she whispered. "I'm not feeling well. Can you give me a ride home?"

"I'm actually not supposed to drive after my accident," he stated.

Cora blinked against the tears and Brock must've seen that she was on the verge of a breakdown.

"We'll go the back way." He slid his arm through hers and ushered her out.

Finally, she could escape and gather her thoughts without an audience.

She was gone. Braxton had searched the entire damn house twice and nobody had seen Cora. It was hard to miss a stunning woman with a dog.

Just as Braxton was about to search the second floor again, Zach bounded down the steps and shot a look to Braxton.

"Have you seen Brock?" he asked.

Braxton shook his head. "Not since I first got here. I can't find Cora, either."

Zach ran a hand through his hair, which was normally messy but he'd attempted to get it under control tonight. He'd even gone so far as to groom his beard.

"He's a teenager. Text him," Braxton suggested. "His phone won't be far."

"I did text him and he didn't answer."

That wasn't like Brock at all. "He couldn't have gone far. Did you check the basement? Maybe he's showing someone the tunnels."

"That's my next stop," Zach stated.

Just then Brock came down the hallway leading from the kitchen. The second Brock's eyes locked onto Braxton's, they narrowed.

"Where have you been?" Zach asked, stepping forward. He'd kept his tone down since there were guests walking around, but the anger and worry were evident. "I texted you twenty minutes ago."

"I had to take Cora home." He answered without taking his eyes off Braxton.

"Take her home? I told her I'd take her. You can't drive, damn it."

Brock nodded. "I know, but—"

"There's no excuse," Zach fumed.

Braxton understood Zach's anger, but right now, there were more pressing matters . . . at least in Braxton's opinion.

"Why did she leave early?" he demanded. "We need her here."

Had she gotten sick? Had she fallen and hurt herself and didn't want him to know? Something was wrong or she'd still be here.

Brock shrugged. "She didn't say anything. I found her outside the bathroom. She didn't look good. She asked me to take her home and didn't want anyone to know, so I took her out the back."

Uneasiness slid through him. "What was wrong with her?"

"She didn't say, really. All she told me was that she wasn't feeling well and she needed a ride home."

It had only been a couple hours ago she'd been in his arms, agreeing to see him later. What had happened in such a short time? Dread slid through, pushing right through the uneasiness.

"Did she say if she heard Anna and me talking?"

Brock shook his head. "She didn't mention Anna at all. I swear. She was quiet most of the way home and wouldn't even let me walk her to the door. So I waited until she got inside. She didn't look like she felt good, if that helps, but I got the impression she was upset more than anything."

Damn it. If Cora thought something was up with him and Anna, that would be upsetting to her. But if that was the case, why hadn't she come to him? Why hadn't she just asked him about it? Did she truly think that he'd be intimate with her and have something going on with his ex?

"We will talk about this after the party," Zach growled to Brock. Then he turned to Braxton. "People are still coming in, but if you want to leave and check on her, go ahead."

Braxton weighed his options. Torn between loyalty to Chelsea, his brothers, and Sophie, and then to his feelings for Cora, he had no idea what to do.

She'd left upset, though, and that told him something was wrong. Had someone said something to her? Surely nobody treated her differently because of her blindness. He'd seen her chatting with guests, laughing, even, and a few times when he'd walked by he'd even heard her going over the types of services she offered.

So what the hell had gone wrong?

"I'm going to head out," he told Zach. "I'll be back, but I have to check on her."

Zach nodded in understanding. It wasn't that long ago that he was in a tough spot with Sophie, was torn between loyalty and love. Damn it, Braxton didn't want to be torn. He wanted his world to be calm and settled, but since Cora had come into his life, he'd been turned every which way and now he had to choose which direction to go in.

"I promise I'll be back to help clean up," he stated as he headed down the hall. Right now, the need to see Cora, to figure out what happened, was taking precedence over the resort and he knew without a doubt that Chelsea would kick his ass if he ignored Cora's needs right now.

Chapter Sixteen

Cora pulled her nightshirt over her head, wanting nothing more than to crawl between her cozy comforter and shut out the rest of the world. When Braxton had taken her aside earlier, showing her how much he'd missed her, making her believe they actually stood a chance, she'd grabbed hold of that hope and had fully believed they'd come back here and put things back on the right track to move forward with their relationship.

He'd given her a promise of another shot at something special, but in the span of a few seconds, when Cora had been coming out of the ladies' room, everything had changed. Cora didn't even know what to think, how to react. She'd been blindsided and she'd run like a coward and now she was hiding in her house.

But more than anything, she'd been given a wake-up call. So many facts revealed to her, facts she'd not wanted to see before.

When her doorbell rang, she knew without a doubt who would be standing on the other side. She could stay in her bedroom and ignore Braxton, or she could answer the door and face this head-on. The end result would be the same regardless and broken hearts were inevitable.

Pulling a deep breath, she held her hand out and felt for the doorjamb as she headed out into the hall. The bell chimed again.

"Cora, I know you're in there. Answer the door so I know you're okay."

The worry in his tone had her feeling guilty, but she couldn't back down on what needed to be done. No matter how much she'd come to care for him—okay, she actually loved the man—she needed to do this. And she'd thought trying to live independently took courage . . . that step was nothing compared to what she was about to do.

Her fingers slid over the lock, hesitating before turning. She wished tonight would end differently, but . . .

There were no buts. Tonight was going to end the way it should and she'd have to take a step back.

As she pulled the door open, Heidi brushed against Cora's bare leg.

"Why did you leave?" Braxton asked. "Are you feeling all right?"

He'd stepped over the threshold, his body brushing against hers. No, she was not okay.

Cora didn't back up. She couldn't let him in any farther. Strength and courage had to become her friends right now.

"I wasn't feeling well." Understatement.

Braxton's thumb brushed just beneath her eye. "You've been crying."

No way to hide that. She'd always been that ugly

crier. No delicate tears for her. She had no doubt the tip of her nose was red, her cheeks were splotchy, and her eyes puffy. She'd cried so hard after Brock left, she now had a killer headache. Stupid emotions. She'd never had to worry about this before, she'd never felt this way, so the whole experience was new and she was about to sever this bond.

"I started thinking about you, about us." Cora gripped the hem of her nightgown, praying she held it together long enough to set him free. "This moved so fast and with the resort opening and you'll be going back to teaching in a few weeks, plus my family . . . I'm just—"

Braxton gripped her shoulders. "What the hell are you saying? What changed from the moment we shared hours ago until you left?"

Cora closed her eyes and inhaled his familiar, masculine aroma. "I had time to think about everything, to fully see the impact this resort would have on the community and how important it is to your family. I want to be part of that, I plan on doing everything to help make this a success, but moving forward with a serious relationship isn't—"

"Bullshit. Did you overhear me talking to Anna? Is that what this is?"

"I didn't overhear you." That was the absolute truth. "I know you . . . talked."

"How?" he demanded.

Cora stepped back, causing his hands to fall away. "It doesn't matter. What matters is that you need to focus on making your sister's dream come true. I need to focus on what I'm going to do about my family and still maintain my life here because I really do love it."

"What about me? Do you love me?"

Her heart clenched. She loved him more than she'd ever thought possible, but after the run-in with Anna, Cora wasn't sure if Braxton was honestly ready for something more.

The fact was he'd been reckless before meeting Cora. What if he grew tired of being with a blind woman? What if he wanted to move on to a woman who was perfect and not flawed? She'd never wanted to think that, but after Anna's jabs, Cora had to face reality and the real possibility that Braxton might not be on the same page she was.

It was better to let go now than to have to later. Too much was on the line, even more than emotions. Cora needed to let him go, she needed to let herself go. It was the only way. Their relationship developed so fast, had become so intense, she had to figure out if this was the right move.

Working for his family would complicate things, but he'd see things her way once he had time to think. And maybe she could move on. Maybe.

"We can't do this anymore," she whispered, ignoring his question. "I'm going back to Atlanta for a few days and I'll be back before the opening day of Bella Vous to get everything in my room in order and ready to go. I need to see my parents, though. I have so much to tie up with them."

"And I'm not invited." His voice had taken on a cold tone, a distant tone. "Why are you doing this?"

"It's for the best."

"Damn it, Cora. Stop being so vague with your answers and tell me what the hell is going on."

"I told you. There's so much going on in each of our lives that throwing in an intense relationship would be a mistake."

His mocking laugh gutted her. "So now we're a mistake."

She said nothing. She couldn't keep throwing out veiled excuses and she couldn't stand here much longer and not break down. She couldn't risk him breaking things off with her later. Rejection wasn't something she could handle. At least this way she had the control . . . and she was hanging on by a thread.

"I never took you for a coward. You came here wanting a new life, a new sense of freedom, and you faced every challenge head-on."

The burn started building in her throat. She had to steel herself against his harsh yet true words.

"I had no idea the thought of a relationship terrified you that much."

Cora bit down on her lip to keep any words from spilling out. She needed him to go, so if he got angry enough, maybe he'd leave . . . and take her heart with him.

"You go home to Atlanta, to your parents who don't care about this new life you have here," he went on, hurt and anger lacing his voice. "You go back to that stuffy lifestyle you tried so hard to break free from. And when you're there, think of this."

His lips came down fast and hard on hers. Cora stumbled a step before Braxton's arm snaked around her waist and held her steady against the hard planes of his body. The kiss was fierce, fast, and aggressive. Before she could get her bearings, he pulled back, leaving her trembling for more.

"You won't find that anywhere else." His footsteps sounded on the wooden porch. "Lock that door behind me and be safe. Because no matter how much you're trying to hurt me, to hurt us, I still care for you, Cora. And deep down you know what we have is real."

She waited until she heard the start of his engine before she closed the door and secured the locks. As much as her heart ached, as much as she wanted to throw open the door and beg him to come back, she wouldn't be that woman. She'd come too far, she'd promised herself too much.

And she firmly believed whatever was meant to happen would happen. She was holding tight to that belief because she'd just pushed away the one person who'd ever made her feel alive.

Braxton checked on one of his previous students, the one he'd tutored briefly in the past few weeks. The grades were in and he'd passed. Braxton was relieved, considering the boy had a less than stellar home life, yet more determination than most.

And, for about five minutes, his mind had been off of Cora and the fact he hadn't heard from her in . . . too many days.

He eased forward on the edge of his sofa, resting his elbows on his knees, and clutched his phone. Last Christmas had been gut-wrenching with Chelsea's death still so fresh. This Christmas wasn't proving to be much better. Chelsea's death still seemed so recent, especially with the resort ready to open. But now without Cora, hell, he didn't even know what he was feeling. Alone, yes. Empty, yes. Confused, angry, and frustrated? Hell, yes.

When his front door opened and slammed shut, Braxton sighed. Only a handful of people just barged into his house and he wasn't in the mood for any of them.

"You look like shit."

Braxton didn't even glance toward Liam. With a sigh, Braxton flopped back against the couch cushions and rested his phone on the cushion beside him. Maybe she'd call. He wasn't too proud to admit he was keeping his phone close just in case. If that made him pathetic, then so be it. He had no clue what truly happened, but she'd been so damn adamant when she'd kicked him out of her house, he had no idea how to move on from here.

"Seriously, dude. Are you going to sit in here and avoid the world? Because I haven't seen you since the open house."

Braxton snorted as he glared across the room to his brother, who still remained filling the doorway. "Are we going to have the pot/kettle conversation? Because you've been hiding from people for years."

Liam crossed his arms over his wide chest and narrowed his gaze. "I'm not here for me."

"So, what, you came here to see if I was drinking? Feeling sorry for myself? Going crazy like I did with Anna? Don't worry."

Liam came farther into the room, shoved his hands in the pockets of his jeans, and stared directly at him. "This is nothing like Anna. You didn't love her. You wanted to because you got caught up in the lust part of your relationship and thought that would transfer to love and family."

Shaking his head, Braxton laced his fingers over his abdomen. "If you only came here to analyze me, you wasted your time. I'm well aware of what's going on inside my own head."

Liam swiped his hand through the air, knocking Braxton's feet off the coffee table. Taking a seat directly across from Braxton, Liam continued to hold his intense stare. "Listen, you've taken a few days to feel sorry for yourself, now tell me what the hell you're going to do."

"Right now I'm thinking about punching you in the face. That should make me feel better."

He hadn't realized how much he wanted that outlet. Rage, frustration, and confusion all boiled deep within him, making for a lethal combo. Liam just happened to be the unfortunate person who crossed his path. But he wouldn't be like his father. Braxton could control the anger boiling inside.

"Hit me, then," Liam stated, holding his hands up and motioning for Braxton to come at him. "Get it out of your system and then you need to figure out what you're going to do about Cora."

"Leave it, Liam. I can handle this."

"Maybe so, but now that I'm in town, I'm not going to let you self-destruct like you did last time." Liam lowered his head, still keeping his eyes on Braxton. "This is more. We both know Cora is special to you. What you and Cora have is nothing compared to Anna. So are you going to go after her or just have her come to work every day and try to avoid her?"

More like she'd avoid him. She'd done a remarkable job so far in the past few days. Granted, he hadn't called her. Hell, no. He had his pride. Unfortunately, his pride might get in the way of the best thing that ever happened to him.

"She kicked me out." The words tumbled from his mouth before Braxton could hold them in. So much for that pride. "I don't know what happened at the open house. Before it started she'd agreed to let me take her home, but she left early and by the time I got to her house, she'd decided we were over."

"Then make her talk," Liam demanded. "If she's worth fighting for, then get off your sorry ass and go do it."

"I thought I'd feel sorry for myself for a bit longer."

The corners of Liam's mouth tipped up, the scar running alongside his face shifting with the smile. Without a word he headed into the kitchen. Moments later he returned with a tumbler of bourbon.

Braxton stared at the glass Liam thrust toward him. "I hadn't planned on getting drunk. I was thinking I would just sit in the dark and pout like the mature person that I am."

With a shrug, Liam downed the amber liquid. He slammed the empty glass onto the coffee table and, with a heavy sigh, sank down on the other end of the couch.

"Is this the part of the evening when I have to ask you what's wrong?" Braxton asked as he watched Liam rub his eyes. "Because I've got my own shit to deal with, but if you want to unload, feel free."

Silence filled the room and Braxton propped his socked feet back up onto the table.

"I think Macy is going to be a problem."

Braxton wasn't surprised that Liam and Macy were going to be an issue now that Liam was back, but he was stunned that he admitted the fact out loud.

"You can't leave us," Braxton stated. "We need you here."

"I'm not leaving," Liam confirmed, a hint of regret to his tone. "I want to, but I'm not. I owe Chelsea, I owe you and Sophie."

"And Zach?"

Liam hesitated. "I hate owing him anything, but we're all in this together."

"What's going on with Macy?"

"Nothing." The quick reply left no room for argument, almost as if he were trying to convince himself.

"Then there should be no problem," Braxton retorted, knowing it would get on Liam's nerves.

"She drives me insane with her dates, her flaunting them in my face."

Braxton knew now would be the worst time to laugh . . . so he cut loose. "You're kidding? She doesn't flaunt them. She dates. You're just home now and hearing about it."

Liam let out a growl and pushed to his feet. Grabbing the tumbler off the table, he stalked back into the kitchen and came back with a full glass . . . and the bottle.

"How much are you planning on drinking?"

Liam snorted. "Not enough to dull the ache."

"I take it you're staying here tonight then?" Braxton asked. They were adamant about not drinking and driving—as anyone with common sense should be— but after the accident that caused so much scarring and landed Zach in prison for a year, they always took precautions.

"I don't want to talk about Macy or me or what the hell she's doing right now or who she's doing it with." He took a deep drink. "I want to know what you're going to do to get Cora back. We don't need that negativity at the resort. Your tension will hurt business."

"And that's all you're worried about is business?"

Liam reached over for the bottle, poured himself another dose, and settled back onto the couch. "I might be worried about you, but only because if you're the reason this resort tanks, Sophie will kill you and then Zach and I will have to dig a hole big enough to bury you."

Braxton laughed. They had the oddest ways of communicating love, but it was so evident. The loyalty of the Monroe brothers, the bond they shared was so deep and resilient there was no way anyone or anything could sever it.

"Her family is loaded." Braxton crossed his ankles, stared down at his phone one more time, willing it to vibrate. "She withheld that from me, but I get her reasoning. I don't like it, but I understand."

"She's not Anna."

Braxton swallowed, almost wishing he'd started drinking, but he'd done that after Anna. He'd wanted to numb the pain. Right now, he wanted to feel the pain, he wanted to know he was alive and ready to fight, not slink into the depths of a bottle. That would be too easy, too predictable. Not that he'd tell Liam that.

"I love her," Braxton said through the lump in his throat. "Damn it, I've never loved a woman like this before and she just threw it away."

"Then pick it up and take it to her. Where is she now?"

"Her parents have some major party at the end of the year for employees and their families. It's tomorrow night. She mentioned going, but she's been so on the fence about her position in the company, I'm not sure if she went or not."

Knowing Cora, she was going to go. Right now she was probably back in Atlanta because she wasn't home. He'd gone over. Three times.

"Then that's where your sorry ass will be tomorrow," Liam confirmed. "Take today for that pity party you need, and wrap up and pull out your tux because I know you have one."

"How do you know?" he asked, thinking to the dry-cleaning bag in the back of his walk-in closet.

Liam threw him a look and Braxton merely shrugged. In the back of his mind he'd known tomorrow would land him in Atlanta because there was no way he could just take her no for an answer. She loved him, he knew it just as sure as he knew his own feelings, and he wished like hell she'd trusted him enough to explain what had spooked her so much at the open house that she'd felt the need to flee, to cut off their relationship without even one word from him and with little explanation.

"You need backup tomorrow?" Liam asked, eyeing the bottom of his glass as he swirled around the last bit of remaining liquid.

Braxton shoved to his feet and blew out a breath, turning his head from side to side to crack the tension from his neck. "I'm a big boy. I can get the girl by myself."

Liam glanced up to him and nodded. "Make sure you do. I don't want to see you like this again."

Braxton smiled. "I knew you cared."

"Yeah," he muttered. "I care."

Chapter Seventeen

There were too many people, people she didn't know and people she did know. Regardless, Cora didn't want to be here. The fake smiling, the schmoozing, the business talk all as if she were a major part of this company simply because her name was Buchanan.

"Darling, that emerald-green dress is stunning."

Cora stiffened at her mother's tone behind her. She'd worn the same green dress she'd had on at the open house for Bella Vous, but this time she'd dressed it up with a diamond necklace and diamond earrings, and she'd piled her hair on top of her head. Well, her mother's assistant had done the hair to make it just perfect and she'd applied more makeup than Cora liked, but here she was all dressed up, wearing an outer shell that didn't suit her.

Cora tightened her grip on the walking stick, just another prop in this world she wanted desperately to break free from. "Thank you, Mother. I need to get some air. If you'll excuse me."

She didn't wait for her mom to say anything. Cora carefully made her way through the crowd, tapping the stick as she went. Each rap on the floor seemed to mock her. She didn't belong here. Yes, she'd been raised in this grand estate, but now that she'd had a taste of freedom, now that she'd settled in Haven, Cora knew Buchanan Chocolates wasn't her home. Oh, she could run that company from a financial standpoint, which was what she was trained to do, but she knew if she was stuck working in an office for the rest of her life, she'd slowly die.

As she reached the other side of the ballroom in her parents' home, she stretched her arm out, feeling for the knob.

"I've got it."

Cora froze. Her heart clenched at the familiar voice. The door clicked open, fresh air instantly enveloped her as a hand she'd come so accustomed to settled on the small of her back.

Once she was ushered outside, Cora knew the rail of the balcony overlooking the backyard wasn't far. Why was he here? How had he gotten in? So many questions. Fear settled in her stomach. She'd pushed him away and he'd come after her anyway, to her parents' home during a major event. This all had to mean one thing, but dare she hope?

As her hand curled around the concrete rail, she stared straight ahead. "What are you doing here, Braxton?"

"Did you think I'd just let you break things off and not fight for what I want?"

She sort of hoped he'd make it less painful by letting her go with some of her pride intact. "I think we both got caught up in the intensity of sexual attraction and mistook it for something more. I'm letting you go to save us both heartache down the road."

"What about the heartache now?" he asked, his hand settling on top of hers.

Yeah, the heartache now wasn't too comfortable, but had she let this go on much longer, the pain would've been worse if he opted to leave. Anna had warned her about just how reckless Braxton had become and just how quickly he turned to another woman. Cora couldn't risk being just another number because at this point her heart had gotten fully involved.

Cora was near positive he didn't do anything with Anna like Anna had implied. That wasn't Braxton's style. He may have been reckless, he may have enjoyed women, but he was loyal. She didn't need to ask to know that truth. Even acknowledging Anna's claim would be a slap to Braxton's face. Still, it had been a wake-up call for how fast they'd come together, how intense things had gotten. How could she trust his feelings were the same as hers?

"I won't have this out here with you," she told him, turning toward the direction of his voice. "I'll be back in Haven in a few days and if you still want to talk, we can."

"How did you get here?" he asked.

"My parents sent their driver for me."

Because they'd been too busy to come themselves. After the phone calls and the texts from her mother wanting to know where she was, Barbara Buchanan hadn't been able to tear herself away from party planning to come see where her daughter was living now.

"Where's Heidi?"

"I was asked to keep her outside." Cora gripped her stick, mentally tossing it over the balcony. "My parents never liked an animal in the house."

"Did they ask what you like or do you always bow to their commands?"

Cora rubbed her forehead and blew out a breath.

"Cora, darling, is everything all right?"

Cringing, Cora straightened her back and pasted a smile on her face. "Of course, Mother. This is Braxton Monroe. He and his family are the ones opening the women's-only resort and spa I was telling you about."

"Ah, yes. The one you want to work for." Her mother's demeaning tone came across loud and clear.

"I will be working for them, Mom. Braxton, this is my mother, Barbara Buchanan."

"Pleasure to meet you, ma'am." With a smile to his voice, Cora knew without a doubt he'd be laying on the charm without even trying. "You have a beautiful home."

"Thank you," her mother preened. "Cora, dear, you need to get back inside to the guests and Eric was looking for you."

"Actually, Cora and I were talking," Braxton chimed in. "Tell Eric if he wants to talk to Cora, he can come out here."

Cora bit the inside of her cheek. She didn't know if she wanted to laugh or cringe at the way Braxton spoke to her mother. Nobody ordered Barbara around like that.

"Eric is Cora's fiancé, so if he wants to talk to her, she needs to go inside."

Braxton grunted. "Fiancé, huh? Strange since she's not wearing a ring and I've known her nearly a month and she's not said a word about getting married. Actually, no, I take that back. She informed me she didn't want to get married."

Cora winced. The evening air wasn't helping her nerves like she'd originally thought. Granted, her nerves were on full alert now and she was even more confused and frustrated than ever.

"Mr. Monroe—"

"Enough." Cora raised her voice, cutting her mother

off. "I'm not engaged to Eric. I'm the only one who seems to remember that, but it's time you understood I'm not marrying him."

"Darling, of course you are. Who else is going to take care of you and help with the company? Don't pull one of your moods now."

Her mother's warning was low, heaven forbid a guest overhear a family squabble. What would that do to the impeccable Buchanan name?

"Mrs. Buchanan," Braxton chimed in. "Cora is the most independent woman I know. I've no doubt if she wanted to run this company she could do so with the team you already have working there. Adding on someone to keep an eye on her because she cannot see is only proving to her that you don't believe in her abilities."

Her mother's gasp seemed so loud, though Cora doubted anyone but the three of them heard it. Stunned at Braxton's words, Cora stood completely still, gripping her cane and wishing she had Heidi at her side.

"I don't mean to disrespect you in your own home," he went on. "But I won't have anyone talk to Cora in a way that makes her feel less than the amazing woman she is."

Cora had to concentrate on keeping a straight face, which was difficult when her chin was starting to quiver and tears burned in her throat.

"I'm well aware of how amazing my daughter is, Mr. Monroe."

"Braxton, please. Formalities aren't necessary since I'm going to be in Cora's life for a long time to come."

Now Cora's gasp filled the heavy silence. Was he saying . . . oh, no. Surely he wasn't. Cora lifted her hand to her head as a wave of dizziness swept over her.

Instantly Braxton slid his arm around her waist and Cora couldn't even resist leaning into him.

"Oh, there you are," Cora's father said, his footsteps scuffing along the concrete floor of the balcony. "Eric and I have been looking all over for you guys."

"You must be Cora's father." Braxton's low voice vibrated through his chest, sliding over her. "I'm Braxton Monroe, Cora's boyfriend."

"Boyfriend?" Victor Buchanan's shock didn't even compare to what Cora was experiencing. "Monroe . . . Monroe. You're the family she's gone to work for?"

"That's correct, sir."

"This whole scene is absurd," her mother scolded in that condescending whisper. "We will discuss this later after our guests have left."

Braxton's hand slid gently up and down Cora's side. "I'm more than happy to stick around and rehash this conversation and clarify any misunderstanding on your end."

"Now listen here—"

"No," Braxton cut off her father. "I'm here for Cora and judging from what I've seen firsthand and what I've learned before tonight, I'm the only one with her best interests in mind. I'm not leaving unless she's with me and I understand your need to have her here, so this is where I'll be as well. Now, tell me where Heidi is so I can get Cora the proper assistance because this cane is absolutely not her."

"I don't know who you think you are," her father boomed, probably making her mother's face red with embarrassment. "But you will not come into my house and control my daughter like this."

"You're right," Braxton agreed. "I won't control her. You've done that enough and I intend to see her happy, living a free life, a life that she chooses, and I promise you that she would rather have her faithful dog at her side. Now, if you'll excuse us, I want to talk to Cora. I assure you that we will both be here after the party and we can all talk then."

Without another word, Braxton held firmly on to her side and guided her back into the noisy ballroom, straight out the other side and into the foyer. It wasn't until they were back outside via the front of the house that she blew out a breath and willed her knees to remain strong.

"Where's Heidi?" he asked once they came to a stop on the wide front porch.

"She's with one of the staff. I'm sure she's out here somewhere because my father told them to see to it that she remained outside."

"Stay right here and I'll find her."

Sure. Where else would she go? She'd take this time to get her heart rate back under control and figure out what in the world had gotten into Braxton that he was so determined to prove to her that they belonged together. Didn't he understand she'd let him go for good reason? Did he not know that having him here, on her turf, only confused her and made her want to go against doing the right thing? Damn it, she could only be so strong before she'd break.

Braxton Monroe was a man who demanded attention, affection, and loyalty. She wanted to give him all three, but he wasn't ready. He may think he was, but there was no way. Not after her little run-in with Anna. Cora needed that wake-up call, not that she appreciated it coming in the form of Braxton's ex, but it had been a necessary evil.

All the pain, all the grief hadn't been from Anna's truthful words. All the angst and heartache had stemmed from the fact that Cora knew she had to make the most difficult decision of her life and let him go.

"We're back."

Just as Braxton's words hit her, Heidi's fur tickled the side of her calf. "Thank you," she said, extending the walking stick for Braxton to take. Once she had her grip on Heidi's collar and that damn stick was gone, she felt so much better. "You didn't have to come here, but now that you're here, I want to know what you meant in there."

"There's no hidden meaning behind any of my words," he told her, taking her free hand and guiding her toward one end of the porch where Cora knew a settee and chairs were positioned perfectly. "Everything I said was true. I came here because I gave you the time you needed to think. I won't let you walk away again."

Cora reached her free hand out, feeling for the arm of the settee. Turning, she eased down onto the cushion and patted Heidi's head as she settled next to her feet.

"I didn't walk away," she corrected. "I released you from this because you're not ready for—"

"What the hell am I not ready for?" he demanded. The cushion dipped beside her, Braxton's arm extended behind her back. "You think you're some rebound? You think I'm just passing the time with you?"

"Maybe not in your mind, but Anna said—"

"I knew it. You heard us talking."

Cora shook her head. "No, I didn't. She actually met me coming out of the ladies' room and the things she said made sense."

She couldn't see Braxton, but the anger seemed to roll off of him. His breathing had quickened, the hand behind her back had fisted, but other than those minor movements, he sat perfectly still as if he were a wounded animal ready to strike.

"She said you guys were going to work things out," Cora hurried on to say. "She told me about how careless you'd become after her and that I was a distraction until you got back with her."

Whispered curses were muttered under his breath. The front door opened in the distance, music and party noise from inside filtered out into the night as several sets of footsteps sounded across the floor. Once the door shut and the footsteps faded, Cora waited. Braxton wasn't going to let this go and she didn't know how much longer she could hold on to her control.

"First of all, Anna is irrelevant to us," he told her in a low, powerful voice. "I don't care what she said to you because she's only out for herself. What I do care about is what you think, why you felt the need to push me away, and why you still think it's a good idea to be apart because I don't know about you, but these past few days have been miserable."

There went more of that resolve crumbling. She wanted to throw her arms around him and be reassured everything would be all right, that this relationship wasn't just something based in sexual tension and chemistry.

"We both have so much going on," she muttered, clutching her hands in her lap. "I've informed my parents I won't be taking over as CFO. My shares are still mine and I will be part of the company because it's my legacy, but I need an out. They're in denial still, but I think they're starting to come around to the fact I'm serious. I need to take my life back."

"And you don't want me in that new life?"

She wanted him in her life more than anything. "I want you to figure out your own life," she clarified. "I want you to find what makes you feel alive, what makes you happier than anything else in the world. I don't want to be the one to stand in the way, Braxton. You've lived your life to please others for so long, when have you done something for you?"

That hand behind her slid up into her hair, pulling her perfectly placed bobby pins out one at a time. "Right now I'm doing something for me," he whispered. "This isn't you. All these diamonds, the hair in some fancy twist, the layers of makeup. Seeing you smile, knowing you're happy, that's what does it for me, Cora. So every day that I spent with you, getting deeper into your world, learning about how amazing you are, all of that was making me happy. Since my engagement ended and Chelsea died, I've not felt too alive. But then you came into my life and, yes, it's been a short time, but damn it, I know what I want and I know how I feel."

"Am I interrupting?"

Cora jerked her body at Eric's untimely question.

"Yes," Braxton growled. "Who are you?"

"Eric," Cora replied.

Braxton's hand slid from her hair as the settee shifted and he came to his feet. Cora pushed up as well because she had no clue what was about to happen and she needed to prepare herself for a fallout. Her mother would definitely never forgive her if there was a fight on the front porch during the Christmas party.

"Cora, may I talk to you? Alone."

Braxton's hand settled on the small of her back and she was utterly shocked he didn't immediately say no. "I'm in the middle of something. Can we talk later?"

"Actually, this won't take long and I don't feel so bad about telling you this now that I know you're going to be okay."

"Why the hell wouldn't she be okay?" Braxton asked.

Cora shifted in her heels, wishing she could take them off and get the hell out of here.

"I just meant that it's clear the two of you have something going on," Eric amended. "I thought her parents required her and me to marry to secure my place in the company. Even when Cora moved, I thought she'd be back, but I knew in the back of my mind she wouldn't. This isn't her lifestyle, as much as I wanted it to be so we could take this company into the next generation."

The tension was back as Braxton's entire body stilled against hers. He was coiled and ready to spring once more. She reached over, placing her hand on his side as she leaned against him, silently offering her support, her loyalty.

"Cora, I know we aren't a good match," Eric went on. "I mean, on paper we're perfect, but I honestly don't want to marry, not for a while anyway."

"Did you meet someone?" she asked.

"No. Actually, I just want to focus on my career. I know I'm secure here and I know your parents were more concerned about you running the company alone than they were with you actually living alone. I went about everything wrong. When I should've stood up for you and what you wanted, I bowed to their commands because I wanted to maintain my position."

Cora was shocked that this was the same Eric who'd been unbending regarding their wannabe engagement. "And now you're not worried about your position?"

"Actually, I spoke with your father yesterday and after the first of the year, they're making a formal announcement that I'll be taking over as CEO."

She waited for the hurt, waited for the feeling of

regret in her decision to distance herself from such burdens, but all Cora felt was relief. Sweet, pressure-releasing relief.

"Congratulations." She offered him a smile because she was truly happy. "Looks like everything turned out for the best."

"Are you sure you're not upset?" he asked.

"Not at all."

"You know I'll still want your input and I'll be calling for opinions," he added quickly.

Cora laughed and stepped forward, her arms out. When Eric hugged her, she patted him on the back. "I want you to call and I want to be part of this company, I just want the freedom and less responsibility."

"You better let me go," he whispered in her ear. "Your bodyguard is glaring at me."

Still smiling, Cora eased back. "I'm happy for you, Eric. Thanks for telling me."

"Yeah, I was looking for you earlier. I'll let you two get back to your talk, I just wanted to let you know where things stood."

Cora nodded her thanks and listened until his presence was no longer evident. Turning, Cora pulled in a ragged breath. Now she was free of the heavy weights that had been on her shoulders for so long. She still had a major clench in her heart, though, for the man who'd come here fully expecting her to leap back into his arms. Was it going to be that easy? Was he fully prepared to be committed to a woman unlike anyone he'd ever been with? Could she hope for all of that and not get hurt in the end?

"What's going through your mind?" Braxton asked softly.

Turning back around, Cora pushed her hair away from her shoulders. "I can't even concentrate on one thought right now. This is what I've wanted for a while. I don't want to leave the company hanging, but there's no way I want to run it and have all of that responsibility simply because I was born with the last name Buchanan."

Braxton's fingers curled around her shoulder, his shoes scuffed against the porch as he shifted closer. "And what's going through your mind about us?"

Cora dropped her head and tried to home in on exactly what she was feeling, but the emotions were so jumbled up she was struggling.

"Honesty," Braxton added. "Don't worry about a right or wrong response. Just tell me what you're thinking."

Those messy feelings all gathered in her throat, forming a ball of tears so thick, she had trouble swallowing. "I want this to be real," she whispered, biting her quivering lip. "I feel like we were almost victims of such intense chemistry. Then I got so caught up with how you made me feel and I worry it's so appealing because this is new."

The pad of Braxton's thumb swiped at her damp cheek as his arm wrapped around her waist. When he tipped her chin up and gently kissed her lips, Cora nearly lost it completely. The party going on inside didn't matter because she felt as if her life, everything she'd been seeking, was right here in front of her. But could she trust the feelings? Trust that Braxton was ready for the type of commitment she longed for? Too many uncertainties.

"You've spent your whole life having everything planned out," he told her, sliding his fingertips along her jawline and cupping the side of her head. "What happened with us wasn't planned and you're scared to death. Whatever nonsense Anna spewed to you only gave you the ammunition to run, which is exactly what her intent was."

Cora nodded. She couldn't argue with the truth . . . that didn't mean she had to like it, either. She didn't want to look like a fool, but she also worried about being so exposed, putting her heart on the line when she was trying so hard to be independent and stand on her own. She had felt so good leaning on Braxton the past few weeks, and maybe that was the crux of all her doubts.

"Maybe we should take things slower," he went on. "I'm willing to do whatever it takes to give you peace of mind, to ensure you know how serious I am about you, about us. I won't let you question what we have, Cora. Not when I'm in love with you and I want you to be by my side so I can tell you every single day."

Cora's breath caught in her throat. The dam of tears burst and she sank forward, her forehead resting on his chest as days of worry and doubt poured from her. She'd wanted this with every piece of her bruised heart.

Braxton's soft chuckle vibrated from his chest. "Not the reaction I was hoping for when I told you I loved you."

His arms banded around her, his hands stroked up and down her back as she clutched his shirt. If people were passing in and out of the party behind them, she didn't care. Cora had all she needed right here in Braxton's arms and with Heidi resting at their feet. In such a short time, this had become her world.

"Tell me you don't love me," he whispered in her ear. "Tell me you don't want to make this work and I'll leave right now."

"I do love you." Cora lifted her head, blinked back the tears, and sniffed. "I don't know how I fell in love with you so fast, so hard, but I did. Maybe it was the first time I had my hands on you. Maybe it was the night at the pond or when you let me drive. But you've given me back a piece of myself that had been missing and when I think of you, when I'm with you, my heart is so full. How did you do this to me?"

He nipped at her lips. "I was going to ask you the same thing. I've never ached for a woman the way I do you. You're part of me, Cora. The next steps in this relationship can go as fast or slow as you need, but please don't walk away from me again. I can't live without you."

Throwing her arms around him, she buried her face in his neck. "I've never been in someone's heart before . . . not like this. I don't know what to do."

"Neither have I, but with your strong will and my determination to keep you happy, I guarantee we can make this relationship thing work."

"Where will we live?" she asked, lifting her head and sliding her hand around to touch the side of his face. She wanted that extra connection, wanted to feel that smooth glide of his strong jawline beneath her palm.

"Live? You mean, you want to live together?" His arms tightened around her as he smacked a kiss on her lips. "I want nothing more than to wake up with you every day. But are you sure you're ready? You've been wanting this independence and I don't want to take that from you."

Cora nodded. "You've given it back to me, Braxton. Don't you see that? You've shown me that I can make it on my own, but I want to be with you as I stand on my own. Does that make sense?"

"Perfect sense." He kissed her again, slowly, passionately . . . as a promise of more to come later. "Your house or mine? I don't care where we live."

Cora shrugged and smiled. "I know a good real estate agent who can help us decide which house we should put on the market."

Braxton's hands slid lower down her back as he pulled her tighter against him. "I love how you think, Cora Buchanan."

Cora's heart filled, the emotions she'd been so afraid of suddenly fueled the next chapter of her hopes and dreams. "Take me back to Haven. I'm ready to go home."

Epilogue

"I learned way more about thread and quilt rings than I ever needed to know," Sophie stated with a long sigh.

Cora laughed and sank down onto the sofa in Braxton's living room. Well, their living room now. Sophie had just put Cora's home on the market the day after Christmas and with the opening of Bella Vous, the Monroe family was quite busy.

"Well, our first set of guests left happy and we're full of all the quilting knowledge we'll ever need." Cora patted Heidi's head as her dog settled in beside her.

"I've been meaning to ask you something," Sophie said. "Actually, Braxton was supposed to—"

"What was I supposed to do?"

Cora smiled as Braxton entered the room. He and Zach had been making dinner. Cora and Sophie didn't care what it was, they were too exhausted to care and the guys said they'd handle it. Maybe they should've called Liam in for this, but the poor guy was even more exhausted after dealing with a weekend of very eager eaters.

"You were supposed to ask Cora about that position," Sophie muttered.

Cora groaned. "Position?"

The couch dipped beside her as Braxton's arm extended behind her back. "We were wondering if you could help with the bookkeeping if we got the proper voice-activated program."

Cora thought for a moment, how she'd only gone to college for her accounting degree to appease her family. The last thing she'd wanted to do was use it, but that had been a different time in her life.

"You don't have to," Braxton went on to say.

"We completely understand if you don't want to take that on," Sophie added.

Cora shook her head. "No, no. I don't mind doing it. I mean, we're all in this together now, right?"

"Oh, thank God," Zach stated, his heavy footsteps drawing nearer. "Because I'm pretty sure I messed something up already."

Cora laughed. Poor Zach. "I'll fix it. Don't touch anything until I can get in there."

"I'm glad to hear that because I ordered the voice program already and installed it," Zach told her. "I researched and this was supposed to be the best one and simple to use."

Cora's heart melted. This family had taken her in as one of their own, pulling her inside their circle to a place where so much love lived.

"I'm happy to look at it, but can it wait a couple days?" she asked. "I may need a day to recover from those ladies."

Sophie's sweet laughter filled the room. "Absolutely. I'll make sure Zach keeps his hands out of the books.

But you need to be warned, we have another large group coming in next weekend."

Cora nodded. "They can't be as exhausting as the quilters."

"Don't bet on it. It's a writing group," Sophie stated. "I've already been told they all plan on taking full advantage of the masseuse because their backs are cramped. They're coming for five days and plan on plotting and relaxing. I've already warned Liam of all the chocolate he'll need to order."

Cora waved a hand. "I'll order the chocolate. I have connections and it won't cost the resort a thing."

Braxton stiffened beside her. "No. You don't need to do that."

"I want to." Cora shifted to face him better. "After everything you all have done for me, let me do this. It will be nice to do something with my family's company that joins both of our worlds."

Even though she didn't want to run Buchanan Chocolates, that didn't mean she couldn't support them. Now that Eric was in charge, and she was still keeping in touch with all the comings and goings, she could easily keep Bella Vous stocked with only the best.

Braxton kissed her temple. "I love you."

She never tired of hearing those words, of feeling that warmth spread through her at his certainty.

"I have some news to share, since we're all happy and things are looking up," Sophie exclaimed.

"What is it?" Cora asked.

"Well, now that Brock is settled in and we are legally his guardians, Zach and I decided to adopt."

Cora jumped up and squealed, her arms held out, and Sophie instantly hugged her. "Oh, my goodness, that's wonderful. This is so exciting."

Sophie squeezed before easing back. "Brock was

pretty happy, too. I worried how he'd react, being a teenager, but I think he is mature enough that he understands the need for kids to have a good home."

"You guys will be the best parents," Braxton chimed in. "I'm really happy for you."

Sophie held on to Cora's arm. "We also plan on getting married in the spring and I'm going to need some beautiful bridesmaids."

Cora smiled. "I'd love to."

Sophie laughed. "I knew you would."

When Cora's eyes started burning, she blinked against the building moisture. "Sorry. I've just never had a sister or even a close girlfriend."

Sophie embraced her once again. "Chelsea would've loved you."

Oh, that did it. Cora lost it. She'd heard so much talk of Chelsea and knew what a staple she'd been to this family.

"And that's our cue to go check the grill," Zach stated.

"Yup. We'll yell when everything is ready," Braxton added.

Cora sniffed and pulled away from Sophie. "Men. They can't handle tears."

"Another reason why the girls need to stick together," Sophie laughed.

All the love inside Cora threatened to burst. The love and happiness that had built within her in such a short time was all-consuming. She couldn't imagine ever feeling more complete, but she knew this was just the beginning and things would only get better from here.

Connect with Us

Visit us online at
KensingtonBooks.com
to read more from your favorite authors, see books
by series, view reading group guides, and more.

for sneak peeks, chances to win books and prize packs,
and to share your thoughts with other readers.

facebook.com/kensingtonpublishing
twitter.com/kensingtonbooks

Tell us what you think!

To share your thoughts, submit a review,
or sign up for our eNewsletters, please visit:
KensingtonBooks.com/TellUs.